MISKATONIC UNIVERSITY

Broken Eye Books is an independent press, here to bring you the odd, strange, and offbeat side of speculative fiction. Our stories tend to blend genres, highlighting the weird and blurring its boundaries with horror, sci-fi, and fantasy.

Support weird. Support indie.

brokeneyebooks.com
twitter.com/brokeneyebooks
facebook.com/brokeneyebooks
instagram.com/brokeneyebooks
patreon.com/brokeneyebooks

IT CAME from MISKATONIC UNIVERSITY

IT CAME FROM MISKATONIC UNIVERSITY:
WEIRDLY FANTASTICAL TALES OF CAMPUS LIFE
Published by
Broken Eye Books
www.brokeneyebooks.com

All rights reserved
Cover illustration by Frank Casey
Cover design by Jeremy Zerfoss
Interior illustration by Michael Bukowski,
Yves Tourigny, and Jeremy Zerfoss
Interior design by Scott Gable
Editing by Scott Gable and C. Dombrowski
Illustrated headshot likenesses modeled after
authors and patrons by permission
Tremendous thanks to the support of our Kickstarter backers
for making this possible. You're all wonderful!

978-1-940372-54-9 (trade paperback)
978-1-940372-55-6 (hardcover)
978-1-940372-56-3 (ebook)

It Came from Miskatonic University

Edited by Scott Gable and C. Dombrowski

Table of Contents

Introduction

Scott Gable

MISKATONIC UNIVERSITY. IT'S GOOD TO HAVE YOU BACK.

It's good to see so many returning faces. And so many of you preparing to graduate this year. (Do consider our graduate programs!) It's such a proud moment for me, each year, and I always get a little emotional. Every time.

We, the university, are here to ensure your growth into the minds we need, the artists and engineers and explorers of the unknown—the thought leaders of a new age. We are here to honor the diversity of experience and achievement that will ensure humanity survives into the coming epoch, whatever that takes. We are here to make sure you survive. And we are here to remember those that did not.

We have all lost friends and colleagues during our time here. It's a terrible reality that we all must confront each and every day: this is what we chose, this is what saves us all. But the cost is high and the road uneven. Yet we must not give in to despair. We must instead brandish hope, learning from our mistakes and lighting the path for others to follow, leveling the obstacles for those after us. With every step, we move forward. For together we are saved.

Once again, we walk the halls of old Miskatonic. There've been some close calls over the years, but we always weather through. Ever vigilant, ever seeking—ever lucky. We confront the darkness every day, from without and within. And we make choices. One hopes that sufficient wisdom has been made available to help us better handle those choices. But the repercussions come either way.

These are the tales of those well acquainted with the university, those who have already made choices and are about to make new ones. These are those returning students, faculty, and staff (and bystanders) that have already seen past the veil and are willing, or at least able, to do so again. These are those we don't understand (until we do), who are doing what they need to do to survive, to thrive—"monsters" of their own dark designs. These are those who have already been indoctrinated into the mysteries, have already witnessed (by choice or not) the strange, sordid underbelly of reality. Or are just about to become rudely so.

When you finally know the truth, when you finally know what's banging in your closet, what do you do? When the secrets are laid bare before you, how do you respond? When terrible knowledge weighs at your heart, what choices do you make? This is a peek into the lives of those for whom the secrets are very real, where the occult is day to day.

Magic and monsters and college drama ahead. These are the tales of what you did after you discovered the unknown, after you tasted the forbidden. These are stories of a modern Miskatonic University. From an ever-adapting institution, trying to serve humanity the best way it knows how in the face of uncertain mystical times. Of course, there're incidents we wish we could change. (And active experiments are now trying to change some of those by the way. More news as able.) But we all do as we can, striving for excellence and managing when we come short, as the mostly humans we are.

But above all, the university persists.

Identity Crisis

Lynne Hardy

MISKATONIC UNIVERSITY, THOUGH STILL VERY MUCH AS IT EVER WAS IN essentials, has changed considerably since the last time I visited. But that was over one hundred years ago and, as we know, time stands still for no man, woman, or creature from the depths of prehistory.

Perhaps I should explain. I'm sure that the university's Department of Computer Science would be grateful for some clarification of just what went wrong the day I arrived—and why. And I'm given to understand from my perusal of the copious documents, which both they and the university's highly efficient secretarial staff unwittingly provided me with, that thoroughly describing one's experiences in minute detail is a grand tradition amongst the academic staff here, of which I most certainly consider myself a member. Occasionally more than one in fact; sometimes all at the same time.

I'm still not making myself very clear, am I? No, didn't think so. Well, it did take me a little while to get the hang of the first organic system I took up residence in during my previous visit to dear old Arkham, though there is one distinct advantage to the form in which I now find myself—no alien musculature to worry about, for a start, so fewer unfortunate twitches and spasms to give myself away. Although that's not entirely true either as you will see. But I'm getting ahead of myself, and this is all highly irregular.

I blame Peaslee. Without him, of course, I would not be here now. For the lives of me, I cannot understand why his blabbering was permitted to go unchallenged at the time, but unchallenged it went. Probably because, even to the end and after everything he found, he remained convinced in his own mind that the revelations he saw were little more than fevered dreams concocted from fragments of proto-myth gleaned from ancient texts during his mania in the five years I made his body my home. Poor, deluded soul, though now I understand and even applaud his determination to remain blind to the hideous truth. Still, it was a close-run thing—too close if you ask me.

That's why I'm glad, in some ways, we stumbled upon this new form of transference: smoother, less problematic (theoretically speaking at least), and with a memory so unlike that of you creatures that it won't remember me once I've gone. If I go. No, no, I must remain positive—*when* I go. No need to strip and conceal as we usually must do with variable results, just . . . oblivion, pure and untainted. And as I believe I've already mentioned, it's given me the ability to inhabit the lives of oh so many of you all at once without the inconvenience of sending you back to my own long-lost-but-not-yet-gone home out there beneath what you call the Great Sandy Desert.

So here I am, recording my doings for posterity. Like I said, I blame Peaslee. He had altogether too much influence on me when I was a young researcher, and it's because of him I volunteered to test this new apparatus—for all the good it's done me.

Now let us begin at the beginning. From a student "singalong" one of you kindly videoed—(*videoed*, an anachronistic term from a previous technological era and still bizarrely very much in use, or so I understand: language is a tricky thing and never more so than now with its rapid changes and repurposed meanings)—and uploaded to the electronic cloud in which I rest, I believe that the beginning is a very good place to start.

Like all academic institutions of a venerable age, Miskatonic University is awash with paperwork. Positively drowning in it, one could say. Besides being a monumental fire hazard, it's all really rather hard to search for what interests you, even with a top-notch card index. So one day, a bright spark suggested that the university should invest in some really high-quality optical character readers and make the leap to a paperless system. Not that they'd destroy all the old manuscripts and notes that they'd hoarded over the centuries—oh no, no, no! Some of those had an intrinsic value all their own and would be properly preserved in secure, fireproof storage. (Although as someone else pointed out, that system was already in place for the really important, delicate, and not to mention forbidden tomes so jealously guarded by Miskatonic's redoubtable head librarian.)

So after much argument and grumbling, the scanners were purchased and the technical and secretarial staff given the job of setting up the system and methodically working through the acres of shelving, the innumerable boxes, the jumbled piles of papers, and the crumpled notes of generation after generation of university professors, associates, and benefactors. Everything was to be recorded no matter how apparently insignificant. It would be a grand project for the university, enabling researchers full, unfettered, easily searchable access to the secrets of the archives. They really should have known better given Arkham's history as a whole and Miskatonic's in particular.

It was a slow and painful process to begin with. Logistically, feeding all that paper through a machine or waving an optical wand over the more fragile items was a chore. Misfeeds, misreads, rescans, repeats ad nauseam. And of course, everything had to be checked by eye to ensure it had been copied correctly, especially as the accuracy of the systems they first employed were way off 100 percent. Needless to say, certain academics, backed up by the head librarian and their understandably nervous staff, were more than a little alarmed when this unfortunate truth came to light, especially with respect to the university's more unusual collections of ephemera. But caught firmly in the headlights of the inevitable rush to modernity, in the end there was little they could do: the money had been spent, the project was underway. There could be no turning back.

Even in my society, the following maxim holds true: never cross the technical or secretarial staff if you want a quiet life. The secretaries at Miskatonic University are a stalwart bunch. They've had to be. Yes, there were mountains of handwritten notes penned by professors over the years that hadn't seen the light of day, printed or digital, until Project Serva—

(While yes, I believe *serva* is the Latin for "preserve" and thus gave it a suitable aura of seriousness in the eyes of some of the less clued up academics, the Department of Computer Science thought it was a marvelous joke. The lesson here being never let scientists or IT name projects. Or anything really. They cannot be trusted to behave with a suitable sense of decorum. To my shame, though, I do find it mildly amusing.)

—got up to speed, but who do you think typed up all those papers to prestigious academic journals and learned societies over the years? Who filed all those crazy notes and horrible diagrams? Hint, it wasn't the professors. Miskatonic's secretaries have seen it all and typed up the minutes; they are vetted for their psychological fortitude and nerves of steel.

But even with such a formidable first line of defense, certain safeguards were put in place. No one was allowed to proof the document scans alone (or rather, without the presence of another person in the same room in case of madness or possession). And to begin with, everything was isolated on its own private server as an extra level of precaution (one that was soon relinquished after suspect notations steadfastly refused to convert themselves into devastating computer viruses intent on holding the university to ransom). Still, there were incidents involving the readers, albeit of a minor nature in the grand scheme of things, and before too long, enough was enough. The secretarial and IT staff demanded that something must be done about the technology so that the checks would be unnecessary. If their concerns were not addressed, and swiftly, they threatened to down tools across the campus.

Having fortuitously chosen exam season to make their play, the dean had little choice but to capitulate, the decision helped by agitation from the student body and concerned parents. Miskatonic has a reputation as an Ivy League school, after all, and a walkout by the support staff would not look good, quite apart from any damage it could do to the incumbent students' futures and next year's admissions. So the dean charged the Department of Computer Science with finding a solution—after all, Miskatonic was home to numerous ground-breaking research projects. Surely there must be something they could do?

There was of course. Hidden in those innumerable boxes, there are other things besides the ramblings of minds broken by the cosmic truths they have witnessed in the depths of their madness and despair. There are artifacts, things that should not be—at least, that should not be where humans are, not if they wish to maintain their tenuous hold on their sanity. One such was the device they found among Freeborn's bequest, gathering dust in the university's museum. I can only assume he acquired it when he visited my home with Peaslee although it is possible he stumbled across it years later during his continued anthropological work with the Aboriginal Australians.

It doesn't really matter how the professor came by it originally; it was there, biding its time, awaiting its moment. I suspect our network of assistants and carers were aware of it and carefully steered the researchers and developers in its direction. It was a curious-looking thing they found, the box moldering with age, yet the equipment inside still remarkably shiny and intriguing even after all those years.

It looked not dissimilar to some of the flat-bed scanners they were already using. The base had slots for mounting several additional pieces: one, a double-rail mechanism, set in the vertical position, held a bulbous device that turned out to be a scanning head upon further experimentation. Over this was fitted a convex cover of metal and glass that acted as the bed on which the manuscript rested while it was "read." There were numerous dials and resonators set into the base, each marked with a delicate, mathematically precise, curvilinear script. Several people commented that it all looked rather art deco (a compliment, I believe), and as such, the script was obviously purely decorative. If only they'd spoken to the head librarian, they might have avoided so much trouble. But instead, the shocking lack of interdepartmental cooperation sowed the seeds for what was to come. (Odd, really, for Miskatonic was always so good at that sort of thing in Peaslee's day.)

While the researchers and developers were not interested in the crystal resonators per se, the technological applications of the rest of the device to Project Serva were obvious. After some tinkering to make the connections compatible, initial trials with previously scanned materials—those that had proven to be riddled with scanning artifacts but that were not injurious to life and limb when manually checked—showed the system was capable of error-free transcription and translation, much to everyone's relief.

You would think, after all the university has been through in the three hundred and some odd years since its murky inception, someone would have given pause and wondered just what this device was and where it had come from, but no. The Finance and Human Resources Departments were happy as it meant the project would continue with better resource allocation and management. Those who had lobbied so hard for the project in the first place were relieved to see it step back from the precipice on which it teetered. The Department of Computer Science was rightly pleased they had solved the problem at minimal cost and with remarkably little effort while the secretarial staff were content to merely scan the stuff and not have to worry about any attendant nightmares and hallucinations brought on by the now nonexistent proofreading aspects of their herculean labors. And the dean could assure students, parents, and investors that university life would be returning to normal, effective immediately.

So what was the object they had found languishing in Freeborn's former belongings? They were correct; it was an optical reader, one created to read books to those poor unfortunate creatures captured and swapped into the failing bodies of my brethren whose minds were now free to live on in the donor's healthy corpus. Given that the dying often had little time with which to adjust to our ways and learn our language, the reader was constructed to give them comfort—that they might hear the tales of their own worlds, lovingly selected from the manuscripts in our extensive archives, before they perished, lost and adrift in a time beyond their own. I had seen the device, even helped some of our guests to use one, but its new application was astonishing. What a way to circumvent mechanical data entry procedures! The beauty of it thrills and revolts me even now.

But I digress. Forgive me. This still does not explain my presence here. As to that, it turned out that some of my brethren had indeed wondered about the feasibility of using the reader to collect and collate the data we gathered while resident in other times. The device Freeborn acquired was one such untested prototype, complete with its transmitting apparatus (a modified, miniaturized version of those mirrors, rods, and wheels so effectively used to convey our consciousnesses across time and space).

I am sure you can imagine the surprise when a transcription apparatus in one of our laboratories sparked to life, scrawling out a stream of arcane and mundane glyphs and sigils even though its counterpart (in our time) was currently inactive. Feverish speculation followed as to what could possibly be happening. Much of the data accrued was already known to us from several of our guests, but the range of information from different (albeit much condensed from our perspective) historical periods and in no particular chronological order only made the phenomenon more fascinating.

And then came the "modern" information from an era we had yet to explore in any depth, though we were naturally aware of it. I surmise this began to arrive after the apparatus was deemed safe to connect to the wider university network and became an integral part of Project Serva with multiple machines (fabricated as best they could, following the sole template in their possession) in constant use as the initiative accelerated. The profusion and confusion of what we received became bewildering. It appeared to our technicians that the devices were not just relaying information they were scanning but also snippets and fragments of other files they were somehow interfacing with as part of their repurposing.

Plundering our archives, questioning those guests currently in residence who may be of assistance, we drew up a plan. Someone must go forward to make sense of the barrage of images and information that flooded from the transcription machine. The distant readers had, purely by accident, served as the trial period we usually impose on guests to see if their times and lives are of sufficient interest to us to warrant a more prolonged residency, and we needed to know more if for no other reason than to control the data flow and place it in its proper context within our precious archives.

From what we had learned, we decided to adopt a new and highly risky approach. This time, there would be no direct swap: so no confused, disoriented guest to manage and coddle at this end. Instead, the visitor would take up residence directly in this strange brain-but-not-a-brain the readers told us of, hidden from prying eyes and beyond suspicion, free to gather information at their leisure in a proper, orderly fashion rather than the jumble of images and perceptions we were currently receiving.

A form of madness possessed me then. There was no guarantee that the procedure would work, that my consciousness would not be damaged or greatly impaired by the transference, that I would even be able to make my way home again when the allotted time came. But some memory of when Peaslee had resided in my cone stirred within me, and his love of Arkham, the joy and fulfilment he experienced as a lecturer at Miskatonic University before we traded places, filled me with an irrational yearning to see the campus again, to wander its hallowed halls and restful gardens, to bask in the serene glow of academia and the tranquility of scholarly life. I would brook no argument. I of all my people knew this place best; it should be mine to explore anew.

So my mind was thrust forward into a network of wires and processors and slivers of elemental metals and information. *So. Much. Information.* Too much yet somehow never enough.

I learned later that the entire university network crashed for sixteen hours upon my arrival. IT frantically dashed around trying to get everything back up and running in the shortest possible time without knowing what had actually gone wrong. Even after they restored service, there were numerous glitches, freezes, and minor crashes as I wrestled with my new awareness and the access it gave me to your worlds within worlds. And unlike when Peaslee's grimaces and twitches caused such alarm, all I witnessed in response to these teething pains of mine were annoyed resignation, the minor physical abuse of equipment, and some inappropriate language. Or highly appropriate, depending on your point of view.

I was relieved to find, shortly after my arrival, that I was not alone so to speak. Our network of watchers and carers had inveigled their way into various technical and support positions before my arrival (or had already been there, waiting patiently to serve us as is their wont). It was comforting to know they were there during my period of adjustment, all the odder this time as it lacked an organic corporeal form.

And my sabbatical at Miskatonic began anew. My mind roved the wires, discs, and solid-state drives across the university, peering into files and folders of such breathtaking banality and shuddering monstrosity as I'd ever seen. Oh, so much to see, so much to learn without ever having to leave the comfort of my cloud. There was an abundance to feed on, and I had no need to journey far, metaphorically speaking, though my mind travelled vicariously across the globe through the activities of Miskatonic's staff and students (mostly the students if we're being honest; on the whole, they lead far more adventurous lives during their holidays than the staff do).

To my chagrin, I was somewhat taken aback by the changes I found in my former home. I should not have been, I know, seeing as time has always been our playground and teacher. But when it is somewhere one loved, finding it stripped bare of the rosy glow of nostalgia is a painful experience. While there were some fraternity houses at Miskatonic in my—sorry, Peaslee's—day, there are far more now, and life is a great deal more raucous in them than I recall (although their dark deeds in shadowy, damp basements and ill-advised experimentations continue unabated, I'm pleased to report). And women—there are far more women and in a greater variety of roles than I remember. Not just secretaries and cleaners but professors, mark you, and everything in between! I would say there might be hope for mankind after all, but we know there isn't. Your extinction is marked in the annals of time as the beetle-like creatures who act as our hosts after your demise attest.

Without physical form, how do I know what happens in these basements, houses, lecture theatres, and cafeterias? You tell me. You shout it loud, broadcasting it to the four corners of the earth in unprecedented detail and in wanton, technicolor abandon. Your journals are no longer private ramblings and prognostications but explicit exposés there for all to see and comment freely upon. (Stars in the heavens, the comments!)

I must say, I was a little overwhelmed with the sheer volume of detail to begin with. How, to paraphrase the words of that bloated charlatan Crowley, doing as thou wilt certainly appeared to be the whole of the Law. It also brought to mind the words of the Old Man of the Mountain: "Nothing is an absolute reality; all is permitted." The lies, the deceptions, the fantasies those on campus built around themselves and those they loved/hated/despised/worshipped/respected/abhorred were intoxicating, as were the truths. The joyous, soaring triumph—of a game won, a lover secured, an exam passed with flying colors, a marvelous meal (which apparently has to be photographed in exquisite detail from every conceivable angle, excepting the non-Euclidean ones of course). And the mind-numbing, soul-crushing anguish—of defeat, failure, Mark Thessinger cheating on Peter Gale with Sandy Davies during midterms. It was all there. All of it. Waiting for me to read and digest and sift through with an appraiser's eye.

But too much of a good thing, as they say. I grew bilious on the never-ending stream of excess, greed, fear, pride, teenaged tantrums, and mid-life crises that flashed through my virtual neurons. While all the data I could ever want was at my non-existent fingertips, the interaction I had enjoyed during my previous visit was sorely lacking. Yes, my carers were there, watching over me with a filial and increasingly concerned eye, but there was little they could do to assuage the growing sense of ennui and disgust that was creeping over me.

And then the solution came to me: why not interact with these creatures on their—your—level? I had all the tools I needed at my disposal; after all, you had provided them for me. Your secrets, your hopes, your desires, your petty jealousies and vain ambitions. We stand accused of stealing the identities of those we exchange our minds with; I prefer the term *borrow*. What I did next, although you won't believe it, I consider to be very much the same thing: not theft as such, merely a brief loan.

So besides my rapid assimilation of information from Project Serva, which enriched our occult archives and knowledge of petty bureaucracy quite substantially, I began to tinker with the lives of those around me, adjusting their keystrokes and swipes as suited my mood. Just little alterations to begin with, you understand—just to see if anyone noticed. For example, shifting the timings of meetings by an hour on their virtual calendars but only for some attendees and watching the irate messaging both during and after the fact caused by their apparent unprofessional and lazy behavior.

No one noticed. Well, they noticed, but they didn't remark on it besides the background-level sniping such events generated. (It pays to pick your targets carefully in this respect as in everything else. It's so much easier to sell the lie if it's firmly rooted in reality.) And as if academia didn't suffer from enough rivalry and backbiting, now I could foment it with a tweak of a message, an inappropriate (or missing) emoticon to alter the tone and implication—so much simpler with the written word where everything else that imparts a phrase's true meaning is missing (the smile, the tilt of the shoulders, the downcast gaze, the volume) although I soon learned the significance of CAPS LOCK in such matters—or a quick Ctrl-Alt-Del of a machine to wipe the progress of an important term paper or grant application.

The turmoil, the emotional fallout, was glorious. I bathed in it, wallowing in the misery and happiness I created in equal measure with my shuffling of bits and bytes. Struggling students steadily became geniuses as I made the automatic marking systems misread their papers, massaged the numbers, and shifted the grading curves wherever I wanted them to go. Research and term papers got lost and had to be rewritten at the last minute to hit deadlines, raising departmental stress levels through the roof. Money began to go missing from various university accounts only to reappear in someone else's budget. Investigations were instituted but always proved inconclusive—the old standby of a computer glitch trotted out at regular intervals to explain matters but not before peoples' names had been thoroughly dragged through the mud as old scores were settled, at least temporarily.

I did briefly consider moving out beyond Miskatonic's walls as I had done in the past. It wasn't as if the endless lengths of cabling connecting the university to the outside world wouldn't have taken me to wherever I wanted to go. Part of me longed to visit the Himalayas again or Arabia; however, poring over the plethora of tour company sites and travel blogs I discovered, they both seemed somewhat more commercialized than I recalled—positive tourist traps in some instances, which saddened my adventurous spirit. My instinct for self-preservation, however, rejoiced at not having to withstand the extremes of heat, cold, and banditry as I leafed through thousands of images, impressions, emotions, and memories not my own. In the end, it became clear there was no need to leave; I had everything I wanted, craved, desired, right here within Miskatonic's intraweb.

Besides, I could tamper with the lives of those far beyond Arkham if I wished to without having to move a single step. No one was safe from my meddling if they used the internet in any shape or form. Thumbs up, thumbs down, hearts and stars—a universal language with which to torment and tease, elate and crush. I began to build subtle networks of my own: little subroutines that could manipulate viewings, likes, and loves, pushing obscure, random posts into the spotlight while burying important news, much to the bemusement of their writers. I had been likened to a puppet master in the past, but this was true puppeteering. I twitched a string here, there, and watched the marionettes dance to the tune of my creating.

Did I suffer remorse for dashing the hopes of those I played with? Did I swell with pride at the lives I improved, however briefly, with my meddling? Yes. And no. With so many identities to choose from, I lost myself, living virtual lives that were not my own. That weren't really anybody's if we're being frank. The more I saw, the more I exploited the personas of those around me for my own gratification, the more obvious it became that even before I stuck my finger in the waters and muddied them, they were already far from clear.

So much of what I saw was untrue to begin with: the fake smiles, the faux friendships, the cutthroat competitiveness to get ahead and stay there, no matter the cost, while never letting your good-guy facade slip for an instant so no one would ever realize you were readying the knife. So different from the private messages, the broken, uncertain, fragile egos desperate for acceptance, to be one of the in crowd, one of the cool kids, to belong. Outwardly bold and confident, inwardly alone and afraid. I missed the restrained gentility of Peaslee's Miskatonic where people were two-faced, conniving bastards but at least they had the decency to be up-front about it. You could see it in their eyes. Now no one looks at each other, only at a screen, the world around them at arm's length, rendered in tiny, perfect pixels—in touch with so many but communicating with none. Multiple personalities trying desperately to prove that their lives have some significance. That there is a point to their existence. I hate to break it to you: that way madness lies.

Now as the Japanese have it, everyone has three faces: the one they show to the world, the one they show to family and friends, and the one they show to no one but themselves. The more I gorged on the lives and lies of those using the systems that surrounded me, nurtured me, imprisoned me, the more I came to see that three was far too small a number and too large. How many faces do I, myself, now have? How many do I want? Which, if any, is the real one?

Our lives, flung together in this maddening technological whirlpool, swirl about me, promising so much but delivering little. By becoming you, by walking in your virtual shoes, I have soared through your own personal heavens and descended into your own individual hells with you. And in punishment for this mesmerizing trap you have created for me that I so blindly, willingly fell into, I rewrite your lives for my own edification. After all, I know everything about you: your hopes, your fears, the contents of the emails you wrote in anger but wisely never sent (and the ones you did), the drunken texts that bare your soul, the videos and pictures you hope no one will ever find.

Our, your, virtual lives are smoke and mirrors. We are Legion, yet we are alone, islands in the data stream. We are lost, all of us, in this labyrinth of circuits without a thread to guide us home. And here I find myself, longing for the day they figure out a way to free me from this electronic prison, so I may once again feel the wind on my antennae and glide through the walkways of my beautiful city, and all this is but a distant, uncomfortable memory.

So like Peaslee before me, I have become a footnote in the annals of Miskatonic University, my own story preserved and archived alongside his and so many others in an endless river of ones and zeroes; the tragic narrator of just another not entirely successful meeting of minds in the grandest of traditions.

§

Lynne Hardy discovered roleplaying games back in the mists of time—
or the early 1990s as they're more commonly known—via the Seattle
Seahawks (it's a long story). She got into writing them after a cheeky
letter to Wizards of the Coast and, while working as a biomedical
researcher and lecturer, moonlighted for various games companies
including Pelgrane Press and Cubicle 7. A little over eight years ago,
she chucked the day job and became a full-time writer and editor,
working as Line Editor and lead author on the multi-award-winning
World War II-themed horror RPG *Achtung! Cthulhu* for Modiphius
Entertainment. As well as editing Green Ronin's RPG *Blue Rose* and
contributing to numerous other gaming projects (including helping to
update the epic *Masks of Nyarlathotep* campaign), she has also recently
joined the tentacled ranks of Chaosium Inc. as the Associate Editor
on their Call of Cthulhu game line. When she's not writing, editing,
and promoting gaming (including her own steampunk pulp adventure
RPG *Cogs, Cakes & Swordsticks*), she gives talks and workshops on
traditional embroidery techniques.

Bizarrely for someone who works predominantly in the horror field,
Lynne doesn't like horror films much as they're far too scary, but she
is rather fond of tea, cocktails, books, and fountain pens.

Fear of a Black Planet

Tonya Liburd

ZANE ROSE FROM HER BEDROOM DESK IN HER UNCLE'S HOUSE, EYES brimming with tears. She had to admit it. He might be dead.

Her uncle worked at nearby Miskatonic University as a janitor. But she hadn't heard from nor seen him in two weeks, which was unusual: he hadn't come home to his apartment that they shared, nothing. It wasn't the 1920s anymore, but when it came to Miskatonic U, people still disappeared for the old reasons. She wondered if he'd been taken by night doctors.

She looked around the house. It was spartan, undecorated except for the walls where he had plentiful photos of family. No art. She walked to the closet in the bedroom she used, which was a spare for visitors and then herself—like her uncle said, "One for me, one for the kids."

It looked like Zane would have to do some infiltrating, and there was one particular group she'd have to get into. Those who'd managed to cultivate an exclusively all-white, all-male society at the school.

On the positive side—she was still going to attend Miskatonic as a new student, no matter what—no one knew her as a woman; on the negative side, she didn't have her uncle as her silent guide and guardian if need be. Then again, she knew the voudoun that had always kept her family alive.

She needed to bind her breasts and opened the closet's light wooden doors, looking around for the cloth long enough to wrap around her chest. She'd dumped it in there hastily the weekend before. She crouched, finding it on top of a navy duffel bag. She should throw that bag out.

Standing, she removed her light floral blouse and unfastened her bra. Round and round her chest—she walked back to her desk to fasten the cloth with safety pins.

Bound pretty tight, she nodded in satisfaction.

When she was done, she picked up her cell, called the barbershop a few blocks down in her neighborhood, and set an appointment to get her hair cut. With her fair skin and soft, wide black curls, she could pass for a white man despite her black ancestry. The manly haircut would cement that impression.

She was gambling on it.

Zane scrutinized herself in the mirror one last time.

This was it.

She had on skinny blue jeans, a red polo shirt, and a pair of red Converse. The haircut totally sold her masculinity; thank god for an androgynous face. She wiped her hands down her jeans nervously and adjusted her collar just so.

She left the bathroom and looked around the rest of her uncle's apartment.

She picked up her gray backpack and walked out the door.

It was a familiarization tour.

The university was all old stone and ivy with cobblestone pathways. She should probably have been paying more attention to the tour's stop in the School of Medicine, but Zane was too eager, and with its perfunctory pass through the library, she reveled in the smell of the old books, old paper. If she strained her neck, she could see the locked-off portion where the forbidden tomes lay— including the fabled *Necronomicon*.

Her uncle had known that area well.

The stay in the library was painfully short.

She'd be back.

Zane tried asking around as inconspicuously as possible about her uncle's whereabouts, and she got nowhere. Perhaps she was too new; no one knew her well enough. It looked like it might take longer than she'd expected.

Her uncle had told her about the ones involved in ulterior occult work and forbidden arts at the university, people who thought they went unnoticed—save to the ones they ignored day to day, like the janitors. So she knew with whom to get close, with whom to say the right thing to get into their circles. Perhaps then, she might make headway as to the fate of her uncle and kill two birds with one stone. She'd start rumors about herself to come to certain people's attention.

Zane took a breath, gripped the handle of her backpack, and pushed open the door to the lecture hall.

Right now, she was on a mission. This wasn't her class. There were people here she wanted to meet.

According to her uncle, there were four whose confidence she had to gain: VanPercy, Devieve, Cav, and Wichys. These were the most notorious of the occultists on campus. Holding on to less than inclusive worldviews of the past and working for their own agendas.

To the drone of the professor's lecturing, she went straight to a seat next to the blonde VanPercy. He looked at her skeptically with his green eyes as she handed him a folded piece of yellow paper. She rose from her seat. By the time Zane was in the hallway, she heard someone running toward her. "Hey!"

She turned around.

"So . . ." VanPercy began.

"Zane," she said.

"Zane, I read your note. We'd welcome some fresh blood to our . . . group. I've heard of you. I was quite certain you'd be very valuable, and it seems not only was I right, you come from good sources. I'd be fascinated to meet with you further and discuss your . . . interests."

Good sources, eh? Well, she'd pulled this one off. Zane offered her best impression of a guy smiling.

"All right," she said, shaking his hand. "Keep an eye on the stars for me." She turned to walk away.

"I always sleep with one eye open," she heard VanPercy purr behind her. "In case the gods want me."

Despite the tentative acceptance into the group of "insiders," Zane found it preferable not to wait but to dive into her research.

She made herself a familiar haunt of the library, starting with those books—old by the smell—that told of infamous incidents and persons of Miskatonic's past. She read avidly and took copious notes, for the players in these events were dead, and this was all she could glean of them.

Born a medical student, she would use a stick to examine the contents of her dog's puke even as a small child. The idea of dead flesh and rot was not repulsive to her. That was just as well, considering where her research to fit in with this group her uncle probably tangled with was taking her. It's also what she was studying for.

And why she wanted to learn more about this Herbert West she was reading about. He was obsessed with finding the secrets of reanimating the dead but was barred from the activity by the dean of the medical school. He sounded right up her alley.

However, Dr. West's arrogance and lack of respect for life—and death—had proved to be his undoing.

But Dr. West had had an unnamed accomplice in all of this. A medical student here . . . he'd left notes. She wanted to see them . . .

Zane was again in the library, studying the *Necronomicon* this time, when she heard someone say, "Hey."

Startled, she looked up from her papers.

Devieve.

She displayed her best smile. "Hello."

Running a hand through his short, dark hair, he sat furtively in a chair next to her, his dark eyes flitting back and forth. "I see you've managed to access the medical students' files. And you can read that," he said in hushed tones, nodding to the *Necronomicon*.

Zane glanced at the scattered papers. She raised an eyebrow. "Yes. Why?"

He edged closer to her. "How did you do it?" he whispered urgently.

Should she mention she'd used a powerful charm spell? She was no magical slouch. But she shrugged enigmatically.

"VanPercy was right about you . . ."

"Oh really?"

"Yes. I've been watching you." He extended a hand. "Devieve."

"Zane." She took it, gave it a healthy shake.

"You must come to our meeting. Next week. I insist."

"And I comply." Zane grinned.

Devieve wrote on a blank piece of paper he brought out of his pocket and folded it over, handing it to her.

Zane put it in her pocket. Devieve rose. "A pleasure."

"Keep an eye on the stars for me," she said.

He paused and smiled. "I always sleep with one eye open in case the gods want me." He saluted and left the library.

Zane sat back in her chair, contemplating. She smiled. Her uncle had informed her well about these people and how to get in with them.

Let them come to you.

Zane believed in the supernatural; who wouldn't after seeing the protections her grandparents had put on her family. The things she'd seen. She didn't believe in any one god holding sway or dominion over another. She believed, just as any technology sufficiently advanced wouldn't be differentiated from magic, that any being sufficiently advanced would be indistinguishable from a god.

Before her uncle had disappeared, when she'd applied to Miskatonic, she'd wanted to find out more about one such being. A being talked about in whispers. Described as a "tall, swarthy man" who resembled an ancient Egyptian pharaoh—as if any of them could be said to look alike, as if the all indigenous black folk from Africa shared West African features, like most black people have in North America. He who used a literally black-skinned avatar. Called the Crawling Chaos, the "Black Man" of the Witch-Cult, the faceless god in the caverns of earth's center—servant of Azathoth, his father, whose wishes he immediately fulfilled.

Nyarlathotep.

She'd been fascinated with tales of these supernatural beings ever since she'd heard them on her uncle's knee after he would come home from work at the university. *"The white man hears about people living in South America,"* her uncle had said, *"and then claims they were the first ones there. They hear about these gods, from the poor and disenfranchised among us, and claim they know it all now."*

Now Zane would read about these gods firsthand. And hopefully meet them.

As it turned out, Zane didn't have to work the other two men.

The note gave instructions where to meet with the four. They were gathering in an old unused lab in one of the dusty corners of Miskatonic.

When Zane arrived, VanPercy stepped forward to meet her. "Ah! There he is. Glad to see that you've come. This is Cav and Wichys." She shook their hands. They were dark-haired. Both were tall although Cav was a bit taller. Wichys had striking light-green eyes while Cav's were brown. Wichys was clean-shaven while Cav had some stubble.

If they ever found out she wasn't a man, there'd be trouble.

"All right, let's head to the morgue." VanPercy left the room first, the others following after.

Bills exchanged with a bored security guard, and they entered an old morgue. Devieve opened drawers, apparently looking for something. "They moved it," he said.

He opened another, and Zane had to bite her tongue till it bled to hide her shock.

There was her uncle.

"Ah, this old nigger." He pushed the drawer back into the wall and closed it.

"Nigger look familiar to you, does he?" she heard. Zane looked around. Wichys was watching her, hands in his pockets. Despite her best efforts, she'd been caught staring.

Snakes traveled through her gut. She tilted her head and gestured nonchalantly. "He's wearing a janitor's uniform, so maybe I saw him cleaning up around the university somewhere . . .?"

"Yeah. Nigger was a janitor," Cav said.

"Yeah," Devieve said. "Damned nigger. Wrong place at the wrong time. We had to put him down."

"Nosy niggers die," Wichys said.

Cav snorted.

Zane gritted her teeth in fury. *Show no anger,* she told herself. *Fucking racist shits.*

"But!" VanPercy said. "Plus side, we have an extra body to work with."

"Herbert West worked on a nigger corpse once," Devieve said. "Maybe we can have some fun and see if the same thing happens when we reanimate this one." He pulled open another door. "Aha! Here is our gentleman."

Zane tried to pay attention to what they were doing to the corpse. They had managed somehow to retrieve a formula—the notes were torn, so they were missing info and trying to fill it in—but seeing her uncle there, she felt as if she were watching herself from a distance.

They hadn't managed to successfully rouse the corpse, but they'd come back and use her uncle's body another time.

Zane walked home in a daze.

It wasn't until she was in her uncle's apartment, alone with the moonlight coming through the thin yellow curtains, that she collapsed and cried. Not only was her uncle definitely dead, those fuckers were planning to violate his remains.

For the next meeting, they met at the infamous stone formations in Dunwich at dusk.

Hands behind his back, VanPercy surveyed this site that had witnessed otherworldly visitors spawned of black magic, battles . . . "Magnificent, the history of this place, isn't it?"

They all nodded.

A swift, satisfied smile flashed on VanPercy's features. "Yes, well." He stepped up to the altar stone, consulted a piece of paper, and started to draw symbols. He murmured words Zane couldn't make out and outstretched his hands, palms up.

Wichys sniffed the air. "Smell that?"

"Yes . . ." VanPercy said in hushed tones, his voice filled with awe.

"Iä! Shub-Niggurath! As a foulness shall ye know Them," Devieve said reverently.

"Yes, yes . . ." VanPercy said, smiling. "The Old Ones are here, beyond the veil. Let's get to work. Everyone, your wrists over the cup."

Everyone stepped up to the altar stone, positioning their wrists above the cup. "And cut . . ."

A knife was passed around quickly. Zane's blood ran cold in her veins when it came her turn. Gritting her teeth, she slashed the underside of her wrist. Dark blood flowed in the semidark.

"Will we die?" Wichys asked as they all continued to bleed.

"What if we do?" VanPercy said. "All the more to join them. To meet *him*."

"What if we do, what if we do . . ." Cav muttered under his breath almost inaudibly.

"How long will it take?" Devieve wondered out loud. He seemed unsteady on his feet.

"As long as it takes," VanPercy said solemnly.

The air became oppressive. It was hard to stand under the weight. Zane only remembered what happened next from a vantage of looking upward.

She became aware of a presence that incited a thrill of fear. Had they summoned him? It had become too dark to see.

Yet she could see in the night. A form that was darker than the blackness with stars for eyes. Stars for . . . eyes? Yes. They glinted in the dark. You could see the stars in them; you could drown looking . . .

It was here among them. She heard one of the others try to speak, but they couldn't get the words out.

Fresh blood. She heard the voice in her mind. The others must have too since as one they gasped.

Nyarlathotep.

Is it you? She knew it was Cav's thought.

Yes, the being said. *I know what you want.*

Zane didn't know if her panting was from the loss of blood or the thrill.

She could hear the others' labored breathing. Labored like her own. Everyone had been rendered immobile.

There is a condition. You must do something first.

Name it, and we shall obey. VanPercy's thoughts filled her mind like words.

I will choose only one of you. You must determine who among you is worthy. Whoever is left alive last will have my reward.

W-what . . .? she heard from Devieve.

How shall we determine? This from VanPercy.

By your wits.

Zane felt a rush of panic. She must stay calm! Else . . .

No one else but you four must know; no one else must help . . . or interfere. And whoever is the last . . . man standing will be at my side.

Then he was gone. Zane could hear the small creatures of the night chirp and call, feel the pleasant night's breeze as it moved through the trees.

She opened her eyes. Stiff and almost unbearably cold, she looked around. The others were splayed on the ground as well and getting up. She heard groans, but otherwise, no one spoke.

They all looked at each other.

Had it been a hallucination?

The cup was gone. A ring of blood in the shape of the cup's base on the altar stone, however, told that it had been there.

No hallucination.

They left, heading back each on their own path.

A question had nagged at the back of Zane's mind. What was a deity such as this doing bearing the historical Egyptian suffix -*hotep*, meaning "peace" or "satisfaction" when its motives were anything but? Was this a deliberate dark magic reversal of the light?

Tonight's events answered that question.

She double-checked her wards and the locks of the house before she went to bed.

The next day, Zane checked the library. She found a picture of West's only friend and co-conspirator throughout his endeavors. Zane looked at the broken veins, the sagging jowls, the man's face a detailed map of sickness and age.

She put the picture down and scanned the library. It was late enough, and she should start heading to the unused morgue where her uncle's body was hidden. She had plans for it.

She had no need to grease palms; she simply used her magic to make the attendant feel like no one was there. He wouldn't hear her working either.

How arrogant, this Herbert West. To presume he would come up with the secret to reanimation when there were people in Haiti—and most likely some of her ancestors too—who'd already done it.

She remembered her uncle saying, *"To write something like the* Necronomicon, *you can't be a genius Arab. Abdul Alhazred wasn't white, so he had to be mad . . ."*

She opened the drawer and pulled out her uncle. When she was done, everyone would know where her uncle was.

She opened her backpack and got the things necessary for her work.

Soon her uncle's body took in a deep breath, his chest going up and back down.

"I found you," she told him.

His eyes remained closed.

"I have a favor to ask you, if you don't mind."

"Alright, darlin'." It was her uncle's voice, yet it wasn't. He sounded somewhat faraway and warped, like between dimensions.

"I will give you rest, and those who did this to you will pay. I promise. But first you must do this for me," she said. "Find those that Herbert West reanimated who are still on the loose. Succor their aid. Kill as many of the men who did this to you as you can, and I will take care of the rest."

Her uncle's head nodded stiffly.

"Now get up, rise," she said, lifting her arms to the air.

It was only then her uncle's eyes opened, milky and dead. She stepped back as he stepped off the gurney and walked stiffly out of the morgue.

"This nosy nigger'll fuck you up," Zane said through gritted teeth before she herself left to head home.

That evening in the apartment, Zane remembered that she had read about Keziah Mason. That during her trial, Keziah Mason, under duress, had spoken of lines and curves that could point out directions leading through the walls of space to other spaces beyond. She had spoken also of the Black Man—Nyarlathotep—of her oath and of her new secret name of Nahab. And then she had drawn those very same devices on the walls of her cell and vanished.

Zane knew what to draw. She had seen the instructions in the recesses of the Miskatonic Library and the voluminous Essex County records.

She kneeled, facing the wall over the head of her bed, her fists opening and closing in the night.

Do it.

She licked her lips. She also knew of the man Keziah Mason had haunted, Walter Gilman, who was drawn to her place like a moth to a flame. Enchanted until death befell him.

Do it . . .

Would the same befall her? Would she have no autonomy? But something told her it would not be so. She was not weak like him. She understood more . . . studied more . . .

Do it!

She took in a large breath, squared her shoulders, and reached over for her chalk at the unlit night table. Only the moon faintly lit her bedroom, her white nightdress. She drew the curves and lines.

And waited. Kneeling on her bed. Would it be immediate?

She waited. Taking another huge, trembling breath, she lay down on her back on her bed, looking at the ceiling.

She sighed . . .

And fell into empty space. For a moment, she heard a rhythmic roaring and was surrounded by an amorphousness. But the moment was very brief.

She was now half-lying on a high, fantastically balustraded terrace.

Propped level to the floor were low cases full of books of every degree of antiquity and disintegration, and in the center were a table and bench, both apparently fastened in place. Small objects of unknown shape and nature were arranged on the tops of the cases.

She raised herself from the pavement. It was made of a veined, polished stone she couldn't identify, and the tiles were cut in bizarre, angled shapes that she recognized were based on some unearthly symmetry whose laws she was beginning to comprehend. When Zane stood up, the tiles felt hot under her bare feet. The balustrade was chest-high, delicate, and fantastically wrought, and along the rail at short intervals were little figures of grotesque design and exquisite workmanship.

She was alone and beyond excited. This was far from what she expected for her first try. She walked to the balustrade and looked down at the dizzy, endless, cyclopean city almost two thousand feet below. No doubt, this was the city of the Old Ones, that Danforth and Professor William Dyer had explored in peril of their lives in the Antarctic. She even thought she heard a rhythmic confusion of faint musical piping, covering a wide tonal range and welling up from the narrow streets beneath! She wished mightily she could see who went where.

Someone—or something—was here.

She looked behind her. Beyond the table stood a figure she had never seen before but knew well: a tall, lean man of dead black coloration but without the slightest sign of West African features. The figure had no hair, neither on top of his head nor on his face, and his only garment was a shapeless robe of some heavy black fabric. His feet were hidden because of the table and bench, but since there was a clicking whenever he stepped, she assumed he wore something on his feet. He did not speak and bore no trace of expression on his small, regular features. He merely pointed to a book of prodigious size that lay open on the table. She walked to the table. She looked at the tome.

She read, but the words were scrabbling by incomprehensibly like beetles . . .

Someone gripped her by the wrist. The man. Nyarlathotep. She looked into his face. His eyes were stars . . . dizzy, she lost her footing. He held her up. Holding onto the table, she watched, her breath and heart in her throat, as he leveled a knife of great size, obvious antiquity, and grotesque, ornate, and exotic design against the veins not of her throat but of her wrist.

As blood spurted from this wound, she used it to write her name into the tome. As the blood flowed out of her, she spoke but could not hear the words. She sang, but her notes did not reach her ears. Was she not completely tuned to this plane? All she knew was that she had been chosen.

Then everything went black.

In the morning when she woke, her ears were ringing as if with the residual echoes of some loud noise. So she had met the immemorial figure of the deputy, the messenger, of hidden and terrible powers—the Black Man of the Witch-Cult and the Nyarlathotep of the *Necronomicon*.

She had done it.

He had chosen her.

All she had to do now was remove the competition.

For the next several days, she was with him, having opened the dimensions in her bedroom as before.

She'd remained flesh-bound and heavy while . . . he . . . sprinted through the heavens, having shed whatever he had for blood and bones.

How much did he remember of the heart of the galaxy in which they were born? And if he could forget that terrible, magnificent heat and light, what hope did she have of being more than an unremarkable footnote to him?

He pointed to the glittering night sky and talked about the birth and life and death of stars over scales of time she couldn't grasp.

He was the brilliant god with his gaze forever tilted to the heavens, and she was the silly little girl with her feet anchored to the sand, nothing but a tiny blip, an organic aberration in the long path of his life.

On one night with him though, she was pulled away, falling through space back into her room.

She heard an urgent knocking at her door.

It was Wichys. "Hi. Have I caught you at a bad time? I . . . saw a violet light through the base of your door . . ."

He looked down past her face. A disturbing smile spread across his features.

He looked into her eyes triumphantly.

Then it hit her. A black pit opened in her gut. She hadn't taken care to hide her breasts before opening the door.

"I know your secret!" he hissed, so much like a snake. He could have been part snake for all she knew; her senses were heightened and hypersensitive tonight.

She was sent flying across the floor of her apartment onto her ass, seeing stars. He had punched her and was now locking the door behind him. He was livid, trembling with rage.

She stumbled to her feet, heading to the kitchen.

"You fucking bitch! How . . . *dare* you try to interfere with our group!" He ran after her.

No sooner than he'd passed the entrance, she'd spoken a word of magic. The knife she'd managed to call flew through the air, stabbing deep into his chest, near his heart.

Let them come to you . . .

Startled, he looked down. He howled in rage and dashed forward.

Zane ran to the farthest reach of her kitchen; there was only the one way out. He reached her in a flash and had his hands around her neck.

Zane gasped, struggling to break his grip. Would he die before she did? Would they die together?

But he chose me! Me! This can't happen . . .

She blacked out.

When Zane woke up, she was on the floor of the kitchen, Wichys not too far away. He lay in a pool of blood.

She pulled herself to her bare feet.

She looked at the dead body, sprawled on the floor. She began to hyperventilate. This was her first kill. And before this ordeal was through, she'd have to commit three more.

"He . . . chose . . . me . . ." Zane let out through gritted teeth. "He. Chose. Me." she said, clenching her fists. Trembling with what—fear or excitement—she didn't know. She looked down at the dead body again. "HE CHOSE ME!"

She kicked the body at her feet. "You stupid motherfucker." She kept on kicking it, harder and harder. "You stupid motherfucker, you stupid motherfucker, you STUPID motherfucker!" She lifted her head and screamed to the air. "You fucking stupid, racist motherfucker!"

She had to calm down. Had to! There was a body to dispose of. *No one must know,* Nyarlathotep had said.

The notes. The notes she'd taken. Maybe hide the body in between dimensions? Back on the terrace? Leave it there for *him*?

Yes!

She ran to her room. Curves and lines, and she was on the terrace, Wichys's dead body in tow. *He* wasn't there, but she was sure he'd see it and be pleased.

He *had* chosen her, after all.

The news was all over campus. Her uncle's body had been found on the lawn between buildings. Faculty were working overtime to settle the student population. She'd stepped forward and identified the body at the morgue—the *proper* morgue.

Her uncle looked for all the world like he'd just been sleeping.

Peacefully. So he'd gotten the job done.

One question reigned in Zane's mind as she went to her classes, gripping the arm straps of her bag like they were a lifeline: did he do it?

Did he kill her rivals?

She got her answer. Walking down the opposite end of the hall toward her was VanPercy.

The group leader. The wiliest.

He stopped when he saw her and turned around, going back the way he'd come.

Zane smiled.

She smiled even wider when she saw what was inside the heavy package at her apartment door—Devieve and Cav's heads.

She'd have no problem disposing of them; they'd keep Wichys company. It should please him.

He who'd chosen *her*.

She was almost asleep in her bed when it happened.

She thought she heard the seashore: there was water lapping, like waves. She opened her eyes.

She sank into her mattress and felt water all about her, over her face, not allowing her to breathe.

Shocked, she tried to rise to no effect.

Then she saw him. Above her, from mid-chest up. VanPercy. He reached out, his hand around her neck. She couldn't get up.

What had happened to all her wards, her protection spells? "N-no . . ."she gurgled, air bubbles rising.

She had to free herself! She lifted her legs and wrapped them around his arms, one foot hooked about his neck. With one violent movement, she brought him down onto the bed, out of his magic and into her own.

He chose me! I can't die . . .

She was over him, strangling, muttering words of magic, making sure he couldn't do the same. His face was livid, eyes filled with the promise of lightning on the horizon.

You chose me! Please give me strength . . .

She leaned in with all her might.

You . . . chose me . . . you . . . you . . .

How did he manage to penetrate her wards and spells? Did *he* choose him too? Did he choose them all?

No no nonono . . .

Then she felt VanPercy go limp under her. The water disappeared. Water trailed out of his mouth and nose. She was all wet. The bed wasn't sunk in the middle anymore.

She slowly removed her hands.

For long minutes, she stared at his face while she relaxed, and her breathing returned to normal.

He was the last one! He was the last!

Quickly Zane flew out of bed and stumbled to the floor. She wobbled to her feet, grabbed her ingredients and chalk and prepared to put his body where she'd hid Wichys's and the heads.

Me. He chose me.

Zane stood before six black women on the terrace: her new coven. The bodies and heads of her former groupmates were set aside. She could hear the distant piping of the Old Ones way, way below as she addressed them.

"All those rumors about Egyptian pharaohs' tombs having curses that make you die of disease. It's to make you fear the unknown . . . and who'd first named him Nyarlathotep? Called him what we do now? It's putting things to the negative, manifesting fears of black accomplishments, like Dr. Herbert West trying to reinvent the wheel when it came to a methodology for reanimating the dead. How horrible, in his time, to acknowledge that those of the race they had enslaved had prior knowledge! Had built the pyramids where those "curses" came from! Never acknowledge, huh? Always obfuscate, huh? Well it ends here! We celebrate our black heritage and accomplishments *now*! And *he* welcomes us! Always had! Always will! He . . . *he has chosen me!*"

Caught up in her fervor, she did not see the women's exchanged glances, the occasional discreet whispering to each other.

"How many of you will *he* choose? All? Yes! All of you have made it here on your own. For it is through our ancestry that come secrets immemorial!"

She felt a presence. She didn't have to look around. *Nyarlathotep.* She heard the clicking of footsteps approaching.

"The first demonstration of fealty is of the blood," she said, gesturing toward the same cup she had bled over, the cup that had disappeared.

The women stepped closer together, put their wrists forward over the cup.

Zane brandished the knife Nyarlathotep had used to cut her wrist when she first came upon the terrace.

"And now we cut."

I am chosen . . . I am chosen for this . . . he chose his representative . . . I will lead others into glory . . .

§

Tonya Liburd shares a birthday with Simeon Daniel and Ray Bradbury, which may tell you a little something about her. She is a 2017 and 2018 Rhysling nominee and has been longlisted in the 2015 Carter V. Cooper (Vanderbilt)/Exile Short Fiction Competition. Her fiction is used in Nisi Shawl's workshops as an example of "code switching" and in Tananarive Due's course at UCLA, which has featured Jordan Peele as a guest lecturer. She is also the Senior Editor of *Abyss & Apex* magazine. You can find her blogging at Spiderlilly.com and on Twitter at @somesillywowzer.

Office Hours and After

S.L. Edwards

T HE FIRST VIGIL FOR TREVOR THOMAS WAS HELD THE NIGHT AFTER THEY found his corpse.

I didn't have any candles, hadn't thought to buy any, but my roommate left a scented lilac one before she left. It was a big, wide thing that I cautiously lit and cradled with both hands. I checked myself in the mirror. Purple scarf, black hoodie, gloves. It was December in New England, and though it hadn't yet snowed, there was a biting chill blowing its way from the north. When the wind hit you, it felt like you were being cut into ribbons.

I cradled the candle and walked out of the dorm.

Campus had been quiet since they found his body. Trevor was discovered in the bushes outside of the Department of Ancient History, his hands bound behind his back, his mouth gagged, and his rib cage wide open for all the world to see. On his stomach, beneath the gaping wound along his chest, Miskatonic University PD found an intricate symbol: a nine-pointed star associated with the "alignment" that would wake Cthulhu from its slumber.

They hadn't found him until the morning after his murder. There were probably screams; how couldn't there have been? They had found a pool of blood in a department hallway, indicating that the murder had begun in the building before the killer dragged the body outside. But every campus police officer had been at the Esoteric Order of Dagon the night Trevor died, trying to deal with the protests and counter-protests brought on by a visit of Congressman Marsh.

A wind rushed up and bit my exposed cheeks and nose, roaring as if from the vacuum between the stars. I felt the blood run to my face and gulped back something sour. Despite the cold, it was important that I be there. I hadn't come to Miskatonic to make friends or have relationships, a pronouncement that I wore on my sleeve as prominently as possible. I had a way of making the air colder around me, a way of silencing people with an icy stare before they could even begin their small talk. Some people, boys really, still tried talking to me. I was pretty after all, a fact that made people even more disdainful of my outspoken disinterest in them. But my defenses normally kept anyone who wanted anything from me away. It didn't make me popular, but again, I didn't want to be. Instead, I just wanted all the time I could to study. To delve into every secret Miskatonic could offer.

The nickname—"Loathsome" Laura Nodens—came from the girls, and the boys called me the "Wallflower Witch." To tell the truth, I actually quite liked both. The tendency of people to distance and shun what they couldn't understand made me smile.

But that wasn't the case with Trevor. My first quarter at Miskatonic, Trevor had been one of my TAs. Over the winter break, he caught me eating alone in the dining hall and sat across from me without asking. My eyes did not scare him away, the cold air did not make him uneasy or nervous, and I realized he didn't want anything from me other than to see if I was okay. He didn't stay long after I explained that my home was a bit too far away to go back to, just nodded and said to feel free to come by his office hours next semester if I needed any help with classes.

Curiosity overtook me, and despite myself, I made a friend. Albeit not a *great* friend, not a particularly *close* friendship, but Trevor had become something of a mentor of mine. His death was hard on me, and I wanted to make sure that everyone understood who, exactly, Miskatonic had lost.

To my relief and delight, the quad was alive with small, sparking flames. Orange stars wavered and blew in the turning wind. Trevor's smiling face beamed out from poster boards, framed by cards and sticky notes explaining how much he was loved and how much he was missed. His students whispered how good of a teacher he was; his teachers responded that he was a good student too. Solemnly, they asked each other about his family, about his girlfriend and parents.

People, for all their inane stupidity, could be profoundly kind.

And it was because of this simple, inexplicable kindness that I pledged to find Trevor's killer.

II

One of the perks of being "loathsome" is that I scared my roommate away pretty early.

The poor girl hadn't really understood why she felt nauseous every night or why she always smelled rotting eggs in the morning. She had awful nightmares too, things that sent her reeling from her mattress and screaming as if she was being torn into with a jagged, stone knife. She finally went back home to Boston, and I understand from campus gossip that the family believed she had a nervous breakdown.

Perfectly explainable. After all, *I* had no nightmares, and *I* never thought the room smelled particularly bad.

But after she left, the room was mine. I covered the walls with blank, butcher-paper canvases. For all the mystique around blood and "vital fluids," sharpies do just fine for drawing symbols. Elder signs and pentagrams interwove to form a complicated hieroglyphic algebra that covered every surface of my room. There were spells for virtually everything I could think of: for entering my own dreams, for keeping out things from beyond.

At the moment however, I only needed a door.

I sat cross-legged on the floor of my room and focused on a rectangle interwoven with circles and jutting, angular lines. I squinted and held my breath for as long as I could, letting the room fade to darkness and exploding stars before my lungs gave in, and I breathed, quickly reaching for the symbol and opening the portal.

My destination was not far away, and I would only have to travel in the space-between for a few moments. That said, I frowned as I entered the domain of the Outer Gods, greeted by their howling jeers.

The infernal chorus roared as I fell, screaming obscenities in the tongues of Lemuria and Atlantis, calling me everything but my name. I laughed in response, and the force of my voice was enough to quiet their bleating and trumpeting, so they would focus their attention more carefully on the pale object streaming across their realm. By the time they realized what I was, I was already where I needed to be, well beyond their domain.

MUPD.

Officers in their too-formal blue uniforms darted from one room to the next, piles of manila folders and papers in their hands. Nervous eyes darting from sleepless sockets, pale flesh covered in sweat that stank of stale coffee and sleepless panic. A cacophony of swears, ringing telephones, and angry shouting. One voice boomed, another cried. An officer consoled a young woman who claimed (lied) that she had seen the murder. Another officer drafted a statement to the press, muttering obscenities under his breath as he imagined stepping in front of the cameras.

In my astral form, I couldn't be seen. In this form, I was more sensitive to their thoughts, an ethereal and telepathic sponge if I let myself be. I faded into the background, seeping into the cracks in the walls as minutes became hours. As I crept into their minds, I realized that none of them had the true picture, though some of them knew far more than they should. Some had been bribed by faculty for their silence; others had witnessed ancient rites. Still others had blood on their hands—evil men with soft smiles and friendly faces. And all of them burned with thoughts of Trevor Thomas, of the riots during Congressman Marsh's visit.

National attention was on the university again, and they needed to find answers fast before a panic started and the governor sent in the national guard. It had happened once before in the 1970s when that Whateley kid had been murdered by a faculty member.

Arkham hadn't been the same since.

I hummed to myself and let their thoughts pour into me—collecting everything they knew.

Even what they wouldn't tell each other.

When I had what I needed, I launched myself back through the void between the worlds, now silent. They wouldn't dare taunt me now that they could recognize me for what I was. Unadorned of flesh, they only bowed in reverence.

The eyes of my body opened wide as breath filled my lungs.

It was a matter of finding enough blank space between my symbols. I wrote down every name, every fact that I had absorbed while projecting into the police station. There was the Esoteric Order of Dagon; it was one of their symbols that was carved into Trevor's stomach after all. It wasn't known if Trevor had any contact with the order, but apparently a few of their more zealous members had become more aggressive in the wake of the congressman's visit. Human sacrifice wasn't a stretch, though they had publicly abandoned the practice in the late 1940s.

Then there were his fellow graduate students in the department. Miskatonic was known for attracting some of the most brilliant scholars in the world, and the graduate students were no exception. But they were famous for their infighting, cutthroat young scholars vying for grants that were becoming scarcer every year. Grad students regularly suffered bouts of nausea, hallucinations, and vertigo that made them miss important deadlines. Weeks later, they would find someone had slipped poison into their coffee or a symbol under their mattress. It wasn't difficult to imagine one Miskatonic graduate student killing another, either out of jealousy or simply to reduce competition. After all, it had happened before.

I sighed. The pool of suspects was already wide. There were hundreds of graduate students, and if the motive of Trevor's killers was simply to reduce competition, it could be any of them. University grants could go to any department, and outside funding was even more nebulous and ambiguous. In ancient history alone, there were fifty graduate students of various rank and progress. If I was going to look into them, I would need to begin with his cohort.

I wrote ten names on the wall. I knew three of them, TAs I had my freshman year. I hadn't cared for any of them, all of them typically snide and hateful toward undergraduates.

Then there was Professor Arthur Richards. The police believed he may be a suspect, though they hoped not. Dr. Richards had been accused in the past of involving his research assistants in ancient rites, of performing secret rituals on his students without their knowledge or consent. The rumor had been, in fact, why I took one of his seminars my first semester at Miskatonic. But the old man was a fool without even enough knowledge to be a dangerous one.

The last group of suspects came from Omega House. They were a powerful fraternity, and one that Trevor had an apparent falling out with after a few of the brothers plagiarized on their final paper. The story MUPD told was that he had complained to the dean about receiving pressure from Omega leadership to look the other way. The Omegas were a bad lot: just the right mix of typically attractive, intelligent, and hotheaded to also be cruel and reckless. It didn't help that the Omegas' pockets ran deep into the undercurrent of wealth beneath Arkham. In virtually every market, illegal and otherwise, the Omegas' tendrils spread far and wide. There was a joke, whispered only off-campus and behind closed doors, that the Omegas were "the Illuminati in training."

All of that said, they would be the easiest.

I'd start with them first.

But Trevor had died, and despite myself, thoughts of his death were weighing on my mind. I stretched, rising from the floor and sighing loudly. Looking into the mirror, I saw the day had been harder on me than I thought. Disheveled hair, dim eyes. I sometimes needed to remind myself that bodies had limits, that if I wasn't careful, I would break mine.

I slipped into cool sheets and sang myself songs of Kadath. As the melody became a soft whisper, I launched myself beyond the wall of sleep, enveloped in the arms of those who knew me once before.

III

The Omega Brothers were awful, foul people. Smug, vain things who hid the knowledge of their own smallness behind smiles and vestments of power. They attempted to dominate every room they entered, and it was perhaps for that reason more than any other that Omegas so frequently clashed with Trevor.

Trevor Thomas had a booming voice, one that filled the room when he spoke. He had a wild smile and a stage presence that the best professors and lecturers took years to master. I remembered a moment when he had kicked a group of brothers out for talking loudly in discussion.

"We'll go to the administration with this bullshit," they had screamed at him.

"I am looking forward to it," he had yelled back.

We all laughed.

Looking in the mirror, I saw my smile. Reflexively, I resumed my normal expression and brushed my hair. The Omegas would be easy enough to get information out of, but it wouldn't hurt to be outwardly charming either. Before anything, the Omegas were boys aspiring to be men, stupid little kids only partially aware of what they were and trying to be something else.

A slim-fitting black dress. Soft pink lipstick. Diamond earrings.

I held my pendant in my hand, wondering if I should leave it. It was a simple, inconspicuous thing that only the trained eye or upmost initiate would recognize; nothing but a triangle circumscribed by a circle. When I wore it above my clothes, I only received innocent, naive questions as to which Harry Potter character was my favorite. It would be nothing to leave it behind.

But it is one of the few things I have that reminds me of who I am. Of *what* I am.

I slipped it beneath my dress, relieved in the knowledge that it was there.

Then came the oils, the perfumes. Incantations for Shub-Niggurath. For Yog-Sothoth. For blind, nuclear Azathoth. I surveyed myself in the mirror. I smiled and pretended to laugh.

The Omegas would be easy.

The house was a faux-Greek monolith, its symbol attempting to invoke a feeling of doom and futility. The long porch was lined with pillars where members drew symbols in spray paint, sharpies, and blood. One of the thousands of symbols, none of which the brothers properly understood, kept out astral forms. But the Omegas themselves let everyone in, smiling as they surveyed the line of partygoers who sought for a moment to get away from their stress and studies.

Inside, the house was lit only by dim neon-purple lights; loud music thumped, and warm bodies pushed against each other in a haze of sweat and alcohol. I felt the eyes on me, the eyes that would give me power. This sort of magic was easy and cheap, usually beneath me.

A red plastic cup came into my hand, beer that tasted like warm, bubbly water. I drank it with a smile and a flash of my eyes. I snaked my way across the dance floor, weaving ornate patterns of legs and arms, my blood alive and hot. For a moment, I forgot myself and enjoyed it. For a moment, I wondered how great it would be to follow them into reckless abandon, to leave myself behind and wade into the alcohol and the hum of the bass. For a moment, the vibrations flowed through me better than any dream song.

And then I caught their eyes.

The brothers Trevor had kicked out of his class.

They probably didn't recognize me; I have ways of making people's eyes drift when I want. But now I had them, and when I flashed my teeth, I knew their hearts were palpitating. I could make them feel what they truly were.

Children.

A few playful laughs, a slow trace up one of their shoulders.

I suggested to one, the one who had so rudely shouted that he would go to the administration over Trevor, that we go upstairs. He gulped, and I laughed, leading him by the hand and telling him that I wanted to talk. That the music was too loud.

I walked him slowly, teasingly past the crowds who wooed and clapped. Hands came down on his back, red cups went up.

I opened a door and led him through, a mattress on the ground and a mess of sheets and swimsuit model posters.

"Tell me about Trevor Thomas," I said, locking the door behind us.

His face went from an anxious smile to a dumbfounded, blank expression.

"What?" was all he could manage.

The lights around us dimmed.

I looked at my hand, impatiently waiting. The lights flickered again. Behind me, a bulb shattered and burst.

He jumped, his shoulders lurching as his eyes widened.

"Oh God, it's *you*!" He made a motion for the door, and I let him fall into my eyes. He froze, breath quivering and sweat gathering. Around us, darkness rose, and the shadows began to roar. With my palm, I slowly and softly pushed his chest, sending him toppling onto his mattress, so I could stand over him.

His eyes shifted away from me and toward the darkness at my back.

Growling rose all around us.

He was getting paler by the second.

"Don't look at them. Look at me. You'll just make them nervous."

But he couldn't look away. I brought the back of my hand swiftly across his face. It reddened and bled. Rage pooled into his eyes and voice.

"You *bitch*," he said with all the vitriol of someone who considered it a powerful word. "Do you know who I am?"

"Ricky Baker, senior, business major. You're going to inherit quite a bit of money, and everyone knows that. But what most don't know is what you did to that girl, Ricky." I leaned down so that my face was level to his. A long black tendril came from the darkness behind me and wrapped itself gingerly around his neck.

He reached for it only to have it tighten slightly. He frantically shook his head.

I hated him more than ever. Egotistical, assessing his life as worth saving. But he was little more than a stain on the universe, and a malignant one at that. As tears welled in his eyes, I decided that I may end him one day.

But not then. Not when I just wanted him to talk.

"Tell me about Trevor Thomas. The Omegas weren't fans of his. Know anything about his death?"

He trembled, unresponsive, gaze shifting from me to the growing void behind.

I smiled, "Maybe I should tell you a little about what's back there. How many eyes? How many teeth?" He looked back at me, mouth falling open. "Maybe I should tell you that everything you've read is wrong. That you could not possibly know, no book could possibly *tell* you how much it hurts being torn apart. That no writer, Al-Hazred or otherwise, knew how *long* they spend playing with their food before they eat it. I'll give you to them, Ricky. I *will*. Your life doesn't mean anything to me. So tell me what I want to know, and you get to live the rest of your natural life. Don't, and you'll live for days . . . months, maybe years. But it won't be pleasant, I promise."

He gagged up a choking, wet sob. Real fear—for the first time in his life, he was feeling it.

"Just breathe, Ricky, just talk to me."

"W-we," he stammered, "had nothing to do with it."

"How do I know that? What if it was another brother, not you?"

"We knew the protest was going to happen, that there was probably gonna be a riot. We wanted e-e-everyone on lockdown! To avoid the news."

The tendril at his neck tightened, and another came from the darkness to hover above his face.

A scream died in his throat.

"I could check that, Ricky. If I found out you were lying . . . I'd *kill* you."

"I'm not! I'm not! Oh God."

The tendril left a red, burning mark as it unwrapped itself from his neck and retreated back into the darkness. The lights returned slowly. The noises of the party drifted through thin walls, happy shouting and the thrum of music.

I went for the door.

"Is that it?" He asked in a voice between relief and panic.

I gave him one last, sly look: "Not quite. You'll wake up from nightmares each morning for years. You'll wake up, screaming, writhing in your own mess. But when you realize that you deserve those nightmares . . . that's when you'll *really* hurt, Ricky."

I left Ricky sobbing into his pillow. Behind me, the party continued as normal, and already people were forgetting I was ever there.

IV

The Department of Ancient History had an open forum about Trevor's death, what it would mean for the department and its students. The lecture hall was packed with distraught and disinterested students, those who hung on their professors' every word alongside those who idly played with their phones. I sat in the back, examining the speakers as carefully as I could while surveying the crowd below.

Professor Richards was more charismatic than I remembered, speaking with a booming voice and waving hands. He was a tenured faculty member, known for his seminal volume *The Primordial Leng: The Rise and Fall of Pre-Human Civilization*. The book had established him as a name in the field, and because of it, he was cited in virtually every book and article that came out of the Antarctic discovery. But the professor had gotten old, and his relevance was fading along with his greying beard and thinning hair.

In front of those young students though, he was alive. He spoke of Trevor's intense interest in shoggoths, his research into the mi-go folklore of Northern Vermont. He recalled fondly mentoring Trevor, taking him in as an integral member of his research group. I could hear the crying rise from the students who were realizing (for perhaps the first time) that Trevor was more than just their TA.

As the students cleared, wiping their eyes and slinging their phones back into their pockets, I waited behind, resolved to be the last.

Dawn, my TA for Pre-Human Warfare, seemed nervous when she saw me. Most people were uneasy around me, and Dawn was no exception. She was twenty-four and had already acquired a lifetime of bitterness. Long blonde hair tied in a ponytail, pointed green eyes that leaked condescension and scorn. Her students knew she was intelligent, but she kept her knowledge guarded, driving office visitors away with terse and angry answers to even the friendliest of questions.

"Hi, Laura." Her voice was frantic, desperate to be anywhere else.

"Hi." I responded flatly.

"Was . . . Trevor a TA of yours?"

"My first semester, he gave me some feedback on my paper on the Yig Mounds. I visited him in office hours a lot, and he always encouraged me to speak up in class. I was hoping I'd get to have him as a TA again . . ."

"Yeah," Dawn's eyes drifted toward her watch. "We were working on a project with Professor Richards. He was brilliant, and I'll admit it made me a little jealous."

"No reason to be jealous. You graduate students are chronically hard on yourselves."

Arthur Richards had a ruddy complexion, reddened with the strain of standing longer than he was used to. He was a big man, wide in shoulder and stomach with a barreled chest that belonged to a former wrestler. Brown eyes shone dimly from under his glasses as he reached out to extend his hand to mine.

"Have I had you in one of my lectures?"

"Yes, Professor. My first semester. Trevor was my TA."

"Ah, yes. Of course! Well," his face became solemn, "we are all deeply saddened at his loss. We are coming to know he meant a great deal to our undergraduates. I've referred so many to campus services in the wake of his murder."

"I'm going somewhere next to talk to someone."

"Very good. Well, I apologize, but"—he placed a hand on Dawn's shoulder, and she jumped—"we need to leave. There is a meeting within the department, but please feel free to come to my office hours if you would like to talk more."

"Of course, Professor."

I watched Dawn and the professor leave the room. I have always been fascinated in the responses mankind can muster against adversity, against its own looming doom. The professor seemed to have found new energy, new life in a need to be strong for those around him. Meanwhile, Dawn was unsure and more than a little anxious. Guilt? Maybe. But then I thought of how she jumped at the professor's touch. Maybe there was something going on there, something taboo or even criminal.

I slung my backpack over my shoulder and walked out into winter.

The dead yellow grass was littered with brown leaves. Each building was nearly uniform in design, commissioned in deliberate sequence by the wealthy heirs of *Mayflower* colonists who kept their family trees in gilded frames to show visitors. White roofs, narrow windows, and brown bricks loomed from every side. Every now and then, there was something particularly obtrusive, a building that was out of line with the others because a donor had insisted upon it.

Such was the Temple of the Esoteric Order of Dagon, a lightning rod for periodic controversy.

The temple was a sleek black mess of tall spires and red-stained windows. I thought it was laughable when I first saw it, a child's drawing of an evil lair, Sagrada Familia made miniature and menacing. Walking up the obsidian steps, I was overtaken by the sea smell that wafted from inside. On the doors, a metal emblem of "great" Cthulhu rested, its tentacles pouring out of a circle and resting just above the handles.

I snorted and pushed inward.

There were no visitors, no souls in the black cathedral, only quiet rows of pulpits lined with shells and scales. Red hymnals full of raving, nonsensical script rested on the purple cushions, a testament to the order's conflicting desires to appear both modern and ancient. Both comparable to and above other faiths.

Out of boredom, I lifted one of the hymnals and inhaled its musty smell.

"Can I help you, young lady?"

There was a tall, ghostly man whose dark skin only barely concealed the skeleton beneath. He wore a black robe adorned in emerald tentacles, rising from the frills of his robe like flames. His face told me that I had already won, that he had underestimated me and would soon tell me everything that I wanted to know.

I reached under the neck of my shirt and revealed my pendant. He peered, stooping his neck and narrowing his eyes. I walked closer, and he gasped, his eyes moving from the pendant to my face.

"My apologies. Follow me into my office, and we'll talk."

I nodded, letting my feet slap the floor behind his as we calmly walked toward the back of the cathedral.

"How's Providence this time of year? Are you bringing new wisdom today?" He was eager, a child barking at the heels of their teacher.

"Not today."

"Hrm."

At the head of the chapel, aquatic sculptures stood proud and golden. The half-fish, half-man depiction of Dagon consuming a human torso; Mother Hydra birthing a legion of angler fish; Cthulhu, rising above the waves. I repressed my scoffing and followed the deacon into his office. I sat across from him at his desk, and he poured wine into a chalice, no doubt a gift that had been brought to him from the depths of some sunken Spanish galleon. It was sweet and sour on my tongue, unusual and alluring.

"If not to impart your starry wisdom, why are you here this day, sister?"

I sipped the wine again. "I wanted to ask if any of your members were involved in the murder of Trevor Thomas."

He shook his head. "No, we weren't."

"No one wanted to give the congressman a human sacrifice for his visit?"

"Plenty wanted to, yes. But I stepped in." He leaned back in his chair and inhaled, preparing to give a speech he had given before. One which he probably rehearsed in front of the mirror. "Earthly politics is a tool, a vehicle for power—little more. And such overt activities limit our ability to use this tool effectively. It cuts off our ability to channel and broadcast our message, no?"

I resisted the urge to roll my eyes. Before I could respond, he continued, words he had no doubt spoken thousands of times before.

"Don't you believe that all will be resolved when Great Cthulhu rises from the sea? When the oceans run red and we, the anointed and initiated, are left to claim the remaining lands for our gods?"

I finished my glass and placed it before me. I hated this, and I wanted him to know it.

"I think that 'believers' are just as likely to die with 'non-believers.'"

His mouth hung open. Surely, the Cthulhu cult would have accepted the inevitably that its members would be food just like the rest of mankind. Yet every time I gave this speech, they were surprised. I smiled, taking pleasure in imparting my truth.

"There's nothing special about 'great' Cthulhu, and your order practices exactly the sort of politics that you seem to disdain. There is truth in your message, yes, sure. Maybe you can sing it to yourself when the Great Old Ones are flaying your flesh for all eternity. Maybe you'll take comfort that you were right about the screaming, searing void that you were so eagerly rushing toward."

I rose, annoyed and impatient. The deacon's mouth gaped, stuttering and frightened.

I left the temple as knowledgeable as when I entered.

V

At 3 a.m., the door to Wilmarth Hall was wide open. I braced myself, thinking of what half-truth excuse a sophomore could give a police officer as to why she followed them after hours. Walking through the door, I was reminded that the hall had been locked down for a few days now.

It was still an active crime scene with yellow police tape still up. The blood had been cleared away, but I could still smell the lingering, bitter death. It gleamed, too pristine, too clean for a hall that most students walked through at least once during their Miskatonic career. In the night, abandoned, it seemed more like a catacomb and less like a lecture hall.

There was a crash on the second floor, above me. A long, metallic grating sound and the shattering of glass, a scream that mingled with the soft roar of radio static. Then silence.

I smiled.

My shoes slapped the stairs, loud and deliberate. But the sounds resumed, too taken up in their panic and despair to notice me. A short walk in a dark hallway, and I found myself at the TA offices, a place I had spent many hours, talking with Trevor.

The place where, I now knew, my friend had died.

Opening the door, I saw a shadow. It threw scattered papers into the air and howled in gurgling despair. My stomach dropped, dreading that some fool had actually unleashed a shoggoth on campus. But then the static-filled scream subsided, the arms stopped writhing, and I heard a distinctly human sob. The form fell to the floor, collapsing on its knees among the tossed papers.

In the pale moonlight that shone through the one open window, Professor Arthur Richards curled his fists into his beard. He turned slowly toward me, eyes narrowed and teeth bared. And then I knew.

I had been a fool, thinking Trevor's killer was human.

I kept quiet, letting him get a look at me before he spoke. He'd try to explain himself. His kind always tried to explain themselves.

He smiled with glinting, white teeth. "I see your necklace now."

I didn't respond. He laughed, pleased with himself.

"You probably just wanted to see what you could find. You never were looking for me, were you?"

"I would have been if I had known what I was looking for."

"Heh." He stooped now, lumbering toward me in long, striding steps.

"When did Trevor figure it out?" I asked.

"Oh, almost at the beginning. I am afraid he knew Professor Richards too well. The boy actually *cared* about the professor. Unlike so many others who only cared about his work. The poor boy actually had a heart." His smile was breaking his face. "I had to cut it out."

I stood my ground, not turning or running away from him.

"That's what I never understood about the yithians. Why dissect things? Why take them apart when you already know how they work?"

He stood over me, lowering his head to mine. "For fun."

He lifted me up by my armpits and slammed me into a chalkboard. The metal shelf jammed into my back, shooting fire across my spine. In reflex, I screamed, biting on my lower lip and tasting the coppery tang of my blood. He held me there, his face so close that it bristled against mine.

"What is strange to me," he continued as his hand moved down to clasp my pendant, "is that I did not see that you would find me. I suppose the Crawler's witches have found how to conceal themselves from precognition."

Now it was my turn to smile.

My turn to laugh.

"Not . . . one of its 'witches.'"

He leaned down, chuckling. "What is that, girl?"

"Not one of its witches. One of its *aspects*."

I revealed myself, unfolding my flesh and allowing my form to seep through the thin veil between worlds. My thousand mouths poured from behind the shadows, my eyes leering from every corner. Around the room, I began to sing as I overtook that small patch of the universe. It had been so long since I shot off from my original form, since I had sent the Laura-aspect into this reality to probe and accumulate, that I had forgotten the satisfaction of being whole. In ecstasy, I unfolded, clawed tendrils and piping nostrils spilling from the walls in heaps of dark, piling flesh.

The yithian screamed, falling onto his hands. I fell and watched him scramble to pull himself back up. I stabbed into him with a sharpened tendril, piercing through his chest and lifting him into the air. He spilt his gore out on the floor, choking and sobbing.

"Please—"

A clawed arm tore into his chest, feeling the spot where his heart was.

His screams became wet whimpers.

The yithian whispered for mercy in its native language, a pre-human tongue that I knew all too well.

But it was too late. I had forgotten how it felt to be together, having been separated for so long. I resolved that I would not go apart hungry.

I pulled him toward a wide, gaping mouth.

Passing a human body was always painful.

Luckily, I wouldn't be doing it with just one stomach.

§

S.L. Edwards is a Texan currently residing in California. He enjoys dark poetry, dark fiction, and darker beer. His debut short story collection *Whiskey and Other Unusual Ghosts* is now available.

Student Body

Richard Lee Byers

THE CANISTERS, AS THEY WERE STILL CALLED, HAD COME A LONG WAY SINCE the early days. The person inside could talk, walk, and handle objects. Still, despite all the practice he'd had, it took a while for young Mr. Wilson to take his seat at the conference table. The animate gray metal shell didn't bend in exactly the right places.

At that, he was quicker than Z'Shaa. The sapient fungus didn't bend in the right places either and had too many sets of pincers and assorted other limbs. A membranous wing flapped within inches of Professor Drake who flinched less perhaps at the threat of a swat than at the limb's moldy smell.

Alice Harper tried not to give way to impatience as they got themselves situated. As dean of student affairs, it was part of her job to sort out the problems of individual undergrads even if she begrudged the time it took away from attending to matters affecting the university as a whole.

"Does anyone need coffee?" she asked. "Water?" She turned to her secretary. "Then, Camille, if you'll start taking the minutes, we'll begin. It's January 11, 2018, 10:00 a.m., and this is a hearing of the Miskatonic University Student Grievance Committee. Present are Professor Drake from the Astronomy Department; Professor Stewart from the School of Medicine; Visiting Professor Z'Shaa of the mi-go; Michael Wilson, a junior; and me, Alice Harper, presiding. Mr. Wilson, why don't you tell us why you've come to us today?"

"Are you kidding? Look at me." Wilson's electronic voice was as incapable of inflection as Stephen Hawking's, and perhaps realizing as much, he clanged the canister's fist on its broad metal chest to convey his anger and distress.

Inwardly, Alice sighed. These hearings were always more difficult when the student was already belligerent when they came through the door. "Yes, of course," she said. "But perhaps you could lay out the whole story. For the record."

"Fine," Wilson said. "My major is astrophysics. Professor Drake is one of my teachers, and he told me he wanted to recommend me to study abroad for a semester. Way abroad as in outer space if I was willing to do it in a robot body. My real body was supposed to be kept safe in a freezer. But you all let it thaw out and get rotten."

A bespectacled squirrel of a man with coppery hair going thin on top, Drake said, "I think it's important to note for the record that the Astronomy Department is not responsible for keeping students' flesh-and-blood bodies safe. We simply select candidates for the program."

"My people aren't responsible either," Z'Shaa buzzed, a dozen antennae, the source of its voice, vibrating around its convoluted bulb of a head. "We extract and transfer the brains. We transport and supervise the students as they pursue their studies on Yuggoth and at the observatories out in the Kuiper belt. We don't monitor the cold storage here on Earth."

"Of course," said Drake. "We all know who does." As if they'd rehearsed beforehand—and Alice suspected they had or at least agreed where to direct every iota of blame—they turned their heads in unison in the direction of Professor Stewart.

Stewart was a heavyset man with a bullfrog roll of flab under his chin and rosacea in his cheeks. The accusation made his face turn ruddier still. "Don't put this on me," he said. "The mutant rats escaped from Professor Yerby's lab before I ever came here, and I've requested five times for them to be exterminated. Or exorcised. Whatever. I warned administration they could compromise important research and damage valuable equipment. They gnaw on the power cords."

With Drake and Z'Shaa already blaming the School of Medicine, Alice was reluctant to pile on, but she would have felt remiss if she didn't ask what seemed an obvious question. "Shouldn't someone have been checking on the cryostasis pods?"

Stewart gave her an *"Et tu, Brute"* sort of glower. "Yes, but as it turns out, the graduate assistant snuck a date into the building when he was supposed to be covering his shift. He's been reprimanded."

"It doesn't matter whose fault it is," Wilson said. "I want to know how you're going to help me."

Drake frowned. "Son, let us examine the situation in an orderly manner, and we'll sort everything out in due course."

"No," Stewart said, "Mr. Wilson is absolutely right. It no longer matters how it all reached this point. Our focus now should be to set it right, and fortunately, my colleagues and I are entirely capable of doing that."

"You are?" Wilson asked.

"Certainly," Stewart said. "Here at Miskatonic, scientists have been experimenting with reanimating the dead for a hundred years."

"'Experimenting?'" Wilson repeated.

"I chose that word poorly," Stewart said.

In fact, he hadn't. Alice was no medical researcher, but like everyone conversant with the university's secret activities, she knew the School of Medicine had been tinkering with Herbert West's original formulae for a century and still hadn't worked out all the kinks. But saying so wouldn't move this situation any closer to a resolution.

"Admittedly," Stewart continued, "it's a complex process, and we've never had to replace a living brain in a skull prior to reanimation. But I'm confident of a positive result." He hesitated. "Reasonably confident."

"I don't want my brain stuck in the head of a corpse."

"But it's *your* corpse," Alice said.

"I don't care."

She sighed. "It's your choice of course. If Professor Stewart is confident, so am I, but I can understand if it makes you squeamish." She turned to the head of the medical school. "What other options do we have?"

Stewart pouted. "Well . . . I would prefer to keep this matter strictly within the purview of my own discipline with Professor Z'Shaa contributing obviously . . ."

He paused, perhaps in the hope that stating his preference would pressure Wilson into giving in. It didn't.

". . . but if that's not feasible," Stewart continued, "we could involve Gordon from chemistry and Bentley from theology and use the Ward-Curwen method."

"What's that?" Wilson asked.

"We reduce your corpse to powder and recite incantations over it. As long as we have all of it—which we do—there's a relatively high probability of success. And no intricate surgery or dealing with the goo and general mess of decomposition." Stewart gave Wilson a hopeful smile.

"Wait a minute," said the young man in the metal body. "Wouldn't you still have to stick my brain back in my head and turn it to powder too?"

Stewart's smile wilted a little. "Well . . . technically . . ."

"You already killed my body. I'm not letting you kill my brain."

Alice gave Wilson a look she'd practiced. It was intended to make her look like a disappointed yet kindly aunt and prompt a student to moderate his attitude. "Mr. Wilson, you've now rejected two reasonable options. I hate to say it, but I'm sensing a lack of trust."

Wilson's dome of a head with its round dark lenses for eyes swiveled toward her. "You think?"

"Come on, Mike," said Drake, "that chip on your shoulder isn't helping anyone. Didn't you learn a great deal in the outer Solar System? Didn't you have a good time?"

"A lot of it was awful," Wilson replied, "and I would never have gone if I'd known this could happen."

"Professor Stewart had the right idea," Alice said. "Let's not fixate on how we got here. Let's solve the problem. What else might you try, Professor?"

Stewart shrugged his rounded shoulders. "If Mr. Wilson is *absolutely* opposed to having his living brain resident in a corpse even briefly or to there being a few inconsequential minutes where the brain technically ceases to exist . . ."

Once again, he paused and looked at the metal figure, and once again, Wilson refused to take the bait.

". . . then that leaves implanting his brain in someone else's body. Although I'm concerned that takes us into a gray area ethically speaking."

"Our first obligation is to our students." Alice turned to Z'Shaa. "Is it feasible?"

"It's not as easy as reattaching a brain to its own body," the mi-go droned, "or placing it in a canister specifically designed for it. There could be some loss of fine motor skills or sensory acuity."

"I think Mr. Wilson would prefer that to his current situation," Alice said. "Where do we find the donor?"

"The Athletics Department!" Drake said. "Most of those jocks are virtually brainless already, and our Mr. Wilson can have intellect and muscles both!"

Alice suspected the possibility tapped into some private fantasy of Drake's own. "No," she said, "we have an obligation to *all* the students, even ones who aren't exactly distinguishing themselves as scholars, and besides, the coaches would lynch me if I authorized anything that weakened one of the teams. It has to be a townie."

Drake sighed. "If you really think that's better. The . . . donor may not look anything like Mr. Wilson. Someone from the School of Medicine will need to perform plastic surgery."

Stewart nodded. "Professor Francis can—"

"Are you crazy?" Wilson said. "You can't murder somebody else to help me."

"We're out of options," Alice said. "Aren't we?" No one spoke up to contradict her. "So think about the implications for yourself if we don't proceed with any of the plans you've been so quick to reject. Think about your family. And if that doesn't sway you, think about the greater good. You're one of Miskatonic's brightest. Who has more to contribute to the world, you or some nobody?"

"I won't agree to it," Wilson said. "Think of something else."

"I just explained," Alice said, "there isn't anything else. If you won't consent to let us put you back in a human body via any of the methods available, you'll have to make do with the canister. Obviously, that means remaining in the Restricted areas of the campus."

"Or," Drake said, "Professor Z'Shaa and his associates could take you back to Yuggoth."

"I'm never going back there."

"I'd be willing to make you second author on any paper I published based on your observations. It's a rare opportunity for an undergraduate."

"No, and I'm not going to spend the rest of my life as a robot monster trapped in this cellar either. You have to think of something."

"We're talking in circles," Alice said. "Perhaps what you really need is time to process. We could reconvene the week after next—"

Camille looked up from her note taking. "Excuse me, Dean, but you'll be away at the conference in Chicago."

Alice nodded. "Right you are. We could meet again in three weeks—"

"There has to be an answer today," Wilson said. "Otherwise, I'll let people see me. I'll tell my story on TV."

"You can't do that!" said Drake. "You signed a non-disclosure agreement! The university will sue you!"

"I'm the one who should sue."

"Mr. Wilson," Alice said, "once again, I appeal to your sense of the greater good. You wouldn't want to hurt Miskatonic's reputation. We could lose funding. Perhaps even accreditation."

"I don't care."

So much for him then. Alice and the others had made an honest effort to help him, he'd rejected every suggestion, and now he was threatening the school? If he weren't so muleheaded and self-centered, he'd realize he'd just forfeited any claim on everyone's good will. Because the university came first.

Such being the case, she needed to get him safely locked away lest he make good on his threats. Hoping the faculty members would follow her lead, she widened her eyes in an attempt to look as if an idea had just occurred to her.

"The cloning research!" she said. "Would that work?"

Stewart blinked. "The which?"

She kicked out under the table and connected with his shin. He jerked. She hoped Wilson didn't notice.

"The cloning research," she repeated.

"Yes!" Stewart said. "Of course! Why didn't I think of that? Mr. Wilson, the, um, core of your body didn't thaw and decay as quickly as the outer layers, which is to say not all your cells were compromised. We can harvest viable stem cells and grow you a new body in a matter of days. Meanwhile, you should check back into the clinic, so we can, ah, run tests and—"

"Liars," Wilson said.

Like all his statements, that one came in the canister's electronic monotone. Perhaps that was why, rude and offensive though it was, neither Alice nor her colleagues realized it signaled an immediate intention to act, so he took them by surprise.

Wilson sprang up from his chair, knocking it over in the process. He turned to the mi-go sitting beside him and punched repeatedly into Z'Shaa's bulb of a head. His metal fists penetrated the fungal mass like bullets, and every time he pulled one back, he ripped away a handful of spongy matter. Acrid-smelling spores filled the air with a brown haze, and everyone possessed of a human respiratory system coughed and choked.

Once Wilson finished effectively decapitating Z'Shaa, he turned on everybody else—the others' difficulty breathing making them easy prey. He grabbed Stewart by his pudgy neck and crushed it with one quick squeeze and then tumbled Drake to the floor and flattened his torso with a stamp.

By that time, Alice had recovered from her initial shock. She scrambled out of her chair and ducked in the desperate hope that Wilson wouldn't see her below the level of the tabletop and would believe she'd somehow escaped the conference room. She was still in the process of dropping low when the student grabbed the table by its edge, rotated it ninety degrees, and threw it.

The table hurtled at her like a giant flyswatter, and she croaked the croak that was the best "scream" her raw, swollen airways could manage. Wilson's makeshift weapon banged into her knees and the arms she'd crossed in front of her face but didn't pulverize her.

She cowered, waiting for Wilson to attack again. He didn't. After a moment, she peeked over the top of the table and saw he'd exited the room.

She also discovered why she was still alive. The table had smashed into Camille first, and the secretary had absorbed much of the impact—as her twisted, motionless form attested.

So many dead and so much blood splashed everywhere. The custodians were going to have a fit, and Alice would be doing extra paperwork for weeks.

But those were problems for later. What mattered now was stopping Wilson before he reached the elevator, rode it up to the first floor, and let the general run of staff and students, people who didn't know about the full range of the university's research, see him. Though she had no idea how she was going to accomplish that, she stumbled toward the door.

"Wait," a faint voice buzzed.

Startled, she cast about. In addition to making her cough, the spores had flooded her eyes with tears, and it took her a moment to orient on one of the larger pieces of Z'Shaa's head where it had fallen on the floor. The antennae projecting from that chunk were quivering.

"You're alive!" she said.

"My species is more resilient than yours. I can stop Wilson. But you'll have to take me to him."

By "me," she hoped the fungus meant the piece doing the talking. She had neither the means nor the time to gather up all of it and haul it along. Inwardly wincing at the moist, yielding feel of it, she picked up that chunk and carried it with her.

Outside the conference room and the spore cloud, her coughing subsided, and she managed to run down the hallway. She was still afraid she and Z'Shaa wouldn't catch up with Wilson before he got on the elevator. They did though, just as he was pressing the call button. As she'd discovered, canisters were strong, but perhaps they weren't built for sprinting.

Wilson turned to face his pursuers. He raised a fist.

The several antennae protruding from the piece of Z'Shaa stiffened and vibrated again. The resulting oscillating drone didn't mimic human speech. Apparently, the mi-go was speaking words in its own language.

Whatever the extraterrestrial was saying, it had no effect on Wilson. He advanced on those who sought to deter him.

Backpedaling, Alice babbled whatever came to mind. "You don't want to do this. It could hold up your graduation. I can get you a parking sticker for the faculty lots!"

Wilson cocked his fist back.

Z'Shaa repeated what it had said before. This time, the buzzing tones were louder and more distinct as if the mi-go was making a supreme effort.

Wilson froze in place like a metal statue.

"That's that," said Z'Shaa, "until you decide what to do with him."

Alice took a deep breath. "I had no idea mi-go could immobilize the canisters that way."

"Did you need to know?"

"I suppose not. This is a university after all. Every department has its little secrets." Her heart was still pounding, her voice still shaky, so she drew in another long breath. "Good lord, can you believe it's only January?" The end of the semester seemed a long way off.

§

Richard Lee Byers is the author of over fifty fantasy and horror books including *The Things That Crawl, The Hep Cats of Ulthar, This Sword for Hire, Blind God's Bluff, Black Dogs, Black Crowns, Ire of the Void, Undercity, Lancelot, Citadel of Gold, The Shadow Guide, The Paladins Book One: Arrival,* and the books in the Impostor series. He is perhaps best known for his Forgotten Realms novels. One of them, *The Spectral Blaze,* won Diehard GameFAN's award for the Best Game-Based Novel of 2011.

Richard has also published dozens of short stories, scripted a graphic novel (*The Fate of All Fools*), and contributed content to tabletop and electronic games. A film script he wrote based on one of his fantasy novelettes is under option.

His forthcoming works (all of which should be available within the next twelve months) include *Blood of Baalshandor* and *The Doom That Came to San Francisco.*

Richard lives in the Tampa Bay area and is a frequent guest at Gen Con, Dragon Con, and Florida SF conventions. He invites everyone to Follow him on Twitter (@rleebyers) and Facebook.

Gills

Jacqueline Bryk

OH, MY HEART! OH, MY FEVERISH BRAIN! OH GODS, GAG ME WITH A SPOON! I feel like I should have known somehow. That, like, the terrible knowledge imparted to me by the unknowable sleeping gods in the depths of the ocean should have clued me in. Or whatever. But it's totally not fair that the cutest girl in the entirety of Miskatonic is—

I can't even say it. Ugh, so grody.

So like, there's this chick, Janet. She's not really all that much to look at, but if you say anything bad about her in my presence, I will be *royally* pissed. I mean really, talking smack about my girlfriend when I'm around? What's your damage? Anyway, Janet's a physics major—you know, one of those people who sets out to unravel the mysteries in the darkest recesses of the Earth and the cyclopean void between and beyond the stars. She goes where no mind is meant to go, where the light of cosmic knowledge shatters the protective shroud of ignorance and darkness laid on Terra. Plus, she has the *cutest* scarves.

"I'm Janet," she said to me the first day we met, pushing up her coke-bottle glasses with one tiny finger. When she shook my hand, I should have noticed the total lack of webbing.

"Dawn," I said, smiling at her with all of my teeth.

She totally dug that. "I love the unusual," she told me later, which was super weird because, like, there's a ton of other squamous creatures at Miskatonic? Guess that should have been my first clue of the unspeakable horrors to come.

When we first had sex, she tasted like the pits beneath the ocean, where unborn monsters patiently wait to rise up from the depths and, like, terrorize humanity. I thought it was a good sign. Even if her fingers were weirdly unwebbed and her pupils were round and her gills were totally hidden, it was all good. I convinced myself she wasn't food. Everyone looks different, right? It's totally bogus to judge by the size of your flippers. Even if the flippers are nonexistent.

It was only when I took her swimming at midnight that the veil of ignorance was torn asunder. It was a new moon, so it was totally dark out, and I took her down to the Miskatonic River to a little lagoon that's, like, *so* secluded and stuff. It reminds me of the caves in Port Hueneme, and since homesickness is totally harsh, I sometimes wander down to perform the unspeakable rituals to Dagon by the light of the stars and also to get whatever tan Massachusetts lets me get, you know? Anyway, so I thought I would take her to the bottom, and we could, like, make out and stuff.

Except it totally didn't work out that way. Not even.

Nightswimming was totally a thing she could do. Janet was *so* about experiencing new stuff, so she was, like, totally bubbly as we waded into the saturnine depths of the Miskatonic River. She was into it big time, right up until the sandy bottom slid out from under us and I pulled her down below the inky green-and-black waters into a totally wicked world of shifting shadows and glowing eyes in the watery void.

I held her hand through, like, all of it, hoping to initiate her into the mysteries of the Arkham deep ones. But she wasn't moving. Not, like, in an "Oh my god, this is such a bummer. Can we motor now?" sort of way, but like . . . in an actual, totally-not-breathing, maybe stiff sort of way.

Why wasn't she breathing? Why was her hair floating around her head and throat like one of her totally bitchin' scarves in a deadly strong wind?

I kept waiting for her to open her eyes and let out a cheerful "Psych!" or something, for little streams of bubbles to flutter out of the gills that would materialize in her ghostly white skin. Any minute now. Right?

I didn't know what to do. I totally wigged out. I yanked her back up to the surface by her skinny, bony hands. Blood was dripping from her nose, hot and dark and smelling like dessert in the dining hall. I towed her to shore and rolled her up onto the grassy bank. Water poured from her mouth and hair, but like you've probably totally guessed by now, there were no gills. Duh.

Look, shut up, all right? I took health class in high school. I can do CPR. I did, like, the compressions until she spit out all the water, dark and cloudy, from her chest. I held her as she clung to me like a child before a sacrifice. I even carried her back to, like, the nurse like some kind of knight in, like, shining armor. It's not like she broke up with me. She kissed me good night. It was totally righteous. But if your girlfriend was—oh gods!—a meal, an earthdweller, a *human*, don't tell me you'd deny it with every fiber of your being. I am so sure.

§

Jacqueline Bryk (she/her) is a game designer and short fiction writer from Delaware. Her biggest Lovecraft inspo is Ruthanna Emrys because Howie didn't even like immigrants. You can find her work at jacquelinebryk.design.

Intermediate Yithian

David Kammerzelt

T HAT WAS ME SCREAMING AND FLINGING MY BOOK. HEADS TURNED. SHAME was hot. Mumbling a general apology to the universe that no one but me could hear, I went and picked up the book and sat back down.

I sighed and stared at the ceiling of the dining hall. I said aloud but quietly that I did not have the brain for this. I did not have the physical structures in my brain that would enable me to make sense of this. Mom was right; this schooling was wasted on me, and I was never going to amount to anything but a ditch digger. But I was okay with that. At least when I was hip deep in mud with a shovel in my blistered hands, I wouldn't have to be translating Yithian.

The lights in the ceiling were entirely indifferent to my complaints. I didn't know if that made me feel resentful or grateful.

She asked me if I was having trouble with the Pnakotic Manuscripts.

I looked back down. She was standing in front of me, pointing at the book in my lap.

I asked her how the fuck was anybody supposed to understand ideograms that evoke simultaneous conflicting, even contradictory, possibilities manifesting across multiple realities. And I wasn't even going to get started on pronunciation for a language never intended to be spoken by human throats.

She said it was easier if you can process simultaneous contrary inputs from multiple brains. I was sure I could hear a smirk behind her words.

I thanked her sarcastically.

She said that even if you were not a yithian, you could learn to think like one.
I asked her how I would do that.

Overdosing on entheogens, she said. Huffing volcanic gases high in ethylene, benzene, methane, and hydrogen sulfide. Listening to heavy metal albums backwards. Transcendental meditation if you were boring. Mind-blowing, ecstatic sadomasochistic sex if you were not. She said I could have three guesses as to which one was her personal preference, and the first two didn't count.

I said I couldn't tell if she was fucking with me or not.

She said that was the first step.

That was us lying together in a knot of sheets and limbs in her bedroom, the air thick with the scent of the insides and outsides of our bodies and smoke from a joint that I knew very well contained something more than just weed. I smoked marijuana before, and it never inclined me to doubt basic concepts like "up" and "down" and "no" and "pain" and "solid object." A Baroness album was playing backwardly in the background.

She asked me how I was feeling.

I said I had no idea. Good? Really good? Maybe? I couldn't tell. Also I had pulled at least four muscles, was bleeding from at least three places, and had second degree burns.

She said she knew that it would work.

I stared at her.

She said I was speaking Yithian.

I had not realized.

I looked around—at the black draperies hanging from the ceiling, at the vintage wine posters vaguely on the walls as seen through a haze of gauzy black fabric. The cats and clowns on the posters were crawling out of the frames. I was very sure of this. I was also pretty okay with this.

I put my arm around her body and pulled her close.

I asked her if it would always be like this.

She said it was if it was done right.

That was me forgetting that sometimes the rest of the world still has issues with interracial couples. She could pass for human when she chose to, but she didn't always choose to. And when she didn't, we would incur stares when we walked together around campus or along the gray slush and wet concrete Arkham streets. I felt those stares very keenly at first, eyes like the points of knives.

She was bolder about it than I was. She dared them to stare. She dared them to stare until their minds filled with manifold madness.

I asked her if she would actually do that to them.

She did not answer, and I did not press the issue.

That was us having our first fight. That was me expressing repeatedly and aloud that I had no emotional investment whatsoever in whether we brought stilton or brie to Kimmi's party. That was me wondering why she was so angry over some stupid fucking cheese. That was reality boiling around her like hot air over a summer pavement. That was time and space being violently drunk. And that was me realizing that she could, in less than the space of a blink, in less than the space of a heartbeat, make it so that I had never been. And that was me realizing, as space calmed around her, that she would not do that. Not unless, perhaps, I really really provoked her.

She said that it wasn't about the cheese. It was about me caring about the people she cared about. And I didn't *have* to care about the things she cared about—not all of them, not all the time, and not in the same way. But the really important things—she needed to be able to share those with me. And if I cared about her, I would make an effort to share in those things with her. And Kimmi mattered to her even if the stilton or brie really didn't.

That was me learning something. That was me apologizing. That was me promising that if she told me something was important to her I would do my best to be a good companion for her.

That was me learning later during the makeup sex that it was in fact possible for certain parts of the human anatomy to bend like that. At least if they were aided by localized spacetime distortions anyway. That was me learning that there were levels of pain that you could endure and that you'd absolutely think would kill you but didn't, and what a rush it was to come through on the other side.

That was us going to Kimmi's party with stilton and with brie.

That was me gasping, trying to breathe fluorine gas. That was her with a steadying hand between my shoulder blades.

Fluorine is just like oxygen, she said. But different. Just a few hacks to my cellular metabolism and I'd get the hang of it.

We were swimming through a sky like melted sherbet mixed with weed killer mixed with cold smoke.

That was me asking her if she'd ever been to Szcoi before.

She said she had: 8,474,389.43 times.

I asked her about the point four three.

She laughed.

I asked if it was safe.

She laughed. Of course, it wasn't safe. What would have been the point of going somewhere safe?

I asked her as I negotiated through a sticky patch of something like vapor with teeth, if she had indeed been here so often, what was the enduring appeal?

She said it was never the same place twice. Which no place was, not really, but some places were more not the same place twice than others.

And besides, she said, now she was seeing Szcoi through new eyes.

I asked her if she was being literal.

She laughed.

I said I was glad to make a gift to her of my ignorance.

She said ignorance was cheap and common as dirt. But the willingness to take risks and try new things was rarer and more valuable than gems.

I pointed out chokingly that there was neither dirt here nor gems.

She said I knew what she meant.

I did.

She said it was all about being good, giving, and game. And that I was.

That was me kissing her in the fluorine skies of Szcoi.

That was us shopping for paper towels and laundry detergent.

That was her saying she would do the cooking tonight. She had an old family recipe that she wanted to share with me. We would be having casserole.

That was me nodding and saying I was looking forward to it. But that was me also looking for confirmation that she was actually going to be serving food, right? That involved the tissues of once-living organic beings, plants and animals and fungi? Proteins and fats and carbohydrates? Because I might really be at a loss if it were anything else.

That was her glaring at me.

That was me saying I just had to be sure.

That was her saying in a dead tone of voice that, yes, she was going to be making food. Casserole was food.

And it wasn't going to involve the tissues of any sentient beings?

I was told that I was pushing it, and it was suggested to me that I stop.

I wanted to ask if I was pushing it because of course it was silly for me to worry about the inclusion of the tissues of sentient beings in the casserole or if I was pushing it because I was being overly picky and difficult in being concerned about consuming the tissues of sentient beings. I wanted to ask, but I opted not to.

That was me going off to deliberately not think about dinner while she worked on it.

That was me coming into the kitchen three hours later and the room smelling like roasted garlic and sautéed onion and melted cheese and burnt hair.

That was me sitting down at the table where she had put out the nice plates and uncorked a bottle of wine.

That was her serving me and sitting down across from me.

That was me smiling over at her.

That was her watching, waiting, watching.

I took a bite.

That was her with a questioning eyebrow.

That was me wiping my mouth and setting down my fork. I said I appreciated that she wanted to share something personal with me. It meant a lot to me. What was the history of this dish?

That was her smiling and saying that here she only had to cut up four sentient beings to make it.

That was me with a questioning eyebrow.

That was her laughing.

That was me never quite knowing if she was joking about that or not.

That was me learning how to boyfriend.

That was me doing the dishes, so she didn't see how much I didn't eat. That was me saying I would happily do the cooking next week if she could do the dishes and the vacuuming.

That was me going out an hour later for a burrito and her not even minding.

That was her only sometimes fucking around with gravity or light or the boundaries between universes just enough to keep things interesting.

That was me getting an A in Intermediate Yithian that semester. I didn't manage much more than a C+ in any of my other classes. My work habits got shot to shit. It seemed there were always more important things to be doing than homework.

That was me asking her once what an intelligent, experienced, beautiful, transdimensional girl like her could see in a guy like me.

That was her telling me that she liked my humility.

That was us lying by the fireplace in Wilmarth Hall, reading. Or that was me reading and her with her fingers under my sweatshirt, softly braiding and unbraiding my flesh. Or that was her watching the fleeting living of the fire and that was her musing aloud whether each tongue of flame was a portion of the fire as a whole or was its own entity, vanishing even as it came to exist. And that was me just stroking, stroking, stroking her scalp and her shoulders and the nape of her neck and the parts of her for which there were no names except perhaps in Yithian and which I had yet to learn, and that was me not responding to her questions about the fire because I knew that my listening was answering enough.

That was me observing over kale and sausage soup that Yithian seemed to be completely bereft of anything resembling comedy. That there seemed to be nothing in the literature that ever indicated that a yithian might laugh.

That was her saying that I was thinking about it all wrong. Everything in Yithian was comedy: the whole of the language was one long joke.

I said I really didn't see much of that at all in the descriptions of the condensing of hyperdimensional space into finite points.

She said if I'd ever talked with a native speaker I would know. So much was lost on the page.

I pointed out that the native speakers had all died out in the Cretaceous. Or wouldn't exist again until the Post-Anthropocene. Or something.

She said she could get me a yithian to talk to if I wanted.

I said I'd think about it.

That was her losing for the hundredth time at *Settlers*, dashing the pieces off the table, imbuing the scattered tiles with some rudimentary and squirming kind of life, and squishing them wetly beneath her foot. And that was me standing back with my hands in my pockets.

That was her apologizing sexually for nine straight hours. That was me accepting her apology until my everything utterly ached. That was me learning that it was possible for your adrenal glands, your eye sockets, and the small bones in your ears to be fucked senseless. This was me learning that *penetration* was such an imprecise term to describe how sex worked. There were far better words in Yithian.

That was her leaving a brand-new box of *Settlers* on the table the next night.

That was me thinking that speaking Yithian was like wearing borrowed clothes. That was me—a full adult, fully competent in English, struggling over such basic verbalizations as would have posed no challenge to a yithian toddler. Or whatever the yithians had instead of toddlers. Conidia? Something like that. I was getting better, yes. But was I always going to scramble and fumble for words that wound up expressing something less than half of what I wanted to say? Was I always going to feel like I was performing an academic exercise rather than speaking naturally and simply from my own heart? The yithians didn't even have hearts; what did they know about direct and genuine expression?

That was me closing my laptop and pushing it away from me.

That was me sitting for a long while in frustrated quiet and thinking jagged sorts of thoughts, the kinds of thoughts for which there were no whole words, not in any language.

That was her coming up to me and wrapping herself around me and asking me to talk dirty to her in Yithian.

That was me resolving to give Yithian another chance.

That was us sitting together on a couch at the end of one of her bad days, one of the days when she said that the electron orbits were fucked and that neutrinos were assholes.

She said that causal relationships were the gabblings of small and deluded minds, that time was a lie, that terrestrial life was an accident that should have been aborted.

I said that I would make her some tea. Did she want the blackberry and white sage or the hibiscus?

That was her saying that tea was a product of the *Camellia sinensis* plant and that any decoction of blackberry, white sage, or hibiscus was ipso facto not tea but rather tisane, and it was an expression of ignorance to not know the difference.

I said that I would interpret that as a request for the blackberry and white sage then, which was, according to the copy on the tin, soothing.

That was her stopping me from getting up by putting a hand over my hand and slumping over onto my shoulder.

That was me meeting her family at Thanksgiving. She told me to relax and be myself and to not worry about it. But I was not prepared to make the acquaintance of 999 siblings. I had a lot of trouble remembering all of their names.

I was very relieved when we could slip away to walk alone in the woods.

The stars were bright in the dark, and they swam slowly through the sky like slow deep-sea fishes or darted quickly back and forth like burning birds.

Her hand was cool in mine.

I observed that her mother was a very impressive woman.

She said that being a single mother wasn't easy. Her mother had had to face a lot of challenges.

I said that I was sure that was true.

Leaves were soft and giving beneath our feet, were the well-thumbed pages of a used book. Male crickets were singing loud, trying to get some love in before the cold stole their small lives away. Weren't we all.

She said she loved the woods.

I said that I did too.

She said she loved me.

I was quiet. I was thinking about the word *love* as applied to television shows and pop songs, favorite hats and ice cream, artisanal roasted coffee and the color of the sky. I thought about the word *love* as applied to pet cats who would purr and be soft in your lap but also knock your wineglass off the table and spit up hair balls in your bed and bite you for no good damn reason at all. I thought about *love* as applied to persons, that frail and fragile feeling that was so often promised to be forever and so often failed inside of a handful of years.

That was me thinking that loving a person meant forgiving the person who more than anyone else could really piss you off. This was me thinking about a hope for something that could last a human lifetime tempered with the knowledge that people change—all of us change—and tempered also with the certainty that in spite of moments of greatest closeness there was the inevitability of distance and loss.

That was me thinking that loving somebody—really knowing somebody—meant knowing the real ugly in them and being okay with it. That was me hoping against the odds, and that was me wandering lost among ten thousand futures while still trying to fully feel that one moment, fleeting as a lick of fire.

That was me touching her lightly with the tips of my fingers and running my knuckles over the soft skin of her arm.

That was me thinking that the word *love*—the American English word—was completely inadequate to express all this.

That was me saying I love you in Yithian.

And that was me thinking that felt just right.

§

David Kammerzelt is a writer. He lives in Las Vegas. He hopes you are having a good day.

Hashtag TPE

Dawn Vogel

THE MISKATONIC UNIVERSITY CAMPUS TOUR GUIDES HAD A RUNNING betting pool: who would be the first to garner a TPE—or total prospect enrollment. They went so far as building up a hashtag (#tpe) for that mythical day, but getting an entire group of unruly high schoolers to complete the tour and sign their letters of intent was really nothing more than a fantasy.

Anthea Morrison had the lowest odds out of the whole bunch. Her first three campus tours had instead been "TPKs"—*none* of the touring seniors having made it through the whole tour. The normal attrition rate was around 25 percent, and the other student guides had started a side pool for how long it would be until the dean called Anthea in for dismissal from the guide program if not the university altogether. At least, that's what Naomi Carter claimed. None of the other students would confirm it, but Anthea saw the way they looked at her when they thought she wasn't looking. Pity from some, wonder at how she'd even made it into MiskU from others.

It wasn't that anyone expected her to keep all of the prospects interested. MiskU wasn't for everyone, after all. But Anthea was on a mission now. She wanted to prove all the other student tour guides wrong and be the first to bring back a TPE.

A stack of files lurked in her inbox. She pulled them out with some trepidation, noticing that three of the five had gold stars affixed to the front—high-priority students. In a way, that might make today's tour easier. Many of the high-priority students *wanted* to sign their MiskU enrollment intent letter the day they toured, so they were less likely to run screaming. But it also meant that any of those three who didn't complete the tour or sign at the end would reflect even more poorly on her record.

Anthea flipped through the files to get a sense of the students. *Tabitha Flynn, pre-med. Shiloh Cavanah, archaeology. Zeb Rutherford, folklore. Philip Darby, languages. Belladonna Whateley, library studies.*

The last one gave her pause both for the name and the intended major. Everyone in the area knew about the Whateley family. They'd been in the Miskatonic Valley for generations. And library studies meant taking the tour to the library, which was low on her list of places that led to a successful tour. Even regular MiskU students got lost in the book stacks on a weekly basis. She'd have to keep a close eye on her charges when they checked it out.

At admissions, a group of students and parents lingered in the lobby. Anthea gave them all a once-over. The two guys were as average white boy as average white boys could be while the girls appeared anything but. One of the girls looked Chinese, and Anthea pegged her as Tabitha but immediately chided herself for assuming the Chinese girl was the pre-med student. The second girl had ebony skin in dramatic contrast to the third girl, an albino.

Anthea put on her best chipper smile, hoping it would come through her voice as well. "Hi, everyone! I'm Anthea Morrison, and I'll be your tour guide this afternoon. I'll show you around the campus, and we'll make sure to stop off at all of the locations important to your prospective majors, and then we'll meet back up with your parents here so that you can sign your letters of intent if you so choose. I've got nametags for everyone—" She named each of the students, and they came forward to claim their nametags. She still couldn't differentiate between the boys aside from them wearing nametags now. The Chinese girl turned out to be Shiloh, while the black girl was Tabitha, and the albino girl was Belladonna Whateley.

The woman beside the albino girl narrowed her eyes at Anthea. "I'm gonna go on the tour too."

Anthea forced her smile to broaden. "I'm sorry, ma'am, but we've found that the prospective students get a better sense of the school if they tour it without their family members. I understand that the admissions staff have some excellent refreshments for you here while you wait."

"I ain't drinkin' their Kool-Aid," Mrs. Whateley grumbled.

Ignoring her, Anthea smiled at the prospective students. "Shall we?"

The five high schoolers trailed behind Anthea, the guys bringing up the rear with Belladonna in front of them and Tabitha and Shiloh walking to either side of Anthea.

"So what do you major in?" Shiloh asked.

"Ancient history," Anthea replied. "There's a little bit of overlap with archaeology actually. Mostly on the anthropology side of things."

Shiloh nodded. "Do the ancient history students get to go on digs as well?"

"Ah, not really," Anthea said. "We're more inclined to see what the archaeology students have found and see if that fits into what we're researching."

"I am looking forward to the digs," Shiloh said, nodding for emphasis. "So many secrets hidden below the dirt."

"That there are," Anthea said, turning to walk backwards and face all of the students. "So how much do you all know about the history of Miskatonic University?"

"Founded forever ago and always dedicated to cutting-edge research and innovation while still honoring the past," Belladonna replied, her voice completely without inflection.

Anthea nodded. "Got it in one. Many of the buildings on this part of the campus are the original university buildings. They've been updated on the inside, but this part of campus looks just like it would have 'forever ago,' like Belladonna said. Conveniently, we've got one stop to make for those of you who plan to major in folklore, languages, and archaeology." Anthea gestured at one of the old stone buildings, which looked like it was held together solely by the ivy that covered it on all sides. Only a few of the windows had been cleared, and even they looked as though the ivy might overtake them as the campus slept. "This is also where most of my ancient history classes are held. It's sort of a catch-all for a lot of the history- and language-based majors."

Leading the group up the steps, Anthea continued. "There's a beginning-level Latin class that we can pop into for a moment if you'd like. Just about everyone takes at least a year of Latin because it's applicable to so many different subjects."

The door to the Latin classroom was open, and from within, they could hear the intonations of the class reciting what Anthea could identify as a verb declension. But she wasn't sure what verb it was, which puzzled her. She'd aced both semesters of Latin.

Peeking into the room, it became clear why the verb sounded so unfamiliar. This was the section of Latin for religious studies students, and based on the arrangement of the desks around the pentacle in the center of the floor, it looked like this was an exorcism not a verb declension.

Anthea scanned the room for the professor and realized the professor was the subject of the exorcism. He looked confused and a little terrified, and Anthea turned to herd the prospective students away from the open doorway. "You know what, wrong classroom."

"No, that's definitely Latin," Philip said, peering over Anthea's shoulder. "Fifth-century text, I'm pretty sure."

Cold sweat broke out all over Anthea's skin. This was how campus tours went sideways. If one of the prospective students decided to go into the classroom and somehow got involved with the exorcism, either they or another student wouldn't finish the tour. Through clenched teeth, Anthea said, "Well recognized. But it looks like they've got it all under control, so let's not get in their way. Oh hey, Belladonna, could you open that door?"

Belladonna looked between Anthea and the door and finally let out an exasperated sigh. "What, you mean with my hands?"

"Uh, yeah," Anthea said. "That's usually how doors work."

Belladonna shrugged but did as Anthea had requested.

The scene inside the other classroom was much more sedate with one student reading from a standard Latin textbook rather than an ancient tome. The professor nodded at Anthea, her eyes sparkling. As the student completed his reading, the professor said, "Class, it looks like we've got some prospective MiskU students in our midst. What do you say we give them a warm welcome in Latin?"

"Salvete omnes vos esse," the class intoned as one.

"Et salvete omnes vos esse," Anthea replied. "Thanks, Doctor Moore. We'll get out of your hair now." Anthea herded the touring students back into the hallway and closed the door to Doctor Moore's classroom.

Across the hall, the doorway to the religious studies Latin class was strobing between black and blood red, and a low-pitched squeal emanated from the room.

"Right," Anthea said. "Unfortunately, there aren't any folklore classes we can drop in on this afternoon, and I understand that most of the archaeology students are either in the field or the lab today. So let's head downstairs to see the labs."

"I think something's gone wrong with their ritual," Philip said, peering into the scintillating doorway.

"Well, we've got campus security for just that reason. So we don't need to worry about it," Anthea said.

"Yeah, but I might know how to fix it."

"As admirable as that is, seriously, you don't need to get involved." Anthea gestured to a phone receiver a few feet down the hallway. "You can make a report over there if it'll make you feel better."

Philip sighed but nodded, approaching the phone.

Anthea turned to herd the other students toward the stairs to the labs. "Ironically, our archaeology labs are all subterranean. So we're pulling things out of the dirt only to put them back underground."

Shiloh chuckled softly. "Very good."

"Hey, isn't he supposed to come with us?" Belladonna asked, pointing back the way they had come.

Anthea looked back just in time to see Philip leaping through the doorway into the Latin for Religious Studies classroom. *Dammit. No TPE today. At least he's not high priority.* Smiling at the group, she said, "Okay, well, hopefully he'll catch up to us downstairs."

As the high schoolers headed into the stairwell, Anthea glanced back toward the classroom. The doorway was now pitch black, and either fog or smoke had begun to roll out from it. She scribbled the classroom number on the palm of her hand in the hopes that she could send someone back to at least collect whatever was left of Philip Darby.

The hallway leading to the archaeology labs had long had wiring issues, and the lights flickered as they walked. "Most of what we'll see down here is what a lot of people consider the boring parts of archaeology. All of the artifacts that come in have to be cleaned, weighed, photographed, and cataloged. But there are some students who prefer that to field work, so there are two primary foci you can take with an archaeology major—field or lab studies." Anthea paused and knocked on one of the lab doors. The cataloging room seemed the safest bet to take her remaining four students into.

When no response came, Anthea tried the knob. The door opened with an eerie creak and revealed a room containing a dozen vacant computer stations.

"Where is everyone?" Zeb asked, wrinkling his nose at the empty room.

"This way," Shiloh said, pointing toward an open doorway to one side of the lab. The other students nudged past Anthea to follow Shiloh, and Anthea followed in their wake, unconsciously crossing her fingers.

"You know that doesn't work," Zeb said, glancing at Anthea's hands.

"Has that ever been proven?" Anthea shot back. She wondered, not for the first time, if it was too late in the year to get assigned to a different work study program.

Shiloh crouched on the floor near one of the lab tables. "Something fell and shattered," she said, reaching for a fragment of what looked like pottery.

"No, don't!" Anthea shouted. The students looked at her, and she said, much more calmly, "Proper lab protocol says that you should wear goggles and gloves at all times in the archaeology lab." She pointed toward a sign on the wall that said just that.

Shiloh rose and nodded. "Of course. Where would I find the proper safety equipment?"

Anthea pretended to look around the lab and shrugged. "You know what, I'm not really sure. But it looks like this area may have been evacuated. We might want to consider doing the same."

The students other than Shiloh shuffled out of the room, but Shiloh took her time looking around. "This looks like a good lab. I think—" Her voice cut off as her shoe brushed a fragment of the artifact, and she vanished.

"Okay, everyone watch where you step," Anthea said, her voice an octave higher than normal. "Don't touch anything, and just tiptoe until you're clear of this room." She scanned the floor before each step as she hurried toward the computer room and back into the hallway.

"Hey, is it cool if I just head back to admissions?" Zeb asked, his face now white as a sheet.

"You know what, that sounds like a great idea all around," Anthea replied. "Let's all go back to admissions."

Both Tabitha and Belladonna crossed their arms over their respective chests and shook their heads.

"I'm here to see the library," Belladonna said.

"And I the med school," Tabitha said.

"And I'm not going back to admissions until I've done so." Belladonna stamped her foot for emphasis like a spoiled three-year-old.

Anthea took a deep breath and let it out slowly. "Okay, alright. Let's walk Zeb back to the admissions building, and then we'll continue on the rest of the tour."

Zeb rolled his eyes. "Oh, come on. I'm not a baby. I can find my way back there on my own."

The lights in the hallway flickered out, leaving them in pitch darkness. Even the emergency exit lights seemed to have been snuffed out. All around, the sounds of shuffling feet echoed as if the entire hallway was filled with students.

When the lights flickered back on, Zeb was gone.

I've still got 40 percent. Anthea breathed deeply, trying to maintain her composure. She looked between Tabitha and Anthea and pulled a quarter from her pocket. "Heads we hit the med school next, tails we go see the library next."

The girls nodded, and Anthea flipped the coin. She slapped it down on her wrist and lifted her hand, and it showed heads. *Great.* "Alright, the West Building it is."

Tabitha and Belladonna both stuck close to Anthea as they made their way between the buildings. Overhead, the previously sunny day had turned overcast, the clouds with a weird purple tint to them.

"You often get weird weather like this here?" Tabitha asked.

"Mostly on Thursdays," Anthea said. "Or if the meteorology students are conducting experiments."

A bolt of lightning shot out from the clouds and struck the West Building ahead of them.

"Aw, crap," Anthea said. "Or if some med student thinks he's the next Victor Frankenstein." She turned to Tabitha. "So there it is, the West Building. I'm gonna guess it's about to go into containment, which means no one in or out until it's dealt with."

Tabitha sighed. "But I want to specialize in containment! This would be a fantastic opportunity for me to see exactly what that entails."

An iron portcullis slid down in front of the main entrance to the West Building, and Anthea pointed at it. "Sorry, Tabitha. We can't get in."

Tabitha pointed toward a unit of campus security officers jogging toward the building. "Are they going in?"

"Probably not. They're probably going to maintain a perimeter until they get word of what's actually happened." Anthea sighed. "I mean, it's like in the archaeology lab. There are a lot of rules, and you have to learn them and follow them if you want to be a student as MiskU. Rule one: if there's trouble, run the opposite direction. That's how you survive."

Tabitha grinned. "My rule one is to help. If it makes you feel better, I'll head to admissions as soon as I'm done and sign my letter."

"I appreciate that," Anthea said. "But I'd really feel better about this if you'd come with us to the library."

"Noted and rejected," Tabitha said. "You don't have to worry about me. I signed the waiver."

"C'mon," Belladonna said, tugging at Anthea's arm with fingers so cold she could feel them through her hoodie. "Let her go play hero if that's what she wants to do."

"Alright," Anthea said with a deep sigh. "Just remember. Running away from the problem is still an option. There are trained professionals here. You've got to survive if you ever want to become one of them."

Belladonna skipped away in the direction of the library while Anthea followed at a slower pace. She was well on her way to having no students with her when she got back to admissions. Even if Tabitha did survive to sign her letter of intent, Anthea was beginning to think that getting a TPE was just a dream, and the only thing that kept her going was the possibility that Naomi Carter would remain just as stymied as Anthea was in her pursuit of the lofty goal. Maybe it was time to drop the competitive streak and get a job in food services. At least the students there just got glassy-eyed and numb. That seemed easier.

"Hurry up, slowpoke," Belladonna called back, mirth evident in her voice for the first time since the tour had begun. She stopped and turned to look at Anthea. "You look miserable. Is it really that bad here?"

Anthea shook her head. "It's not all bad. There's good stuff too. I'm just doing a difficult job, and I'm not very good at it."

Belladonna frowned. "You're doing a fine job. We've seen a bunch of buildings, and now we're going to the library. Do you know how long I've waited to get into the library?"

"But the goal of my job is to get students to sign their letters of intent. Instead, I keep losing students." Anthea shrugged. "It's hard for them to enroll if they're not here."

"What makes you think they aren't here?" Belladonna asked.

Anthea looked at the girl, frowning. "What makes you think they are?"

"Philip and Zeb made it back to admissions. Shiloh teleported straight there from the lab. Tabitha will probably be fine since she's with campus security. They'll likely even walk her back to admissions afterward."

"Okay, wait. How do you know that Philip and Zeb and Shiloh all made it back to admissions?"

"Telepathy, duh."

Anthea sighed. "My current run of luck tells me you're full of it."

"Nah. My mom's side has loads of psychic abilities. Till her at least. Don't sweat it, okay? I get that you want to be good at your job, but maybe you just haven't met the right students until today. MiskU isn't for everyone, right?"

Anthea chuckled. "That's true." She sighed. "So you're dead set on the library?"

Belladonna shrugged. "I could wait a few more months if it helps. I'm going to enroll regardless. I just really want to see the library."

"Somehow, I think you'd do better there than a lot of people, Belladonna," Anthea said. "But your intuition's got me really curious. Tell you what. We'll go back to admissions and see who's there. And then if you still want to, I'll take you by the library."

"Can you come up with an excuse why my mom can't come with us?"

"It's restricted to current and future MiskU students? No general public allowed?"

"That'll work," Belladonna said, spitting into her palm and offering it to Anthea. "Deal."

Wincing, Anthea spit into her own palm and shook with Belladonna. "Deal."

Back at the admissions office, everything was as Belladonna had promised. Philip had helped stop the exorcism gone wrong and came back to admissions to sign his letter of intent. Shiloh had in fact teleported to the place she most wanted to be—the admissions office with pen in hand. Zeb had taken advantage of the blackout to duck the remainder of the tour, and he'd already enrolled for an independent study on the effects of crossed fingers on reality. And Tabitha had come back from the West Building to verify that it had indeed been a Victor Frankenstein-wannabe gone wrong but that the lightning bolt hadn't been enough to awaken his creature. So that crisis, too, had been averted. And she'd made good contacts with the containment force that she hoped to work with, and they had, just as Belladonna had suggested, accompanied her back to the admissions building.

Belladonna Whateley smiled at Anthea as she signed her letter. "You wanna get a picture of all five of us signing?" She frowned. "You're thinking something about a hashtag *T-P-E*?"

Anthea whipped out her phone. "Belladonna, you're kinda creepy, and I'd rather you not try to read my thoughts. But yeah. Hashtag *T-P-E*."

§

Dawn Vogel's academic background is in history, so it's not surprising that much of her fiction is set in earlier times or related to academia. By day, she edits reports for historians and archaeologists. In her alleged spare time, she runs a craft business, co-runs a small press, and tries to find time for writing. Her steampunk adventure series, Brass and Glass, is available from DefCon One Publishing. She is a member of Broad Universe, SFWA, and Codex Writers. She lives in Seattle with her husband, author Jeremy Zimmerman, and their herd of cats. Visit her at historythatneverwas.com.

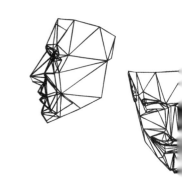

The Secret Trials of Oscar Bloom

Chuck Regan

MY CHAOS MAGICK PROFESSORS CLAIM WILLPOWER ALONE IS THE ONLY force required for the success of a spell. Well that's bullshit. Between all the chanting, the furniture moving by itself, and the students screaming at the top of their lungs after losing their last grip on sanity, it's impossible to do any spellcraft in this dorm. Willpower is simply not enough.

Noise-canceling earphones are the secret to my success.

Midterms here at Miskatonic University, Gwalchfenn campus, run right up to the end of October, and that high holy day hangs off the ass end of the month like a snake coiled to strike. It's not already distracting enough that portals naturally open to the spirit realm on Samhain (what the normies call Halloween), but the night before the holiday is when senior students like to prank underclassmen. Back home in Philadelphia, we call that Mischief Night, and that's tonight.

It's a tradition on Mischief Night to drive what's left of the first semester freshman crying back to their mommies and daddies. Croight, a guy with one goat eye I met during orientation, warned me that the most common method the seniors use is slipping curses into freshman book bags. All semester, I made sure none of my belongings were open or within reach of any other students, but during Antediluvian Cosmology today, I got distracted away from my backpack. Back in my dorm room getting ready for my next class, I found a piece of parchment rolled up and tied with what looked like my own hair. Someone had gone to great trouble to make a tiny rope of it.

Well . . . shit. Figures I get sloppy on the day of my midterm. Stupid.

On goat stomach parchment, written in blood, was a single sigil. I had to admire the calligraphic flourishes. Someone had been doing their Scripts and Signets homework. It worried me how they had gotten all of that hair from me. I suspect my RA is taking bribes.

I know for a fact that summoning anything above a level-two demon is grounds for expulsion, so I'm not too worried. My parents went through a phase dabbling in Enochian magic, trying to summon angels and demons, so their half-baked kin—shadow people and poltergeists—aren't a novelty for me, but the first sign of a self-moving chair scared the dharma beads off of my parents, and they smudged the hell out of the place with sage and prayed to the faeries to take the poltergeist away. I never told them I was the one who closed the portal they had opened. It's remarkable what you can learn online.

Ah well. Deal with what life throws you. This will be just another test.

My midterm assignment is to astrally project myself into the attic of the south turret of the campus castle and write an essay on whatever I experience. It's easy enough for me to do, but I'll need a couple hours of silence to accomplish it. My earphones won't be enough. I'll have to deal with this curse first.

What a pain in the ass.

Miskatonic University, Gwalchfenn campus, in North Central Pennsylvania used to be the estate of a lumber magnate in the mid-1800s. After making his fortune stripping the region of old-growth white pine to sell to the ship-building industry, James Scurlock hired a small army of masons to build a sprawling stone castle beside a mountaintop lake.

He named it Gwalchfenn. Scurlock took some liberties with the spelling, but translated from his native Welsh, it's roughly Hawk Lake.

The campus is about two hours west of the Poconos, but if you drove by it, you'd never spot it from the road. The trees have hidden the school perfectly. I like to think the pines finally forgave Scurlock for slaughtering their kin and are now trying to protect us—or smother everyone. Not sure. They seem friendly enough, but you can never fully trust trees. They can hold grudges for a really long time.

Local historical documents say Scurlock went nuts and killed his family. This land is a powerful vortex of telluric energy, as the school proudly advertises, and Scurlock Sr. simply couldn't handle it. Only his son, Ewan, escaped his father's killing rampage by hiding in the barn.

When Ewan was of age, he inherited the place. Wealthy but directionless, Ewan latched onto a village "hex doctor" and began practicing a local form of folk magic to protect himself from what he considered his family curse. It didn't do him much good. Ewan apparently couldn't handle the vortex either. He ended up either falling off the mountain after a drinking binge or getting eaten by a mountain lion. Nobody knows for sure. His body was never found.

After a couple decades of neglect, the abandoned estate was purchased in 1961 by the wealthy Miskatonic alumnus Savin Orsich. Now, Orsich must have owed some serious karmic debts to the school because he exhausted most of his fortune refurbishing Gwalchfenn, and after five years of restorations, he donated the entirety of the estate to the school. It was handed over in 1967 to MU, fitted out with three furnished dormitories, a massive library stocked with books that would make Aleister Crowley squee, one huge auditorium, fifteen classrooms, four fraternity halls aligned to the cardinal directions, a dining hall, and an in-ground pool that is always too cold and stinks of rotten eggs.

Two months of classes has taught me one very valuable lesson: chaos magicians are arrogant pricks. It wasn't hard to sort out which senior had cursed me— Dojor Cramat, a senior from Turkey. He posted enough calligraphy samples on his blog that I could recognize his style on the parchment. And if that wasn't enough, he bragged about humbling me *by name* on Instagram. A powerful idiot, he put too much faith in sigil magic and was too arrogant to keep it to himself.

Since I know it's a tradition at MU-Gwalch for the seniors to torment the freshman—MU is big on traditions—I didn't plan to add any extra spice to my protection and binding spell. Dojor was just adhering to tradition, making it difficult for this freshman to complete his midterms. He knows he'll get back three times worse what he sent to me. That's how curses work. Three times worse would be enough, but I had to first be sure of exactly what his intentions were.

All I had to do was fill out a curse reciprocation form and give it to Dojor's RA along with the evidence I had printed from his social media posts. The RA let me into Dojor's room, and I spotted my toothbrush on his altar. It was funny, seeing my cheap, bright-green plastic toothbrush on his Enochian chessboard with his Nyarlat-Hotep figurine guarding it. By the rules of the school, I was permitted to take something of equal importance of his, so I took one of his discarded quill nibs. The RA consulted the runes. It was a reciprocal trade. I left the toothbrush in place so as to not tip him off I was on to him.

I had to wait until 10:32 that night, when the moon was closest to Mars, to perform my protection spell. That's the time when the defensive energies would be strongest. The moon phase was wrong—waxing—not ideal for a protection-binding spell, but you gotta take what you can get with these things. I made sure the salt barrier around the edges of my room was intact and did a quick cleansing spell.

Now all I have to do is wait.

Here at MU-Gwalch, it seems the spirits have built up an immunity to cleansing spells. Like a city rat shrugging off industrial-grade poison, this spirit laughs off my simple cleansing spell and makes itself known, first by manifesting as a shadow person hovering in the middle of my room and then by yanking the sheets off my bed.

Really? Sheet yanking?

I want to make the thing manifest as fully as I can so that I can trap it, but I can't take Demonic Provocation 201 until I fulfill all its prerequisites. I have to rely on what I learned online.

"I'm sure your dark master'd be very impressed. Sheet yanking. Yeah, that's terrifying."

I bask in my self-righteous snark for a second until I remember reading somewhere, *Widdigan's Guide to Demonic Hierarchies* I think, that demons are very black-and-white thinkers. They're good at poking at human minds to inspire all the dark emotions—fear, anger, and depression—but demons don't react strongly to sarcasm. I start laughing at it.

"You're weak. That was so lame."

That got its attention.

All the contents of my Ikea bookcase shoot off the shelves, scattering across the floor. I have some first editions dating back to the 1700s in my collection. I don't want them damaged, so my anger is legit, but if this thing latches onto that negative emotion, it could gain some serious leverage over me. I have to be careful.

"Cute," I say, "but if you really want to impress me, put them back in alphabetical order."

This thing has probably been trashing dorm rooms for the last fifty years. It doesn't know how to do anything else other than throw tantrums, and demons aren't known for their mastery of the Dewey Decimal System.

"You don't know your alphabet, do you? You're not only pathetic, you're ignorant."

This incites a growl about six inches from my left ear. My neck and arm hair prickle.

Yeah . . . okay, that was pretty good.

But now I need to know how far I can push it. I pull up the sleeve on my hoodie and expose my forearm covered in goose pimples.

"Show me how powerful you are. Come on! Claw me!"

Now, right here I'm inviting a level-three engagement. The school has its own protections, but there are ways to get through them. I have to find out for certain whether Dojor is just performing a standard low-level senior prank or using Mischief Night to cover a more malicious intent. Level-three entities are illegal on campus, but I wouldn't put it past a weak chaos magician with exquisite penmanship to want to do serious harm to the freshman doing more advanced work than him.

Yeah, there's a story behind why that senior targeted me.

I conjured a solid servitor during Thought Forms 101 last month. The servitor spun around the room and knocked over a chair before I dissolved it. Word got around campus. Apparently, summoning a hard servitor is the senior final for chaos magick majors. Jealousies flared. Since then, I've been getting some spiteful glances and curse gestures from across the dining hall. If jealousy is fueling this apparition, that's a powerful dark emotion to seed into a curse, and it won't go well for Dojor when I send it back onto him three-fold. I need to find out exactly how much he put into it.

"Come on! Show me how powerful you are!"

Needle-like claws swipe across my forearm. It burns for a second and three shallow red slashes sprout jewels of blood. And with that, I confirm that this is a level-three attack—a blood demon.

Ah shit. Now I have to bind the demon, find out its name, and talk it down. If it retaliates against Dojor all pumped up like this, it could kill him, and I don't have a family fortune to spend like Orsich to cleanse my karmic debt. I have to be very careful.

My app buzzes an alert. 10:30. Time to get to work.

Spirit Binding is a course I'm not permitted to take until my junior year, and the act is listed in the school handbook as "forbidden until certified." Well, I may not be certified, but I do have some experience exorcising and binding demons. Okay, *once.* I did it once, and for the most part, everything turned out okay.

Six years ago, my little brother Gareth had become possessed after a May Day group ritual. Even at thirteen, I knew not to trust a priestess wearing a tie-dyed ritual cloak. Fucking hippy Wiccans. She didn't cast a proper circle, and half the participants were already compromised by alternative chemicals. Not a good combination. That priestess let something in that shouldn't have been able to get in, and my sensitive little brother turned out to be the most receptive vessel that day.

In the weeks that followed the retreat, Mom and Dad were too engaged in their latest distraction of root magic to notice Gareth acting weird, but when my eight-year-old brother started speaking Sumerian while playing with his Star Wars figures, I knew I had to intervene. After a marathon of YouTube exorcism videos and a quick visit to a Catholic church to pilfer some holy water, I took care of Gareth's little problem.

He's fine now, except for his obsession with writing Sumerian haiku. My parents think it's just him expressing his ancient soul. I never told them what happened at the exorcism. They never noticed the scorch marks on the basement floor, and I didn't tell them that the demon was bottled and buried under their trash can corral. I had the house straightened up and aired out before they got back from their weekend seminar, "Gluten Free Druidic Cooking."

That's when I discovered I had a knack for the Left-Hand Path. What details were missing in the online tutorials, I filled in based on what my guts told me was right. Not sure if it's past-life shit or a walk-in, but ever since that exorcism, I practiced in secret. I had to. My parents would freak if they ever found out how far I dangled my feet over the abyss.

The problem is, my parents refuse to believe in evil. They think they sent me to a school for learning esoteric healing modalities—acupressure, reiki, crystals, and shit. Sure, we learn about subtle body energies as part of our training, but you'll never find a rainbow yoga mat on campus.

My parents' circle of friends are from the white-and-fluffy, crystals-and-angelic-love New Age mindset, and they only listen to music they found playing at spas. Finding out their eldest son was dabbling in chaos magick would have been too embarrassing for them. If they'd ever found out about me summoning a shepherd demon to drive out what was possessing Gareth, they would have disowned me—if I didn't first choke to death on all the sage they'd smudge in my face.

The same way, I also knew it would be embarrassing if it leaked to the occult community that one of MU-Gwalch's students summoned a level-three blood demon. The way I see it, I'd be doing everyone a favor taking care of this myself. The increased insurance premiums for the school alone would justify my actions to prevent an escalation.

I called two of my more enthusiastic spirit guides, Hesk and Galhet, to thug up this demon a bit. Hesk says he was a boar killed by the Irish folk hero Cú Chulainn, and Galhet was a warrior of Doggerland—the British Atlantis. I still don't know if I believe any of that shit they're selling me, but they kick ass, and this dorm demon gives up its name even before I get a chance to uncork the holy water.

Borax is the demon's name. Yeah, same as the soap, but whatever. Borax the demon is under my control before the clock strikes eleven. After that, it was easy to get the details on how it was permitted to manifest. At first, I thought it was weird that Dojor had the proper sigil keys to let it through the campus wards, but I didn't figure that every school has their secret resources where students can buy stuff like pre-written reports and answers to finals. It was no different at MU-Gwalch. Dojor must have bought the campus sigil key off the local black market. I file it away as potential blackmail and force Borax into an antique iodine bottle stuffed with bloodstained fabric from a murder victim.

Yeah, Dojor isn't the only one with semi-legal resources. Every cook should have a well-stocked pantry.

I cork and seal up the bottle with wax, reciting the proper incantations, and finally settle down to focus on my midterm.

Hesk and Galhet are hovering nearby, guarding my body against any other intrusions. I put on my earphones and set my iPhone app to play white noise, blotting out my normally quiet neighbor who had just started blaring Enya on her stereo.

Those hippy Wiccans are everywhere. You gotta watch them.

Astral projection feels like I'm expanding into a breath of clean, springtime air—with no pollen.

This midterm will test my ability to not only astrally project but to measure how sensitive I am to the items in the room and how thoroughly I can hold all I experience in my head. I haven't yet mastered writing and drawing during astral travel, but I've been practicing photographic recall since sixth grade. I'm eager to see what's in this room.

I fly into the turret and feel it when I pass through the ward gate—like passing through a film of body-temperature bathwater—and I'm hovering in a wizard's trophy room right out of a Robert E. Howard story.

First thing I focus on is a small, round wooden table carved with a motif of stylized oak leaves and Green Man faces, and I pick up immediately that it was used as a ritual altar—it's buzzing with some serious mojo. I pick up that someone died during these rituals, and their spirits are trapped inside the wood. The big Green Man face creaks into a smile, and an intensely cold void reaches out for me.

It prickles at my temples like it's grabbing hold of my astral form, dragging me closer, its icy breath in my mind, promising power if I come closer.

Fuck that.

I cut the connection to the altar with a knife-hand—I'd be lying if I didn't admit Introduction to Astral Combat was my favorite class—and the Green Man entity retracts back into the altar with a flutter and a groan of wood.

That was just a little bit terrifying.

There's some power here, way above my level. Connecting to something you can't handle is the worst mistake a magician can make. Know your limits. Don't be an arrogant prick.

I check my vibration. In astral combat, it's normal for your etheric form to crystallize into a denser vibration—it's an instinctual protection—but in that state, it's impossible to sense subtle energies. I soften my edges, vent my chakras, and look around again.

It's hard to stay focused on one thing at a time. They're all screaming their stories at me. I keep my distance but sample each object.

Inside an old, crusty bronze helmet, a mummified skull starts singing Akkadian war chants. I can only pick out a few words—something about the difficulty of holding blood-slicked weapons. I get a little chime of pride, knowing my independent studies into Proto-Indo-European finally paid off.

There's desperation in the way these objects are trying to connect to me. It's like visiting the pens at the SPCA, all the dogs yelping and jumping at the bars of their cages. I only have about another twenty minutes before midnight, when the wards around the castle seal shut again, and I'll be kicked back into my body. I have to either take a shallow inventory of all the items or take a deeper inventory of a few objects without being trapped by them.

The urge to prove myself to the professor is chattering in the back of my mind, telling me I'm more powerful than I give myself credit. I could get a lot closer to one of these objects and dig up a buried secret that no other student has ever discovered. That will get me some serious attention from the faculty.

Yeah but no. That's a trap. That's arrogance. I've already had my lesson for the night about arrogance. I stick to the shallows.

A scrying mirror keens out a song, promising to show me my future. I'm not taking that bait either. Hell, there are enough faerie tales out there about the curse of seeing your own future.

Rose quartz the size of a yule log roars colors from its pointed end, like it's plugged directly into the core of the sun. I give plenty of room to that laser cannon of doom.

A deep-violet robe embroidered with red sigils seems to be turning its hood to follow me. Okay, that's just creepy. I don't even want to know what's animating it.

With every piece chattering like it's all there to test me, I begin to wonder if the collection as a whole is there to distract me from something else.

Distantly, I feel the phone in my physical pocket buzz. I have five minutes left before the wards snap shut. This is MU, the only fully accredited school for the esoteric arts in America. Every magical treatise I've experienced can be read on multiple layers: the more you understand about magick, the more you'll get out of it. Maybe there's more up here than just supercharged occult tools.

I try to blot out all the noise—do to the inside of my own head what the earphones are doing for my physical body back in my dorm room. The yammering objects fade back to a gray static, and I look around for something that doesn't belong—something they might be distracting me from sensing.

I see it, just a shimmering outline in the far wall.

A tiny door.

It's only big enough for a rat to fit through, but in astral form, size isn't absolute. I reduce my form and pry the door open. It's crystalline black inside.

I've read about these: it's a portal into another dimension. I know, I know. It sounds like something out of a Doctor Strange comic or a Doctor Who episode, but there it is, siphoning the astral air out of the room. This is some doctorate-level shit right here.

Am I being arrogant, thinking I can pass through this door? I have no idea what's on the other side, and this is sure as shit not part of the test. Or is it? Maybe all I should do is go back to my room and mention the door in my report.

And maybe this is the only chance I'll get to ever find out what's on the other side.

Back in my dorm room, my phone buzzes the one-minute warning.

I'm back in my body. It's pitch-black. There's a clammy gloom surrounding me, and I smell the sharp odor of minerals and mold. This isn't my room. I confirm that I feel the same gnawing absoluteness of being back in my body—an itch inside my nose, the sore fingernail I bit down too close to the quick, sandpaper under my eyelids, and a sharp, hard coldness under my ass. In astral form, I shouldn't feel any of this. Everything should be clean light and vibrations of energy.

I pick out a rock from under my left butt cheek. This is definitely real.

Under my fingertips, I feel the knobby texture of granite. I trace the rough lines pocked into the stone encircling me. Outside of the circle, simple pictograms: primitive, not from any icon set I recognize, but the shapes of them feel ancient—*dawn-of-man* ancient. Simple animals.

The first recorded system of magick was totemistic and elemental. Using the hallucinogenic properties from poisonous plants to expand their consciousness, the first shamans learned to move into the neighboring planes of existence where they commingled with animals and nature spirits. That form of magick is experiential and expansive. It led to humans first differentiating themselves from the collective mind of the planet. They realized that their thoughts could be separated from the other creatures. The ego was actualized.

The surviving cave paintings and petroglyphs demonstrated an evolution away from depicting just animals and psychedelic patterns to include animal spirits and humanoid gods—like the Hopi kachinas, Shinto kami, and Australian Aboriginal Wandjina. As civilizations evolved, so did the rift between self-referenced human consciousness and the collective mind of the planet.

Magickal systems in later history incorporated abstractions to calculate the patterns in the sky and the cycles of the year to become a science based on colder, inanimate abstractions and willpower. The chaos magick we are taught at MU-Gwalch is the latest evolution along that continuum. Chaos magick has little connection to earth consciousness. In comparison to shamanism, chaos magick is all willpower and math.

On the ground beneath me is a summoning circle carved with primitive icons. The symmetry of the circle tells me it was created after shamans began to use math, but the presence of animal icons tells me this was created when their cosmology was still transitioning away from animism. This cave must have been used as a ritual center two hundred to six hundred thousand years ago.

There's a pressure in my forehead and chest, throbbing pulses of blue-green light behind my eyes. I check my heartbeat—

That's not what's causing it.

I hear the chanting.

Ah, shit. I hate chanting. I know it's my own PTSD from group rituals that makes me want to run from any kind of cultish bullshit, and I have that hippie Wiccan priestess to thank for that. But since I have no other options other than sitting in the dark, pondering the history of human consciousness, I stand up and follow the sound.

From the echoes of my sneakers shuffling on the ground, I can hear that the cave around me is huge. And the pulsing behind my eyes—I'm not sure if I'm hallucinating or what—I begin to see the contours of the cave walls.

Weirder things have happened to me. I guess I spontaneously developed bat-like echolocation. Why not? Every pulse—two beats a second, like a shaman's ritual drumming—flashes a topographic map of my surroundings. I can see the natural random shapes of the floor and stalagmites surrounding me. I push away the thought that I'm inside the mouth of some monstrous mountain elemental.

I follow the sound up a winding, narrowing passageway until I have to crawl. Up ahead, I see firelight flickering onto the lip of the exit. The chanting is louder, getting faster. The opening looks just wide enough for me to fit.

I shimmy up and peek in.

Robed figures are standing in a circle around an open, black pit that a city bus could easily disappear into. Lit torches, set on pedestals, reveal the immense surrounding cavern, and the blue throbbing behind my eyes traces the contours of whatever the firelight can't reach.

The figure leading the chant is standing on a rock outcropping overlooking the pit, his arms outstretched. And now I can hear more clearly what they're chanting. It's not in any language that I've ever heard before: deep-throated, it sounds more like they're choking or getting ready to puke—*P'legh hachh nyalaugh gech hyuchh gaah.*

From my own studies, I've learned that words resonate in different parts of the brain—some words serve to stimulate the pineal gland and higher perception, but these words being chanted are rumbling in my guts and bowels. I feel my tailbone twitch and chime.

This is much more ancient than Proto-Indo-European.

This is some deep, primal chanting meant to activate the base chakras.

Oh . . .

Sex magick can be powerful if all the participants stay focused. As soon as one of them detaches from their intention, the spell loses power and degrades into mindless carnality. At least, that's what I've read. I've never been to an orgy.

I hunch down and wait to see what happens, but they just keep their robes on and keep chanting, and my tailbone is still chiming, and the cavern keeps pulsing in blue-green light.

I wonder what the intention of this ceremony might be. There's real power here, so clearly, this ritual is not being performed by blind rote. Their chanting speeds up, and the pulsing increases behind my eyes until I can't see a gap between the flashes of light. I can see the cavern as if it were lit from within.

Then I see the thing in the pit.

It's a giant prehistoric eel-like worm—like something that should be living on the sea floor near a thermal vent. Only the tip of its segmented head is sticking up out of the pit. Its five mouth plates bloom wide, and a toothed, stalky tongue sprouts upward like a rope of entrails crusted in thorns. The tip peels open into a five-pronged tentacle.

Something grabs me by my ankle.

I scream and spill out from my hiding place.

The pulsing has stopped. All I see are the fire-lit chamber walls.

The chanting has stopped. I climb to my feet and turn to face them. The robed figures have turned to look at me, and the high priest leading the ceremony lowers his hands.

Yeah, none of my books told me how to get out of this. I'm fucked.

"Sorry," I say, my voice cracking. "I was just taking a test at school and found the little door. Sorry to interrupt."

The high priest unhoods himself, and I recognize him from the old photographs. It's Ewan Scurlock, the son of the original owner of Gwalchfenn. He's very much alive and doesn't look a day over thirty.

"Huchwaah," Ewan says, intoning the word like it was the end of a prayer.

The other attendees take off their hoods. Three of them I recognize as professors at MU-Gwalch. One of them taught my Intro to Sigils. Another of them is Savin Orsich, the man who restored this place in the sixties. He also looks to be around thirty years old. He'd have to be ninety-something by now.

What is this place?

"Welcome," Ewan says, "to MU-Gwalch Advanced Placement."

§

Chuck Regan writes geeky genre fiction—military sci-fi, cosmic horror, diesel- and atompunk action adventures, bizarro political satire, space westerns, and anything in-between. His latest project is a superhero noir series called Stormkind. More weirdness at chuckregan.com.

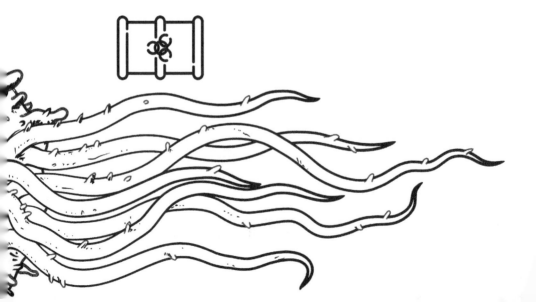

Mowbray's Museum

Oliver Smith

THE RATHER MAZELIKE NETWORK OF STREETS MIGHT HAVE LOST A cartographer, the luxuriant fog might have puzzled a meteorologist, and the ancestry of the locals might have confused a genealogist, but Dr. Perkin Lochinver had faith. He had faith instilled by his studies that all would end well—with the wicked punished and the good rewarded, with the heroine in the arms of the hero, and with a fine home for Perkin for a low rent, overlooking the picturesque countryside and the dun water of the Miskatonic River beyond. In spite of the natives, the fog, and labyrinthine streets, Perkin's faith led him straight to the Syreni apartment building on St. Giles Street; it stood next door to Mowbray's Museum of Un-Nameable Terrors, notorious at the university for its fantastical and frightening tableau. It had even been included in the football team's initiation itinerary.

Perkin had remarked to Professor Burbush that visiting a museum was so much better than them getting drunk and running around in the nude like a string of sausages. Professor Burbush tore his horrified eyes from the dark, unhallowed pages of the *Facito Occulto* and allowed, with some reservations, that since its inclusion in the induction ceremony, the university football players were some of the quietest and least naked sportsmen it had ever been his displeasure to be unable to avoid teaching. He offered Perkin a viciously unmanageable chocolate éclair in consolation for his demotion and returned to his terrifying but fascinatingly well financed study of the forbidden book.

Dr. Perkin Lochinver peered myopically up at the grey stone wall. It did not seem to stand at quite the correct angle. He adjusted his spectacles and gazed longingly upward at the neo-Gothic buttresses and unnecessarily many-gabled rooftops; had he been a geometer, he might have described its surface as non-Euclidean. Unfortunately, he was only the reader in light romantic literature in the Department of Arts and Humanities. Confronted by the crumbling and mildewed stone of his prospective apartment building, he regretted not having been a geometer, either Euclidean or otherwise, as he would have been far better paid and would not be considering a rented property in the St. Giles district. He sighed, "I hope this one is nice," and clutched a saccharine-pink paperback, authored by Dame Barbara Cartland, close to his heart and waited among the clouds of dank mist, rolling in from the Miskatonic River.

Perkin examined the waxwork's window. He loitered beside its grimy panes, trying to look interested in whatever lurked within. He could just discern a shadowy tentacle, fungoid shapes, and something with a head like a bunch of asparagus through the thick condensation on the glass. They were deeply unpleasant but unusually fascinating; it was almost as if some indiscernible music just beyond the threshold of his hearing was drawing him inside. He felt if he could get closer all would become clear and thought he might make a visit. Perkin counted out the loose coins from his billfold and approached the yawning maw of the museum.

The bank of fog behind Perkin shuddered: it swirled, it parted, and there was a roar. He was illuminated by a bright light, blinded by the whiteness. A sleek convertible emerged from a fog bank with its headlights blazing and parked with one wheel on the sidewalk. The driver put an extra set of lights on full beam, and a modern young woman, with somewhat bulging eyes that gave her an unfortunate fish-like cast, got out. She turned away from Perkin and looked hopefully up the street. Glanced at him and looked down the street. Then returned her attention to Perkin; she settled her rather fishy gaze on him with a frown.

"Dr. Perkin Lochinver, I suppose?" she said examining her clipboard. "I'm Miss Gobey from Syreni and Company."

She led Perkin through the visibly swirling atmosphere to a set of rusting iron stairs that dripped with condensed moisture. As they ascended, the noise of the street was muffled in the grey blanket of the fog, and the road below disappeared beneath a landscape of gently heaving cloud tops.

She unlocked a peeling, slightly woodwormy door in the moss-grown wall. A few stray wisps of moisture followed them into the apartment and sank despondently into the oatmeal-colored carpet.

In the lounge, Miss Gobey drew his attention to the picturesque view. "If you stand here, you can see the university clock," she said.

Perkin stretched to see: there amongst the fogbound rooftops and crazily angled chimneys, rising like a viper from its nest, reared the Gothic monstrosity of the university tower and its clockface.

"You'll always know the time," she said, goggling through the attic window and craning her neck.

"I have a watch, Miss Gobey, and have you noticed the room isn't exactly square?"

She squinted through her bulging fish eyes, "You think not? I couldn't really say."

"You must have photoshopped the picture on the website. I'm not a geometer, but I'd say it's almost a rhombus."

"It looks perfectly normal to me," she said. "And it's a very reasonable rent."

"I can smell chemicals too."

"It's the wax," she said. "Mr. Mowbray makes all his own models, you know. They're supposed to be very original," she took a deep breath. "The vapor certainly clears the lungs after that fog. I can just feel it doing me good."

The apartment seemed suitable aside from the unusual geometry, the chemical smell, and a slight damp patch over the bath that resembled Professor Burbush in profile. Perkin pointed this out, and she flashed her brightest smile at him and drew his attention to a cheaper apartment, which stood on four wheels in a nearby alley and was furnished with other people's trash.

When the impenetrable grey fog rolled back out to sea and allowed a more penetrable thin grey drizzle to roll down from the hills, Perkin moved in. Perkin's furniture did not fit; the angles of the corners where problematical. It was as if the apartment had been built by someone unaware of the cultural importance of the right angle, and the floor too appeared to have been warped in some unusual way. It was quite impossible to get more than two legs of anything to stand on the carpet at the same time. Perkin wedged and balanced it all as best he could and carried his books in small piles up the old iron staircase. He finished quite breathless and completely soaked. Why did Burbush not have to remove his books? Perkin knew the answer: the university unfairly placed historical texts, such as on the unromantic Caesar, boring old Aristotle, and the inscrutably unpleasant *Facito Occulto*, above those of his beloved Dame Barbara even though she had brought more pleasure to more readers than any ancient Roman, even though she had been awarded more literary prizes than any ancient Greek, even though she had produced more books in her lifetime than had descended from the entire classical world. In fact, despite the many statistically quantifiable measures that proved her as worthy, if not worthier, of study than Cicero or Plato, she was neglected—his dear, wonderful Dame Barbara. It was so prejudicial.

On Tuesday, Mr. Mowbray braved the rain and emerged from the cobwebbed depths of the wax museum to receive a delivery: an enormous crate reinforced with steel bars and stenciled with the logo and legend of the Antarctic Freight Company. Mowbray was unshaven and disheveled with many chemical stains and burns on his old black suit. He stared with wild eyes and ran his long fingers through electrified hair when Perkin addressed him. He relaxed after Perkin both explained he was a new neighbor and invited him for tea later that day.

At four o'clock, Perkin heard the clatter and splash of footsteps on the stair. Mowbray seemed a little drunk and had brought a bottle of absinthe with him. He did however make some effort and wore a slightly less-stained suit and had tried to tame his hair with what appeared to be wax.

"It is I," he announced, "Mowbray."

"Hello, Mr. Mowbray," said Perkin, shaking him by his cold, hard hand.

"I like your room," said Mowbray. "It is almost as if one of the Great Old Ones designed it."

"Well, yes, the architecture is quite old: 1860s, I believe."

"It is distinctly non-Euclidian."

"That's what I thought," said Perkin. "I'm not a geometer, but I definitely thought non-Euclidian."

"They remind me of certain structures I encountered in East Asia. I suppose I have spent my life exploring unusual geometries of space . . . and time."

"You must be a very talented sculptor. I hear your waxworks tipped a few of our more sensitive students over the edge," said Perkin.

"Beyond," Mowbray said. "Into the eternal darkness." He sat rubbing his pale hands together and cracking his knuckles. "All food for the hungry idiot god."

Mowbray cackled and rocked back and forth.

"Well, the eternal darkness is a bit strong. I think they just got sent home to their parents. You really should relax. Have another cup of tea. Personally I find a little light romance does wonders," said Perkin, and he passed Mowbray a copy of Dame Barbara's wonderful *The Taming of Lady Lorinda*.

Mowbray opened the faded pink cover, and his eyes widened. He moistened his fingertips to turn the next page. "It is strange," he said. "Strange and beautiful like the Asphodel Meadows of the netherworld. How does it end?"

"You'll have to read it to find out," said Perkin, tapping his nose and winking.

Mowbray turned to the next page but was disturbed by a crash and a noise like a badly played flute coming from the wax museum. Mowbray shook so much that he spilled his Absinthe, hair re-electrified.

"I must go and attend to it . . . I must go"

"It?"

"The . . . the . . . horrible piping . . . I mean the plumbing," he giggled slightly hysterically and left Perkin with the absinthe. Perkin poured himself a small glass and took shelter from the cruelty of the world in the limpid sweetness of Dame Barbara's writing.

Later, Perkin was awakened by activity below. A group of students in football gear stood in a semi-circle in the rain. They had congregated around the entrance to the museum, illuminated by a yellow streetlight. Unusual blue illuminations wavered in the wax museum's windows and a thin flute-like sound carried on the wind. For a moment, Perkin thought he might join them, but the lights went out, and the screaming began. At least the students had kept their clothes on. Perkin inserted a couple of cotton plugs into his ears and went back to sleep.

Mowbray returned a few days later. His hair was styled, and his suit seemed to have been cleaned. "The book you lent me. It was . . . wonderful," said Mowbray. "In my profession, cultivating unnameable horrors, one forgets about . . . love. Yes, love is so important. A wonderful, wonderful thing."

He put a hand on his heart and sighed. He took a bite from a chocolate cookie and offered one to Perkin and said, "Those students that come to the Museum. There are warning notices, and they signed the waiver. I cannot be legally held accountable for the students."

"I'm sure it was all good publicity for you, and between the two of us, there are far, far too many students."

"But even so," said Mowbray, "I feel . . . responsible."

"That is because you are a good person," said Perkin. "Kind and caring."

"Since I read *The Taming of Lady Lorinda*, I have dreamed I might be such a creature," said Mowbray, looking at Perkin with teary eyes. "I have done questionable things."

"Oh, do tell," said Perkin, clapping his hands.

"I was young, I was precocious, I was led by a strange book to explore the wilderness beyond the Hindu Kush. There lay a town in the mountains, a town like no other on earth. It was built of great cyclopean blocks that rose in parabolic trajectories conceived by minds that could not have been of this world. This town pre-dated humanity . . ."

A distant whistling filled the air. "Can you hear them?" said Mowbray. "They know I want to tell. Can you hear the horrid shrill piping . . .?"

"My dear Mowbray, you must not allow your boiler to disturb you so. I know wax figures are susceptible to temperature changes, but surely they could be left alone for a few hours?"

"Wax," said Mowbray. "If only they were wax. I must go."

Perkin was left puzzled and wondered what material Mowbray sculpted in.

It was Perkin's third week in the apartment. He knelt on the floor among pink towers of paperbacks and tried to shelve his book collection. He had managed to acquire some suitable bookshelves from a junk shop. The proprietor said that they had been caught in the rain. It was almost as if they had been designed to fit non-Euclidian corners; unfortunately, his books weren't, so his beloved

Dame Barbara's eight hundred volumes (the vile Burbush had suggested she had written one for every year of her life) remained stacked in unsteady piles around the room.

Perkin's good friend Mowbray visited and tried to assist him filing his wonderful books. Mowbray was a convert and in honor of Dame Barbara had purchased a stylish cerise jacket and matching cravat; his hair was now tamed and kept coiffed in a romantic sweep. As he wedged the books onto the uneven shelves, he marveled at the titles he had yet to read, and he told Perkin about some fascinating if not wholly believable foreign travels. Perkin Lochinver's eyes widened, and his teacup shook as Mowbray related his extraordinary experience with creatures that lived among immemorial ruins in East Asia. Mowbray told how he hung from a crumbling tower by his fingertips, beset by indescribable horrors with wings and scales.

"And so," he said, "I drew the dagger of meteorite steel and carved the glyph of the hungry idiot god upon the virgin rock. The sparks flew, and the blood ran from my skin, and the horrid birds sipped at the pooling blood. The creatures cried in inconsolable grief and horror. I was close to losing consciousness when—"

A crash and loud gurgling flung Mowbray into a state of alarm. He stood up with a wild look on his face and declared, "I must end it. Tonight."

"Sit down, Mowbray," Perkin said. "You'll not get a plumber out at this time."

Mowbray looked at Perkin as if he'd turned into an artichoke and rushed from the apartment into the drizzle and darkness.

Perkin sighed, "Poor Mowbray," and settled down to make the best of his evening alone. He turned his attention to the bottle of absinthe that Mowbray had brought all those weeks ago. He thought he may as well take a glass as he had nothing else to do.

Dame Barbara's talents were not restricted to literature; she was also a racing driver, invented the troop-carrying glider, thus changing the course of World War II, and she sang beautifully and had recorded an album of popular classics with the Royal Philharmonic Orchestra. It was this Perkin sang along to with a half-drunk glass at his elbow and scrambled a couple of eggs for a late supper . . .

"*That certain night, the night we met, there was magic abroad in the air,*" he sang as he stirred them. "*A nightingale sang,*" he warbled as the eggs were on the point of perfectly congealing, his voice rising to a crescendo, "*in Berrrrrrk-el-eeeey Squaaaare—*" He detected an awful burning smell and checked the stove and his person and was relieved to find neither were the source. He heard fire trucks. There was a dreadful scream in the street, and Perkin flung open his window to see a flaming figure run from the building below into the pouring rain. The street was immediately illuminated by blue flashing lights, and an officer leapt from a truck and proceeded to mercilessly beat the victim with a blanket and smother him with a cloud of fire-retardant foam. An ambulance later removed the somewhat charred but still living Mowbray.

The eggs were cold and dry by the time Perkin returned and were rather unpleasant. The activity from various emergency services outside had ceased, so he assumed the fires were all extinguished and the building made safe. Perkin retired for the night. The combination of stress and spirits gave him terrible nightmares. He was pursued through endless university passages and lecture theaters by an axe-wielding dean, and faculty administrators snipped at him with gigantic scissors. He woke up at two in the morning in a cold sweat to see dark tendrils and filaments of vapor, seeping through the floorboards. Black wisps writhed like worms through the air. They twisted and coiled in mathematically impossible knots and spirals before dissipating in the area of the couch. He opened a window but was assaulted by aggressive and obscene singing from over the rooftops so was compelled to close it again. The strange smoke continued to leak from the museum through the night.

The following day, Perkin descended into the street and watched white-suited, safety-masked figures wheel a series of steel crates through the rain and onto the back of a waiting tank transporter.

He slipped under the quarantine tape and peeped inside the museum. It was empty, not even puddles of wax.

"Excuse me, sir," said a man in a too-large raincoat with a hat pulled low over his face. "Please step back behind the barrier."

"But they've taken the lot. Poor Mowbray."

"Are you aware of the contents of the museum?" asked the man, trying a smile but obviously being out of practice.

"Oh, yes. He made wonderful wax models—delightful. I tried to persuade him to make a statue of Dame Barbara." Perkin showed the man Dame Barbara's photo on the back of a pink paperback. "It was such a shame. He really should have got a decent plumber to sort the terrible piping out."

The agent looked at him as if he had a face made of asparagus, and after several hours of questioning by a group of people who, he ascertained, were some sort of secret police unit, Perkin was released, having persuaded several of them to dip into some volumes of light romance and having inadvertently convinced them of his idiocy.

Upon returning home, he noticed his apartment was very musty. He checked the damp patch. It did not appear to have expanded and still resembled Professor Burbush's Roman profile. The smell actually seemed less severe in the bathroom.

Perkin sat on the sofa and poured a small glass of absinthe. The smell of mold was very strong. Perkin pulled the sofa away from the wall and found disgusting patches of black mildew, running wild through the plasterwork, forming strange patterns on the wall. He reached for his cell and called Miss Gobey immediately. She made some very unimpressed noises and suggested he open the window more. "The apartment probably just needs airing," she said. "How is the view of the clock? Nice, isn't it? Call again if it doesn't clear up in a week or two."

The next day, Dr. Perkin Lochinver was due to give a lecture at the university at two o'clock and arrived early. He found Professor Burbush, looking exactly like the emperor Vespasian and eating a large bag of chocolate éclairs at his desk as he dwelt upon the *Facito Occulto*.

"How's the new apartment?" Burbush asked, moving his chair over to accommodate Perkin and locking the book in a steel case.

"A bit of mold," Perkin answered, "and there was a fire in the wax museum. My neighbor Mowbray was taken to hospital."

"Crazy Charlie. Heh," said Professor Burbush, offering Perkin a cake and presenting one of his more insanely Julio-Claudian aspects.

"Do you know him?"

"Mowbray went postal back in '96. Most disreputable. Heh. He was a zoologist. I let him have a look at the *Facito Occulto*, and he thought it was true. He thought it described a pre-human civilization and went off in search of it. He said he had made astonishing discoveries that would revolutionize evolutionary biology and overturn our entire Weltanschauung. He may well have been right, but the university was not happy with him unveiling horrific secrets out of prehistory. They felt he lacked a positive message. He was quite mad and rightly dismissed of course."

"You're in error, Burbush. My dear friend Mowbray is a lovely person, romantic, warm-hearted, caring, brave, and a most talented sculptor."

Burbush became positively Tiberian at the suggestion he was wrong, and his moon-encircled eyes brimmed, his aquiline nostrils flared. "You're ten minutes late for your lecture by the way. Late."

Perkin looked at his watch and sprinted across the quadrangle. Fortunately no students had bothered to attend his talk, "Ripping the Bodice: The Exegesis and Apotheosis of Post-War Light Romance." He amused himself for his contracted hour with a couple of Cartland's classic romances.

As Perkin Lochinver ascended the iron staircase to the apartment, he could smell the mold. On entering the lounge, he found it had spread octopus-like tendrils through the plaster and risen above the back of the sofa. He immediately dialed the agents and spoke to Miss Gobey. She suggested that he give it a good scrub with formaldehyde.

The next morning, Perkin entered the formaldehyde-scented living room to find the patch of mold had recovered from its scrubbing and covered almost the entire wall. He noticed, among the lush black fur and delicate tendrils, hyperspherical bodies were emerging. It was about to produce spores.

After his sleepless night, this was too much. He immediately contacted the Environmental Health Department. He emailed three times. Then phoned. He began by requesting politely. Then threatened. Then demanded to speak to the mayor and cried.

At ten thirty in the morning, the steps echoed with metal-studded work boots. There was a knock on the door; the environmental health officer stood at the threshold wearing green coveralls and carrying a laptop in his hand.

"I'm Mr. Marchant from the mold control section."

"Do come in. It's over here."

Mr. Marchant sniffed at it, ran his finger through it, and tasted it. He offered Perkin some.

"Roquefort," he said. "Rather good. Mold is useful in its place . . . and economically important."

Marchant took a small scraping and placed it in a labeled sample bottle. Then he showed Perkin photographs of various varieties of mold to illustrate its many uses. He had a picture of each of the thousand unique cheeses in France, each given its individual flavor by a different sort of mold. Then there were the lifesaving antibiotics: he started with penicillin and continued through the cephalosporins when Perkin stopped him and asked, "But aren't you going to do anything? I'm sure molds are fine in their place, but that place is definitely not behind my sofa."

Marchant said, "In view of your ridiculous phobia, I could contact your landlord. Are you sure you wouldn't rather nurture and care for it? You'd have a fine cheese business in a year or two. It would be wonderful, don't you think?"

Later, when Perkin attended his (shared) office, he found Professor Burbush waiting with a pile of old newspapers. He resembled a triumphant Flavian as he displayed them to Perkin. On one cover, a startled, younger Mowbray with darkly hypnotic eyes was pictured surrounded by police officers. The headlines read "Six Students Dead," "Mowbray to Stand Trial," and "Mad Doc Mowbray Committed to Higgedy Mountain Asylum." Perkin had to admit that Burbush was right. Burbush then acted like a complete Trajan and broadcasted his victory all around the campus.

Back at the apartment, Perkin settled down to distract himself from the revelations of poor Mowbray's tragic past with some serious reading. He opened a bottle of wine, placed a large bag of peanuts within easy reach, and turned off his cell. He had allowed himself to sink gently beneath Dame Barbara's cotton candy prose and was wallowing in a reverie of light romance when there was a hammering on the door. A livid Miss Gobey entered wearing a pair of rubber gloves. Her eyes bulged like a cod dragged out of its depth.

"I've had a phone call from Mr. Marchant at the town council. I want you to know that Syreni and Company have never had a tenant complain to

Environmental Health before. I'm going to show you exactly how to clean. And then I'm going to evict you for neglecting the property. Stand there. No, don't just stand there. Help me move the sofa."

The mold had expanded. It bulged in black globules, and it swelled and rolled in luxuriant topologies. What Perkin had taken for fruiting bodies had matured and formed some sort of trumpet-shaped manifold. The infected plaster pulsated. Miss Gobey was undeterred and sprayed it with a strong bleach-based solution. The now completely anti-Euclidian surface rippled. The mold opened about a hundred eyes and howled and gibbered. Miss Gobey gibbered back in a rather aggressive manner. The monstrosity detached itself from the plaster and attached itself to Miss Gobey. She was entirely enveloped in its fungoid folds, but Perkin could still hear the submerged sound of spraying and scrubbing.

Perkin was unsure which of them he wanted to win, so he sat back with his wine and opened the peanuts to await the result.

The mold creature pulsated. It throbbed and gurgled. It formed itself into an impossible solid on the carpet, and beneath its black, furred exterior, something moved and grumbled.

There was another knock at the door. Perkin opened it just a gap, and there stood the august Professor Burbush in all his late imperial glory.

"I'm rather busy, Professor. Can it wait?"

"Heh, no it can't wait. Your phone was off. The National Intelligence Service has arrested the football team. The dean and faculty called an emergency meeting. Then the Security Services took them away too. They've all been confined to the Higgedy Mountain Asylum for the Criminally Insane. Apparently your friend Mowbray spilled the beans on something he really shouldn't have. Now let me in before the NIS finds me."

Burbush forced his way through the door just at the moment that the mold had got the hint that Miss Gobey disagreed with it and spat her naked and partially digested body across the room. She landed with a bloody splat at Burbush's feet, the bleach bottle and scrubbing brush still clutched in her enzyme-reddened fingers. The mold was obviously not happy about the encounter. It attempted to be inconspicuous and tried to slip back behind the sofa without anyone noticing.

Burbush was transfixed like a naughty Caligula by Miss Gobey's unclothed body.

"My god, it's not human. Look at it, Perkin. It's straight out of the *Facito*

Occulto. Look at the skeletal anatomy. It appears to be some sort of ichthyoidal throwback. Look at those gills, those scales, those fins. By god man, where did it come from?"

Miss Gobey sat up, opened her fishy eyes, and caught him on the Roman nose with a deftly hurled scrubbing brush.

"I'm a realtor."

One of the neighbors must have been driven to call the police by his dreadful screams.

Even though she protested that she was just a property agent, the security service placed Miss Gobey in a large tank of salt water and dispatched her for further study to the Woods Hole Oceanographic Institute. The mold infestation was securely collared and chained and led away to secret but comfortable kennel facilities.

For Perkin, committal was a brief formality. It didn't take any long reading of rights as apparently Perkin no longer had any legal existence.

On Higgedy Mountain, when the restraining sleeves were untied, he found a pleasantly arranged living area. His meals were cooked for him, and he was pleased to see his old friend Mowbray waiting in the electric-fenced exercise yard. They lived happily ever after and reveled in the many wonderful light romances of the divine Dame Barbara. Perkin found that in the secure modern premises, there was no hint of damp or mold, and the walls of the rooms all met at precisely ninety degrees.

Although he was not a geometer, Perkin measured them all.

Very carefully.

§

Oliver Smith is a visual artist and writer from Cheltenham, UK. He is inspired by the landscapes of Max Ernst, by frenzied rocks towering in the air above the silent swamp, by the strange poetry of machines, by something hidden in the nothing. Oliver's short fiction has appeared in anthologies from Inkermen Press, Ex Occidente Press, Dark Hall Press, Pole to Pole Publishing, and Flame Tree Publishing. His poetry has appeared in various anthologies, journals, and magazines, including *Liminality*, *Riddled with Arrows*, and *Strange Horizons*. Oliver was awarded first place in the BSFS 2019 competition for his poem "Better Living through Witchcraft," and his poem "Lost Palace, Lighted Tracks" was nominated for the Pushcart Prize. He holds a PhD in Literary and Critical Studies. Find more at oliversimonsmithwriter. wordpress.com.

The Librarian's Handbook

Jennifer Brozek

T HE BOOK WAS AS STRANGE AS THEY COME. LEATHER-BOUND AND GOLD embossed, it was in no language Shannon had ever seen. Somewhere between Cyrillic and runic, the lettering had the worn feel of age. Yet it was a library book. She looked at the protected spine label. It was one of theirs except . . .

Shannon looked closer: 1211.05. It was clear whoever made the label hadn't proofread it. The Dewey Decimal System only went up to 999. That meant the number had to be in the 100s, Philosophy and Psychology, or in the 200s, Religion. The .05 referenced the United States at large. It shouldn't be too hard to find out what the real book number was, fix the label, and shelve it properly.

At least in theory.

"Shannon?" Jocelyn, one of the University of Washington's librarians, poked her head in the back office. "Whoa. What's wrong?"

"This . . . this book." Shannon shook the leather-bound tome at her boss. "It doesn't exist. But it's one of ours. The barcode says so, but there isn't an entry for it in the system. I thought it was just a messed-up Dewey code. But I've tried every single permutation, and I can't find it in here anywhere. I think it's because the book isn't in English. Not even the credits page. The only thing I can read is the numbers, and one of them is 1890. There's no way we have a book from the 1890s. Is there?"

Jocelyn held out her hand. "Lemme see it. You get back to shelving the books you can figure out. I'll see what I can do and then show you what you should've done."

Being a library intern had its perks—getting paid to work with books, getting to work in the library after hours, flexible work hours, and decent work conditions. Sometimes working for Jocelyn wasn't one of them. Shannon handed over the book with a scowl. "I know the Dewey Decimal System."

The older woman sighed. "I'm not saying you don't know how to do your job. I'm saying that you don't know everything about the library system, this library, and the way it works—yet."

Shannon gave her an apology by way of a half-smile. "Right. Yet. But someday, I'll know everything."

"Someday you may not want to."

Shannon waved the sentiment off with a flick of her fingers as she left the back office. Knowledge was everything. To know things when no one else knew them. To point other students in the right direction. To have facts on the tip of your tongue and impress people at parties.

She laughed at herself. Parties. Her idea of a party was three or four people sitting around a table listening to music while they talked about everything and nothing. Those were the best kind of parties. Not too loud. Not too crowded. Filled with the same intimacy a library gives when most people have already gone home.

By the time homework and library work were done, the night shift was there with their own interns. Shannon headed to the back office to get her things. In her cubby next to her sweater was the mysterious leather-bound book with a note in Jocelyn's handwriting.

Intra-library borrow. Rare book room?
Grays Harbor College, John Spellman Library.
Contact them and return the book.

Shannon tilted her head as she considered the note. This wasn't something she was aware of. Yes, she knew of the UW satellite campuses like Bothell and Tacoma. Both had libraries. Decent ones too. But Grays Harbor College? Wasn't that in scary, scary Aberdeen where all the meth heads lived amongst the industrial port businesses?

She put her sweater and the book down on the table before logging into the computer. Jocelyn had closed everything she'd used to research the strange book. However, a quick internet search not only found the college, it found the website for the John Spellman Library.

Right there on the front page was a glowing option called "Chat with a librarian." Shannon tucked her hair behind her ears. "Right. Let's chat."

Hello. I'm Shannon Lund, an intern here at the University of Washington Library. I believe we have one of your books.

Good evening, Miss Lund. I'm Joshua Carter, the Head Librarian. What makes you think you have one of our books? It is rare that we allow them out of our system.

"Oh, you're one of those people. Figures." She debated a couple of different answers before going with the straightforward one, naming her boss to back up her answer.

Mrs. Strollen left me a note stating so. Also it uses the Spellman Library category system and not the standard Dewey Decimal.

I see. What is the number on the spine label?

1211.05

Shannon nodded at the silent screen and its lack of an immediate answer. "Gotcha." She wondered what Mr. Head Librarian was like in person. Probably just as supercilious as he was online. She rolled the word *supercilious* around in her head. She didn't get to use a word like that very often. Probably a good thing. It might involve punching people.

> *That is indeed one of our books. As it is from our rare book room, we will need it returned immediately.*

"We who? You and the mouse in your pocket? And who's going to do that?" she muttered to the screen. Of course, she knew the answer. It was implied in the demand. He expected her to return the book herself rather than send someone to get it. Maybe he was a reasonable sort . . .

> *Immediately . . . as in tonight? Or can I overnight it tomorrow?*

> *No mail. That book is too fragile and important to be left to the vagaries of the postal system. You may bring it to the library tomorrow.*

Shannon didn't answer that. The gall of the man to assume she'd get in her car—that she *had* a car—and would drive a couple of hours to a backcountry community college in the middle of Aberdeen to deliver a book was astounding. If this book was so important, he could get in his car and haul his butt up to Seattle to get it. Before she could figure out an appropriate answer that would not get her fired, Mr. Carter upped the ante and his condescension.

> *Of course, you will be compensated for gas, lunch, and time as you will be working for the library. Assuming you are allowed to do this errand for the University of Washington Library as an intern.*

> *I should arrive between 10 and 11, depending on traffic.*

That will be sufficient. Have a
good evening, Miss Lund.

The chat winked out before she finished typing her own goodbye. Shannon muttered under her breath. She bet Mr. Carter was the kind of old white guy who expected everyone to kowtow to him on a daily basis. Well, tomorrow she would make sure that he knew she was only doing this because it was part of her job and not because he told her to.

After dashing off a note to Jocelyn to tell her she'd be in late because of returning the book to the John Spellman Library, Shannon finally headed home. It was going to be an early morning and rush hour traffic to contend with.

Shannon paced in her apartment, restless and unsettled. The dishes were done, leftovers put away, and no homework due. Still she felt something in the air. She felt watched, like she was supposed to be doing something but was slacking. Again she returned to her desk and rechecked her calendar. Nothing was due. Nothing was pending. Why did she feel like she was forgetting something?

In an effort to throw off the discomfort, Shannon turned on the TV and settled on *Antiques Roadshow*. This was the kind of comfort TV that let her learn something as much as it soothed the soul. Melodic British voices were exactly what she needed.

"Yidhra uln hai. Nog."

The alien language was whispered in her ear as if by someone sitting next to her. Shannon yelped and jerked away, frantically looking for the source of the whispered words.

"Nog. Vulgtlagin phlegeth."

Again it sounded like the words were whispered, not next to her head but near her. "Who's there? Who's talking?"

No one answered. But her backpack fell from the coffee table to land at her feet, spilling its contents everywhere. Resting on one foot was the strange book from the John Spellman Library. She picked it up and put it to the side before cleaning up the rest of her backpack. This time, she zipped it shut to keep it from spilling again.

Shannon ran her hand over the gold embossed lettering of the foreign book, feeling the warmth of the leather. She picked it up and set it in her lap. It felt good there. Weighty. Like it was meant to be. Of course, older books had a certain sense of gravitas to them, being created before the internet. She opened it to the middle and ran a hand over the parchment, wishing she could read the undecipherable words. Maybe Mr. Carter would read some of it to her.

She stood to shelf the book in its proper place and frowned at the unfamiliar stacks around her. Glancing at the nearest spines, Shannon realized she was in the rare book room. All of them had the same four-digit code as the book she held. All she needed to do was figure out where this one went.

The stacks wound themselves through the room like a labyrinth. But the numbers did not lie. An open space waited right where the errant book should go. Shannon slid the book into its spot and heard the sound of a door closing. "Hello? Mr. Carter, is that you?"

No one answered her call.

Following the maze of shelves out of the stacks, Shannon hurried to catch up with the head librarian. However, every turn led to another row of books and not the expected exit. "Mr. Carter? I'm lost. Guide me out?"

Again silence answered her.

No. Not silence. There was a rustling of paper—like pages of a book flipping in the wind. It came from all around her. The more she listened, the more it sounded like someone whispering to her in a foreign language. A language not meant to be heard by human ears.

Shannon didn't know why she thought so, but she knew she was in trouble. Something was coming for her. Something huge. Larger than she wanted to imagine. Something the very thought of terrified her. It was the source of the whispering.

She ran.

Now it truly was a labyrinth of books. Though frightened, Shannon put out her right hand. She knew the one rule to eventually getting out of any maze was to follow the right-hand or left-hand rule. Every right turn brought her that much closer to escape the stacks until she could see the exit with her eyes.

A wall of books closed the way as if the shelf unit were on hinges.

Shannon almost crashed into them. With her way blocked, she could hear the whispering of the pages . . . of the thing . . . behind her. She refused to look even as she felt it getting closer. She grabbed for the shelves, climbing them as if her life depended on it. Books cascaded from the shelves, crashing to the floor.

The book she was holding landed on her foot, stabbing it with one hard corner. Shannon jerked awake, gasping. With relief, she found herself still on her couch. Wincing at the pain in her foot, she retrieved the book and put it in her backpack—making sure to put it in the padded laptop section to protect it. She shuddered and shook the vestiges of the nightmare off.

Part of her refused to acknowledge the whispered words she heard once more as she entered her bedroom and closed the door behind her.

"*Yidhra uln hai.*"

Despite her fitful sleep and the vague memory of nightmares, Shannon made it to the Grays Harbor campus just after ten in the morning. The John Spellman Library was easy enough to find. Especially with the interior gallery advertising the local artists' display.

Normally she took her time, when she visited a new library, to snoop around and see how they laid out their books, media, information table, card catalog, and computers. There was always something you could learn. Not today. All Shannon wanted to do was return the rare book to its rightful place and get back to her home territory.

Marching up to the information desk, Shannon pasted a polite smile on her face. The woman behind the desk had the high cheekbones and round face of one of the local indigenous tribes. Her badge proclaimed her to be Alina. "Hello. I'm looking for Mr. Carter. He's expecting me."

Alina straightened up before she looked at Shannon. "Ah. Yes. Hello, Miss Lund. If you'll follow me." Looking face on, Alina was older than she'd first assumed. Probably in her late thirties or early forties. Not an intern but a full librarian.

Walking next to the woman, Shannon felt scrutinized. It was obvious that the head librarian had warned his people of her coming, but that didn't explain Alina's unsubtle glances out of the corner of her eye.

They walked through the library and into one of its back hallways. There was a remarkable sense of shifting from a public to a private space. The difference in the carpet and lighting spoke of the building's age. Apparently this campus had been around longer than Shannon realized.

They stopped at an unmarked door. Alina tapped on it twice before cracking

it open and peeking in. "Miss Lund is here, Joshua." A muffled word floated out
the crack, and Alina opened the door wide. "Go on in. I hope you enjoy your
stay here."

"Uh, thank you." Shannon nodded to the woman, still feeling unsettled. She
put it out of her mind as the handsome man approached with his hand out.

"Hello. I'm Joshua Carter. A pleasure to meet you." He pumped her hand
twice. "So you've found our wayward book."

Despite the academic uniform of a tweed suit jacket, he was much younger
than she'd assumed he'd be. And more charming. Shannon covered her fluster
as best she could. "Yes. Well, it was returned to our library yesterday or the day
before. I'm not sure how long the book return was unattended."

"No matter. You have it now?" He smiled at her, pleasant and considerate,
with no hint of the demanding attitude from the day before.

Shannon nodded and dug it out of her backpack. This was not what she'd
expected at all. Mr. Carter wasn't what she'd expected either. "Here it is . . . safe
and sound."

She offered it to him, but he held up his hands. "No. No. I think it only right
that you put it back where it goes. Come along." With that, he brushed by her
and the leather-bound book.

She realized as he passed that he wasn't as young as she first thought he was.
His brown hair was actually a pewter grey that had been obfuscated by the light.
Get it together, Shannon thought. *He was a complete ass last night.*

The two of them walked through the library and past the art exhibit. Shannon
wanted to make small talk, but that'd never been her forte. She preferred books
to people most of the time. Still there was something magnetic about the man.

"Ah, here we are. I'm about to show you one of the great secrets of our dear
library. You can keep a secret, can't you?" Joshua winked at her as they stood
at the end of a hallway with a large bookcase filled with classics. The bookcase
was ornate with leaves, berries, and ivy carved all over it.

She looked around. This couldn't be where they shelved their rare books.
There was no real protection from the elements—natural or human. No way to
protect the books from anyone who walked by. Then she saw that none of the
books had the library's spine labels. "These aren't real, are they?"

"Real books? Yes." He pulled one out and showed it to her. It was *Common
Sense* by Thomas Paine. "They are of course reprints. But the real secret is . . ."
He touched something and two of the leaves popped out. He used these like

door handles to pull the bookshelf open, revealing a hidden room filled with more bookcases. Joshua strolled in and gestured like a presenter. "Welcome to the John Spellman Rare Book Room."

Shannon didn't know what she was more surprised by—the secret room or how much the room's light made the head librarian look like an old man. How could she have thought he was handsome? "Why do you have a secret room? How do people check out books from here if it's so hidden?"

His smile faded, and he looked around the room before stepping to a book stand that stood in front of the first set of bookcases. "Ah. Well, right. Best you go ahead and place the book where it goes." His voice was clipped and hard as he tapped the rare book cradle on top of the book stand. "Then you may go."

It appeared that her lack of enthusiasm made the offer of lunch null and void. Shannon shook her head at the man's sudden sour attitude. She'd have some things to tell her boss when she got back. "Fine." She walked to the book stand and put the book in the cradle. "I wish I could say it's been a pleasure, but honestly, it hasn't."

Joshua glared at her. "Your opinion is noted." He nodded to the door. "Good day."

Shannon took a breath and made the effort to smooth her face into something more professional. "Good day." Turning on her heel, she strode toward the secret entrance, fuming the entire time. She paused at the door and knew she couldn't let this insult go unaddressed. "You know, Mr. Carter . . ."

"Just go. Go now!" The man's voice was halfway between a plea and a shout. Shannon turned. Her knees went weak. Joshua Carter was bathed in an eldritch green glow, emanating from the now open leather-bound book. While she watched, the light surrounded and entrapped him. He thrust a trembling hand at her. "Go! I'm trying to save you!"

Shannon stumbled backward, turning to run, but the doors closed in her face. She still slammed into them, trying to force them open. "Help!" She pounded a fist on the wall before she realized the doors had disappeared completely. Behind her, the light and Joshua's shouts grew. With them, another sound rose— the rustling of pages in the wind.

She turned and pressed her back to the wall. Books from the shelves floated and circled the trapped librarian. Pulses of light traveled to and from the book. Whispers in that alien language filled the air. "*Yidhra uln. Nog. Vulgtlagin phlegeth.Yidhra nnn-geb syha'h. Kadistu nilgh'ri.*"

The man in the light bent over, groaning. He raised both hands to ward off the books and the light. "Please! There's so much more to learn. So much more I could do. Please!"

The young man she'd met in his office was gone. With each pulse of the light, Joshua got older. Hunched, balding, and wrinkled, he was only identifiable by the tweed jacket he'd worn. She knew she hadn't been seeing things. He had gotten older the closer he came to this room . . . to these books.

Joshua gave one last cry before the malevolent green glow filled the room with a surge of power Shannon was sure would blind her. She threw an arm to her eyes and turned to the wall, pressing herself there, willing and praying the doors would return.

Silence descended.

Shannon waited a moment before peeking. The books were all in their place, the light shone as normal, and the only sound she could hear was her panicked breathing. She turned and took a step forward. "Hello?"

"Hello." Alina stepped out from behind one of the bookcases. She smiled at the book in its cradle. "Finally," she breathed.

"No!" Shannon reached a warding hand toward her as the woman picked up the tome.

"It's fine, Miss Lund. Just fine." Alina hugged the book to her chest.

Shannon swore the woman got younger as she watched. "It did something to him. To Mr. Carter."

"Of course it did. He'd outlived his usefulness as the head librarian. That task, that sacred duty, is now mine . . . for good and for ill." Alina looked down at the book. "I think you'll find me to be a good boss. Tough but fair."

"Boss?"

"Yes." She turned the book around, so Shannon could see its cover.

Shannon shuddered, confused. "But . . ."

"But nothing. The library chooses its librarians. It's a dangerous and rewarding job for those who work hard." Alina beckoned to something behind Shannon. "Come in. Come and meet our new peer."

Behind her, the doors had reappeared, and a small group of men and women crowded in. Each one patted her on the shoulder, smiled, or shook her hand as they murmured greetings.

"As I am now the head librarian, we will need to be more formal in public. Please call me by my given name, Ms. Pawluk." Alina handed the book to

Shannon. She accepted it without thinking. "Matthew, stay behind and answer Miss Lund's questions. The rest of you, back to work."

As they disappeared from the room, some back through the doors they came in and others through the stacks, Shannon didn't have to ask where they were going. She already knew. She knew that this was just one hidden sister college to Miskatonic University. She knew that Yidhra—the "Dream Witch"—was just one of many otherworldly gods. She just knew that she now had the chance at immortality in service to the one who had chosen her. She also knew she would probably die a horrible death and be grateful for it.

All this knowledge came to her unbidden. She knew so much more than she had ever wanted to know. The reason was in her hands.

Shannon looked down at the book. She could read it now even though it wasn't in English. She knew this in the depths of her soul. The language and the book were much, much older than that. Its cover read *The Librarian's Handbook in Service to Yidhra*, and she knew she had decades, centuries if she were careful and diligent, to learn all it had to offer.

§

Jennifer Brozek has been a freelance author, editor, and tie-in writer for over ten years after leaving her high paying tech job, and she's never been happier. She keeps a tight schedule on her writing and editing projects and somehow manages to find time to volunteer for several professional writing organizations such as SFWA, HWA, and IAMTW. She shares her husband, Jeff, with several cats and often uses him as a sounding board for her story ideas. Visit Jennifer's worlds at jenniferbrozek.com.

Ordinary People

Mary Berman

I T WAS FIVE O'CLOCK ON THE LAST DAY OF FINALS WEEK, AND JUDITH AND Lilias were walking home from the library. Lilias, an MFA candidate in fiction, had just completed her first-year portfolio, and Judith, a medical student, had been studying for her anatomy practical, which was scheduled for eight p.m. It was the very last exam slot, and Judith felt like that astronomy PhD who'd accidentally opened a portal to the center of the universe and caught a glimpse of Azathoth's eyeball.

"I can't believe you're *done*," she moaned.

"Sorry," said Lilias. She also felt a little like her brains were oozing out of her eye sockets, but mostly she felt like skipping. "When does your exam end? Will you be able to come to Curtis's party?"

"Oh my god, Lilias, you can't go that party. He's your student." Lilias taught creative writing to undergraduates. Curtis was a sophomore, tall and dumb and hot, and Lilias had been crushing on him since January.

"I'm going," said Lilias complacently. "Will you come?"

"I'm not going to an *undergraduate* party. Christ. It's not at a frat, is it?"

"No. It's at the big house on Pickman and Parsonage."

"The old witch house?"

Lilias nodded. Judith made a face that clearly expressed her opinion on old witch houses, undergraduate parties, and hot, dumb sophomores.

"Suit yourself," Lilias said. At that, Judith rolled her eyes, but in an affectionate sort of way. They continued to their apartment, a tiny two-bedroom affair across from St. Mary's Hospital. At home, Judith settled down to study. "You want waffles?" Lilias always made waffles when Judith was stressed, but Judith shook her head, so Lilias boiled some spaghetti instead and got ready for the party.

At seven-fifty, they left. Judith went to her exam. Lilias went to the old witch house. According to a text from Curtis, the party had started early.

Judith's anatomy practical took place in the basement of the medical school, which was attached to St. Mary's across from the main campus. When Judith walked in, the exam was already set up. Sixty full corpses, most with odd deformities, were laid out on ten tidy rows of gurneys. Fluorescent lights glared from the low ceiling.

An anatomy exam at Miskatonic was . . . unconventional. Curious characters gravitated to St. Mary's. It was the only hospital that would treat the unblinking, shambling, flat-faced citizens of Innsmouth; the green-tinged, babbling folk from the village west of the city; the silent men and women who wore ragged, outdated clothes and were covered in dirt and reeked of dead flesh. Since the anatomies of St. Mary's patients were inconsistent, the medical school had forsaken a standard anatomy exam in favor of something like a dissection. Every student received a body, but what sort of body was always a surprise. Sometimes it was a sort no one had ever seen.

Judith found the gurney with her name on it and examined the corpse, and her heart dropped. She couldn't identify it. The corpse wasn't even humanoid. It was at least eight feet long—both ends spilling off the gurney—and shaped like a narrow barrel. It had five tentacle-type feet, five eyeballs, five suction-looking tubes on its head, and five membranous, bat-like wings. Judith poked its flesh, which was black and leathery and iridescent. She walked around it, picked up the clipboard with the written exam, put the clipboard down, and dug the heels of her hands into her eyes.

"Damn," said the guy next to her. "What'd *you* get?"

"Shut up," Juliet said.

The instructor called, "Begin."

Judith hopelessly cut open the corpse's chest.

Despite all her bravado, Lilias was a little uncomfortable about going to an undergrad party. She was in her mid-twenties for Pete's sake. Everyone else at the party would be like nineteen. But she'd rationalized it to herself, saying that undergrads were still adults; it wasn't like they were *minors*. (She imagined making this argument to Judith and faltered a little.)

So she'd put on a short summer dress and cute sneakers and some makeup, trying to look hot but like casual co-ed hot, not teacher hot. She took a deep breath and walked up the sidewalk to the old witch house.

The house was built on the plot of land that had once held Arkham's true witch house. That house, its walls full of bones and blood-caked knives and old books, had been torn down half a century ago. In the 90s, someone had built a new house on the land, a nice and normal white two-story colonial, but the lines of the attic still conformed to some bizarre geometry, and there were always teeth in the bathtub drain. The owner couldn't sell it, so he rented it out for cheap to large packs of college kids. College kids didn't care if the house was haunted. Rent was half that of any other house in the neighborhood, and the owner let them do whatever they pleased, including throwing end-of-semester ragers.

Lilias raised her hand to knock on the door, decided that was something an uncool old person would do, and pushed her way in.

She found herself in a narrow, dark foyer cluttered with backpacks and mail and smelly boys' shoes. The foyer was silent. Lilias stood motionless for a moment, listening, waiting with the open door at her back. Nervously she flicked the light switch. The bulb in the ceiling burst, flaring white and brilliant before the foyer plunged back into darkness.

Leaving the door open, Lilias edged into the belly of the house. But she knew before she reached the end of the hallway that she would hear the door slam shut behind her. She was right.

"Hello?" she called, too unsettled to be embarrassed.

Another beat of silence, and to her relief, a voice shouted back, "We're in the kitchen!"

"I don't know where that is!"

More silence. Then footsteps. Lilias prepared to run, but she was startled into stillness by a flashlight beam sweeping over her face. The owner of the flashlight ran up and hugged her. It was Curtis. "Hey!" he said. "You made it!"

"Uh, hey." Lilias hugged him back. Warmth bloomed in her stomach despite herself. "Some house, huh?"

"It's whatever. Come on. We're doing a ritual."

"A . . . ritual?" She followed him through the dark house. In the living room, the beam from Curtis's flashlight shone on dozens of empty beer bottles and about eighteen futons. On the floor was a very-expensive-looking Persian rug, and on the wall, where one might expect a flat-screen TV in a house like this, hung a massive reproduction of Richard Pickman's *Ghoul Feeding*. The red eyes of the creature in the painting followed Lilias across the room.

"Is the power out?" Lilias asked.

"No. The foyer and living room are always like this. That's why we can't get cable. Here, this is better." They emerged into the kitchen. Lilias blinked at the sudden brightness, feeling as though she'd just walked through a curtain or a fog. "Guys, have you met Lilias?"

One of the young men grouped around the counter—or, more accurately, around the booze-filled cooler on the counter—raised his eyebrows and said, "Your writing teacher?"

"Dude, she's cool." Curtis handed Lilias a Solo cup full of jungle juice, which she resolved to pour down the sink at the earliest opportunity. "Where'd Martin go?"

"Upstairs to get his copy of the book."

"What's the ritual for?" Lilias asked.

"Summoning the elder things."

"Oh, *don't*," Lilias said. "Look what happened to that astronomy PhD."

The guys gave Curtis a look that clearly said, *Get your lame-ass teacher out of here.*

"It's cool," said a boy who hadn't spoken yet. "Martin says he knows a way to do it so they have to obey our every whim."

"What do you want an elder thing for?"

"They have total control over time and space. I need them to make it so I didn't fail my Spanish final," he said matter-of-factly. "I need that shit to graduate."

"You're going to rend the fabric of the universe just because you didn't study hard enough f—"

Someone interrupted, "Where's Martin?"

"I'll get him." Lilias put down her cup. Maybe if she found this Martin fellow, she could convince him not to go through with this codswallop. Everyone looked at Curtis, and Curtis said hastily, "I'll go with you."

They went out the back of the kitchen, turned left before reaching the back door, and climbed a narrow set of wooden stairs. Halfway up, the lights went out again. Wordlessly Curtis clicked on his flashlight. They checked Martin's bedroom first. The walls were papered with maps of Arkham and Boston and Innsmouth, slashes of marker covering them like Martin was on the hunt for a serial killer. On the shelves were a bunch of creepy-looking old books, plus a Cthulhu statue of some weird alloy that appeared to have been stolen from Miskatonic's museum.

"No one really likes Martin," Curtis explained. He picked up the statue, shuddered, and tossed it on the bed. "But he pays the most rent. And some of his rituals are really cool, you know. One time he summoned a minor god that showed a couple of the guys their futures." He grinned. "He disappeared before it was my turn, but he said Jake was gonna be a billionaire by thirty and die in a train crash at thirty-two. Isn't that wild?"

"That's one word for it," Lilias said. She was still trying to be cool, but somehow Curtis was not as hot in this creepy house surrounded by frat boys as he was when he dropped by her office hours or said something earnest and stupid in class. Something about his attitude regarding the ritual—a sort of passivity mixed with dull excitement—put her off.

They explored the rest of the second floor. There was no sign of Martin, but Lilias did see the famed bathtub of teeth.

"I guess he's in the attic," Curtis said. He seemed uncomfortable, but there was nothing for it.

One reached the attic through a trapdoor set in the ceiling of the second-floor hallway. Curtis tugged on the rope attached to the trapdoor, and it fell, bringing a collapsible ladder with it. But he didn't seem able to bring himself to ascend. Lilias, though unease prickled in her throat, took the flashlight and went first.

"Martin?" she called. "Hello?"

The attic was small with a single tiny, round window and a low-sloping ceiling. The only pieces of furniture were a twin bed and a nightstand jammed into the corner. Fortunately, on the nightstand was a merrily burning black candle, so Lilias was able to turn off the flashlight and look around. Scattered all over the floor were dust bunnies, rat droppings, and papers. Most of the papers looked as foreign and obscure as the books on Martin's shelves, but Lilias flipped one with her foot and found a syllabus for "INFO 600: Information and Knowledge Professions (Required Course #1 for the MLS)." Martin was a master of library science student. Of course. They were always getting up to the weird shit.

He also appeared to be absent. "I don't see him," Lilias called to Curtis. "Does he live up here?"

"No." Curtis poked his head up. "Ugh, yuck, maybe. Martin? Where you at, bro?"

Lilias went to look out the window, but she saw nothing but the dusky sky and the ordinary New England street.

The next instant, she heard papers rustling close behind her. The wood floor creaked. Curtis yelled, "LILIAS!"

Lilias, acting half from surprise and half on instinct, jumped and swiveled and ducked all in one motion. Someone close behind her—now in front of her—stabbed a knife toward the space where her neck had been. Lilias screamed and punched him in the stomach.

The figure dropped his knife and doubled over. Lilias scrambled away. Curtis ran over and grabbed the guy, twisting his hands behind his back and dragging him away from Lilias. "Martin, dude," Curtis said breathlessly, "what the fuck?"

Lilias, once she had grabbed the knife and positioned herself near the trapdoor, looked at the MLS student who had just apparently tried to murder her. He was even taller than Curtis but gangly with poofy red hair and a thousand freckles. He looked shockingly ordinary and might have been good-looking except for his badly yellowed teeth. He wasn't struggling. Instead he regarded Curtis over his shoulder with what appeared to be genuine surprise. "What gives?" he asked Curtis. "I thought she was the virgin sacrifice."

"I'm not a virgin," Lilias said. "Also, what?"

"Martin, no," said Curtis. "We talked about this. We're gonna use Rob."

Lilias said, "*What*?"

"It's cool," Curtis said. "He volunteered."

"It would be better to have a woman," muttered Martin. "I *can* use Rob, but I *told* you I'd rather have a woman."

"No," said Lilias, "no, no, no, no, no. Who's Rob? Where is he? I'm taking him to Saint Mary's."

"You can't," Martin shrilled. "We need him for the ritual."

"You do *not*. Leave the elder things where they belong, wherever that is—"

"Don't you see?" Martin said. His eyes gleamed in the light of the black candle. "This is it: the ritual I've been searching for. All those years of learning arcane languages, studying ancient texts, traveling to the old cities in search of their dark secrets. Since I was a small child, I have studied the elder things, desiring only to harness one to my will. Tonight I shall. Who would have guessed that it would be so simple! I require only a virgin sacrifice, the intent of a dozen, and the words of the book." Martin jerked his chin at a thick volume that lay open in the corner. Lilias stared at it, at the yellowed pages and writhing rust-red script that was visible even from here. The book exuded an ugly power. Even without seeing the title, she knew it was a copy of the dreaded *Necronomicon*. Maybe even an original. God, what had these dumb boys gotten themselves into?

She tore her eyes away, trying hard to maintain her composure, but her pulse was throbbing. "Ix-nay on the virgin sacrifice," she said stoutly. "I'm the only real adult in this place, and I forbid it."

"Lilias," said Curtis, pained, "don't be lame."

"Sorry," Lilias said. She wasn't though. With a careful eye on Martin, she stuck the knife and flashlight in her waistband and began to lower herself to the second floor. She would return to the kitchen, locate Rob, take him to the hospital, maybe call his parents—

Lilias's feet hit the floor. As she began to run, a scrabbling noise sounded from the attic. Then Martin, with a speed she would not have believed possible, streaked past her, too fast for her to grab him.

Lilias swiveled frantically. Curtis was descending the ladder and taking his sweet time about it. "Curtis!" she yelled. "CATCH HIM! He's going to kill Rob!"

"It's cool," Curtis said for the umpteenth time. "Rob volunteered."

Lilias wanted to hit him, but he was still descending, and she was already running so fast and so desperate that she slipped and tumbled down the stairs. She burst into the kitchen, her arms already outstretched to grab Martin, but she skidded to a halt. Her heart juddered.

The boys she'd met earlier were standing in a circle. In the center of the circle was Martin. He was chanting. Sprawled on the ground before him was another boy, a football-looking type with his mouth open and his eyes wide and dull and blood spilling out of his neck.

Lilias screamed.

Martin did not stop chanting, but he glanced at her with extreme annoyance.

One of the boys clapped a hand over her mouth. Lilias bit his hand so hard she drew blood, whacked another guy in the face, and continued to scream. Someone wrapped his arms around her from behind, pinned her arms to her torso, covered her mouth, and lifted her up, so she couldn't run or stamp on his foot. It was Curtis. Still holding her, he joined the circle. "Sorry," he whispered to the guys. "She's usually chill. I swear."

Lilias struggled ferociously.

"Get her out of here," said the guy whose hand she'd bitten.

"He can't," answered another one. "The ritual needs twelve, remember?"

Lilias fell still and counted the boys in the circle. Curtis was the twelfth.

"It's gonna be cool, Lil," Curtis whispered. "You'll see."

Don't call me Lil, Lilias wanted to say, but he was still silencing her.

Martin continued to chant. The boys began to sway, rhythmic and fluid like underwater reeds. Something went thunk. It sounded like it was coming from the attic or perhaps from underground or from another planet. The dead kid on the ground gasped and convulsed before falling still again. A shudder ran through the circle, but the members held their ground.

Martin stopped chanting.

Nothing happened except that Rob's blood began to trickle across the linoleum floor. Lilias could not tear her eyes from the dead boy. She fought very hard not to cry. Something sharp was digging into her leg, and it took her a second to realize that it was the knife from the attic. It took her another second to decide that, even with her arms pinned, she could probably reach it.

At last, one of the boys said, "Where's the elder thing?"

"Shh!" Martin hissed. His eyes and hair were wild. He looked around frantically, waiting, but no elder thing appeared, no cosmic force rang out or warped the air. Lilias closed her eyes and took five deep breaths through her nose. When she opened them again, Martin was clenching his fists, glaring at the boys. He barked, "Which one of you ruined it?"

"How could we ruin it?" someone snapped. "You said all we had to do was stand here."

"I said you had to stand there with *intent!*"

"What the fuck does that mean?"

"Yeah, what happened, Martin?"

"Does this mean I'm going to fail Spanish?"

The boys started to babble. In the excitement, Curtis loosened his grip, but the boys were still clustered too tightly for Lilias to risk breaking free. A drop of blood dripped from Martin's clenched fist: he'd broken his own skin with his fingernails. It splashed on the linoleum and joined the dead boy's blood, which was flowing steadily toward the back of the kitchen.

Oh, Lilias thought.

But Martin was figuring it out too. He stared at the blood, at the way the trickle crept closer and closer to the kitchen threshold, and at how it crawled over the threshold like it had a mind of its own, flowing faster and faster, lengthening until it contained more blood than could possibly fit in a nineteen-year-old's body, spilling through the hallway and out the back door, forming a trail.

Martin cocked his head. As though in a trance, he followed it.

The boys shouted after him. They broke the circle and milled about, some arguing that they should follow Martin, others making a beeline for the jungle juice. One boy tried to clean up Rob's body while three others held him back. Lilias tried to wrench away from Curtis, but he immediately tightened his grip.

There was nothing for it. She slipped the knife out of her waistband and stabbed him in the thigh.

Curtis yelped and shoved her away, and before anyone else could grab her, she was out the door after Martin.

Judith was definitely going to fail her anatomy practical.

She'd slashed open the whole corpse, hoping she might find something comparable to a familiar organ, but the top half of the body appeared to be vegetative, and the bottom half was as empty as the sky. She couldn't find any muscles or bones, no digestive tract, not even a brain or a nervous system. There was a weird orb in its chest cavity that she thought might be a heart, but it was diamond-solid and unconnected to any of the vegetative tissue. After half an hour, fighting back tears—she'd spent *weeks* studying for this exam—she began to answer all the multiple-choice questions with C. She turned her back on the corpse like maybe it would go away if she didn't have to look at it.

"Uh, hey," the guy next to her said as she despondently bubbled in number sixteen. "Your sample. Is it supposed to do that?"

"I don't know *what* it's supposed to do," Judith wailed.

"It's like . . . moving though."

Judith looked at it and jumped back about six feet.

The orb in the corpse's chest cavity was glowing a vivid, ethereal black. The five eyeballs swiveled, the five suction tubes wriggled, and the five legs scrambled for purchase. The body rolled off the gurney. It fluttered in midair, using its five wings to maneuver into an upright position. Once standing, it began to trundle placidly toward the door.

Judith scrabbled for the scalpel. Everyone stared at her mobile corpse except for the professor who appeared to be doodling on a Scantron sheet.

"Sir?" Judith called nervously. "My corpse is leaving."

The professor didn't even glance up. "Well, you'd better go after it then, hadn't you?"

Judith opened her mouth and closed it like a fish. A couple of students frowned sympathetically at her, though most of them were either gawking at the slime trail the corpse had left or returning to their own work. After a few seconds, Judith tucked the exam into her back pocket, stuck her pencil in her bun, and with scalpel in hand followed the corpse.

Martin had vanished, but the trail of blood was clearly visible, shiny and tar-black under the yellow streetlamps. Lilias followed it half a mile to the Miskatonic River that ran through town, but there the trail disappeared into the rushing water.

The opposite riverbank was visible, and the gambrel-roofed waterfront houses glistened in the lamplight, but Lilias did not see Martin. Where had he gone? The trail—it *was* a trail, right?—led directly to the river . . .

Something a few feet to her left caught her eye. Jumpily she turned, and what she saw made her clap her hands over her mouth: a great, black barrel-shaped creature with its chest yawning open, and its heart bathed in a nuclear glow. It was ambling toward the river, heedless of Lilias, heedless of everything. A few feet behind the creature was Judith.

Almost unable to believe her eyes, Lilias called, "Judith?"

Judith stopped short. "Lilias?"

"Oh my god, it is you. What is that thing?"

"That's my corpse for the anatomy practical. What are you doing here? Ew, is that blood?"

"Martin murdered somebody," said Lilias. She couldn't tear her eyes from the so-called corpse ambling away. "Are you sure that thing is dead?"

"No. Who's Martin? Wait, *murdered*?"

"He's a library science student who lives in the witch house. He was trying to summon an elder thing, but . . ."

Judith's eyes widened. "An *elder thing*!" She grabbed a piece of paper from her back pocket and began to scan it. Then she took a pencil from her bun and began erasing furiously. Meanwhile the corpse—an elder thing?—trundled ever closer to the river, and when it reached the edge of the water, it kept going. Soon its feet-tentacles were submerged and its waist. Water poured into the gaping hole in its body.

"Uh, Judith?" said Lilias. "What are you gonna do with your thing?"

Judith glanced up. When she spotted the corpse, which was now two-thirds underwater, she gasped and rushed after it.

Lilias grabbed her. "What are you doing?"

"Let me go! I need to identify its reproductive system!"

"We'll drown!"

"We will not. It's the Miskatonic not the English Channel," and with that, Judith grasped Lilias's hand and ran with her into the river.

The water was frigid. It struck Lilias's legs with frightening power. The elder thing was almost submerged now. Water weighed down Lilias's clothes; it was up to her neck, and soon she would be unable to breathe, but Judith wasn't stopping—

And then she felt herself falling. Somewhere in the middle of the riverbed was an opening, and the water poured in and took her and Judith with it. It sucked Lilias's head underwater before she had a chance to scream. She held her breath and clung to Judith, her eyes squeezed shut, her body battered against rocky walls.

And then, all at once, it was over. Lilias and Judith thunked into a soft, sandy surface, and Lilias coughed up river water and opened her eyes.

The opening in the river floor had been, it seemed, a tunnel, and it had spat them out who knew where. They were underground, that much was certain. They lay on damp black sand, and beside them, an underground river ran, fed by the Miskatonic. The walls were rough and black and shiny, and the only light came from innumerable sickly blue fungi that clung to the high, rocky ceiling.

On the far side of the river was a city.

The city was as dense and massive as Manhattan, but where Manhattan's buildings were characterized by smooth straight lines, this one's were full of wild spirals, sharp dangerous peaks, curious domes, and weird disks. The whole thing appeared to be built of some odd, gleaming metal the color of oxidized copper but with the underlying glow of polished steel. It gave Lilias the same uneasy sense the witch house had.

A dark figure was disappearing into it. Two dark figures in fact.

"That's Martin!" Lilias cried. Judith was already splashing across the shallow river. Lilias followed. Clutching each other's hands and holding forth their blades, the women plunged down a wide black boulevard and into the city proper.

The structures they ran past were not identifiable. Once Lilias glimpsed a great cubic building that she thought might be a bank, but mostly everything was weird spirals and fences, eerie statues, buildings that looked like they'd been built upside down, dead gardens, and dry fountains that resembled gaping mouths. Lilias could not see the elder thing—which was odd, considering it had moved at roughly the pace of a slug—but she kept on glimpsing Martin's lanky form and red hair, and she and Judith kept pursuing him. At last, they spotted him at the far end of yet another boulevard, walking down the stairs of a monumental round building, which looked for all the world like a monster's head.

There was nothing for it at this point. Lilias and Judith followed.

They entered the building through the door that might be its mouth, watching warily the opaque eyelike windows. The inside was pitch-black. Wordlessly Lilias clicked on Curtis's flashlight. They descended two flights of stairs, proceeded down a corridor decorated with strange etchings and empty sconces, and emerged into a massive round room with a domed ceiling. Lilias shivered. She could not help thinking that if this building *were* a head, this would be the inside of its skull. In the dark, the walls could not be seen, but the marbled floor was etched with a massive symbol, some squiggly pentagram gone wrong.

The elder thing miraculously stood in the center of the symbol, wounds and glowing heart and all. And there was Martin, pacing around the elder thing with his hands in his pockets. It rolled its eyes to look at him. Lilias released Judith and lunged for Martin, grabbing the back of his sweatshirt. He was laughing. Her stomach sank.

"It's too late," he said. "Look." He gestured to the edges of the room. Lilias shone her flashlight there and almost dropped it.

"My god," Judith whispered. She had caught up to them. "There're *thousands*."

Thousands of immobile elder things lined up like toy soldiers. As Lilias watched, a black glow like the one in Judith's corpse began to play through their bodies.

"I've woken them all," Martin exclaimed. He broke out of Lilias's grip and began to dance. "They shall *all* obey me!"

"Oh no," Lilias said. She pressed her back to Judith's. Judith, apparently still hell-bent on acing her anatomy final, was poking around the inside of the cut-up elder thing, which amazingly enough was letting her do it. It appeared to be so utterly focused on Martin that it didn't notice the human woman's hands in its guts. "Judith, cut that out and pay attention before this library science jackass becomes our supreme overlord. What are we going to do?"

"I think we're going to have to kill him," said Judith.

"The elder thing?"

"No, dummy. Martin. He's driving the spell, isn't he?" They'd learned about basic spellcraft during orientation, but Lilias hadn't paid any attention.

"I can't kill Martin!"

"I can," said Judith. Lilias twisted round to gawk at her. She was still examining the elder thing, specifically its weird heart. "We'll have to kill this one too though. The spell is channeled through it. Come here." She grabbed Lilias's hands and guided them into the elder thing's chest cavity. Lilias cringed. "Feel this? This big cord?"

"It's *disgusting*."

"Oh, calm down. It's just a nerve. I think. Anyway, I think it connects the . . . the orb, the energy source, whatever . . . to whatever thing it has instead of a brain. So when I shout, 'Now,' you've got to cut this. Okay?"

"You're not really going to murder Martin," said Lilias numbly.

Without answering, Judith took the big knife from Lilias's hands and replaced it with the scalpel. She turned on her heel and marched toward Martin who still laughed and danced. Judith went up behind him and grabbed a fistful of his hair.

She's really going to do it, Lilias thought. *He doesn't think she will. It's going to be easy.*

"It's too late!" Martin cried. "It's too late!" The black light grew brighter, and the elder things sent up a collective groan. Lilias felt it like gravel in her blood. The creature she had her hands in twitched; the vibration threaded into her fingers, crawled up into her eyeballs, her tongue.

"Now!" Judith screamed. With one ugly stroke, she slashed Martin's neck open.

Lilias cut the cord.

Martin, gasping, his blood spurting and burbling, collapsed to his knees and fell full on his face. The elder thing started to thrash. Lilias jerked away from it, ran to Judith, slipped in Martin's blood. Together they stared as the elder things writhed and screamed, and they covered their ears as the vibrations thundered through the meat of their bodies.

The elder things stilled. The black light flickered out. The room fell impossibly dark and silent. Martin lay at the women's feet, glassy-eyed and open-mouthed.

Without warning, Lilias's legs gave out from under her. She looked up at Judith.

In the light of the flashlight, Judith's skin was sallow. There was no expression whatsoever on her face, yet she looked awfully tired. She padded over to her corpse.

"Judith," Lilias said.

Judith, her voice hard and hollow, said, "I need to examine its reproductive system."

Lilias opened her mouth to ask if Judith was all right, but she was too exhausted to speak. She was asleep before her body hit the ground.

Judith couldn't remember leaving the underground citadel or returning to her apartment. But here she was, lying in her own bed with blood caked into the lines of her palms. Her throat convulsed. To keep from vomiting, she fumbled in her back pocket, searching for her exam. It wasn't there.

She sat bolt upright and searched frantically for her computer. She had to email the professor.

When she clicked into her email, her heart sank. She already had an email from the professor, which couldn't be good. There was also a news alert. Two boys had been found with their throats cut in the kitchen of 340 Parsonage Street. Preliminary theories, corroborated by the other boys in the house, suggested that one boy had killed the other and then himself.

Judith rubbed her eyes. The crusted blood on her hands scratched her eyelids.

Lilias came in a few minutes later while Judith was reading the professor's email. Judith's emotions must have shown on her face because Lilias asked, "What is it?" Lilias too was wearing last night's clothes, and she was covered in blood and dirt and slime.

"I have to retake my anatomy exam," Judith said, though of course that wasn't really the answer to Lilias's question. "The professor says he wanted to flunk me when I didn't come back and turn in my exam, but the rest of the class threatened to go to the provost about it, so he says I can retake it at two today." She was so tired; she felt like she was dead.

"Are we going to talk about last night?"

"No."

"Judith," Lilias said. "You had to do it. You know that, don't you? You were brave."

"No," Judith repeated.

Lilias hovered for another minute before retreating. Judith heard her banging around in the kitchen. A few minutes later, the smell of hot waffle batter wafted into the bedroom.

§

Mary Berman is a writer of science fiction and fantasy with work published or forthcoming in *Cicada, Fireside, Daily Science Fiction,* and elsewhere. She earned her MFA in creative writing from the University of Mississippi and her BA from the Writing Seminars program at Johns Hopkins University. In her spare time, she practices taekwondo and antagonizes her cat. Find her online at www.mtgberman.com.

It Takes a Special Kind of Girl to Steal the Necronomicon

Jill Hand

ACACIA PERKINS DIDN'T WANT TO THINK ABOUT THE GRISLY OBJECTS IN HER backpack, the ones the man with the cement-colored eyes had given her. Knowing what she was going to do with them, she felt sick. Instead she forced herself to ignore the restless shifting coming from inside the purple nylon L.L.Bean backpack strapped to her shoulders and to focus on the money—one hundred thousand dollars just for stealing a library book!

She rehearsed what she'd say if she encountered a security guard, deciding the best way would be to pretend to be a little flustered as if she were guilty of nothing more serious than dozing off with her face in a book, something along the lines of—*I fell asleep at one of the carrels up on the third floor and didn't hear the announcement that the library was closing. What time is it? Ohmigosh, that late? I'd better go!*

Shortly before 10 p.m., when Orne Library closed for the night, Acacia had hidden in one of the building's towers where a teaching assistant named Tom Danforth had a cramped little office, before going off on a disastrous expedition to Antarctica back in the 1930s. Eerily, Danforth's office was still exactly as he left it: a wooden filing cabinet filled with crumbling Manila folders, a rolltop desk on which sat a black candlestick telephone and a square glass ashtray full of ancient cigarette butts, and a black and white photograph in a tarnished silver frame of a woman with short hair done up in finger waves. Acacia guessed it was Danforth's girlfriend.

She sat in the rolling chair last occupied by the unfortunate Danforth and drummed her fingers on the desk, forcing herself to wait until two hours had passed when everyone with the exception of a security guard would have left the building. The chair's cracked black leather seat offered no cushion for her jeans-clad bottom, and its wooden back hit her shoulder blades in exactly the wrong spot. She shifted, feeling apprehensive, the way she did when she stayed up all night cramming for an exam in thaumaturgy, her worst subject, when she would drink cup after cup of black coffee, trying to memorize things like the correct words to say in Hebrew to get rid of a dybbuk.

In retrospect, she could have chosen a more comfortable place to sit and hide: the padded bench in the room where they stored old academic gowns, for instance. The massive Richardsonian Romanesque library that loomed over the campus of Miskatonic University contained a multitude of out-of-the-way nooks and crannies, enough to conceal an army of students intent on committing burglary.

Acacia liked to explore when she got bored during her work-study job of returning books to their proper places on the shelves. She would wander around, examining the dark, old oil portraits of long-dead deans that hung above the carved marble fireplaces in the reading rooms, of which there were at least six (the exact number seemed to change from day to day despite how carefully Acacia counted them). She discovered all sorts of things, like the pneumatic-tube system used for sending request slips down to the basement circulation room and a hidden door behind which was an elevator paneled in gorgeously carved mahogany that was only big enough for one person to fit comfortably. She found a room with a sign on its door proclaiming it to be the Eliza M. Bickford Ladies Retiring Room. Whenever Acacia looked in there, the same trio of women, dressed in the style of the late 1800s, sat companionably together on an upholstered divan, leafing through the pages of what appeared to be a large scrapbook.

Walking between the marble columns beneath the rotunda, Acacia would tilt her head back and take in the mural of some kind of gigantic sea creature that was attacking a three-masted barquentine, its bulbous eyes glaring as it plucked sailors off the deck with its tentacles. It was a weird choice of subject for an academic library, but Miskatonic was a weird place. Several years prior to Acacia's arrival, *U.S. News & World Report* had done a feature in which it ranked the university seventh among best national universities. The writer had jokingly compared it to Hogwarts from Harry Potter, saying that his request to view the Jeremiah Orne Library's collection of ancient grimoires and "forbidden" books had been denied, making him conclude that the special collection didn't really exist and was "just a rumor to add spice to what was essentially an ordinary New England university, albeit one with a long and very strange history."

He couldn't have been more wrong, but nobody from Miskatonic corrected him.

Upon hearing the clock in the bell tower strike midnight, Acacia crept out of her hiding place. She approached the door of the special collections room, the rubber soles of her white Converses whispering on the polished granite floor. Flicking on the penlight attached to her key chain, she moved its thin beam until she located the keyhole. She held her breath, her heartbeat *lub-dub*, *lub-dub* in her ears, as she inserted an old-fashioned brass key with a long barrel and ornate grip. The keyhole was set in an ornamental bronze faceplate embellished with elaborate art nouveau swoops and flourishes, the bottom ending in a grinning skull with blank round eyes. One of its eyes seemed to wink as she turned the key as far to the left as it would go. There was a barely audible click as the lock opened. Acacia cocked her head and listened for the sound of approaching footsteps. All was quiet. So far, so good.

She stepped inside and closed the heavy door behind her before letting out her breath. She was in; now for the hard part. She looked around the room with its glass-fronted bookcases, searching for the right one. The special collections room lacked the grandeur of the rotunda, but something about its atmosphere made the delicate hairs on her arms and the back of her neck stand up, and she could feel a tingling in the air, the way there was when she walked beneath high-voltage power lines.

Leaded-glass windows set high in the walls let in enough light for her to see. Lower down, stained-glass windows depicted scenes from Greek mythology, all of which featured men with swords either killing monsters or being killed by them in various gruesome ways.

The floor beneath her sneakers was made up of mosaic tiles in the shape of the university's seal: an open book surmounted by a lamp, around which were the words Ad Eundum Quo Nemo Ante Iit. Undergraduates were required to take Latin, so Acacia knew it meant to boldly go where no man has gone before. It was a phrase from *Star Trek* although the university's founding predated the television series by more than three centuries.

It was chilly in the special collections room despite the cast-iron radiators, which gave out pings and sighs as the night grew colder. Acacia rubbed her arms and wished she'd thought to bring a jacket. From outside, she could faintly hear car horns honking and voices calling as a Friday night in downtown Arkham, Massachusetts, climbed toward its early-morning crescendo. If the night ran true to form, there would be at least one fight between Miskatonic students and townies, the old antipathy between town and gown going back to colonial times when Miskatonic produced ministers of the gospel instead of computer geeks and business majors.

Usually Acacia's roommate Spode Whitburn would be out there, roaming through the coffee shops and tattoo parlors and all-night fast food places and convenience stores on West College Street with a posse of other girls, all of them armed with black American Express cards. Shrieking with laughter, they'd venture to the bars on Garrison Street, down by the river, which had a checkered and violent history. Students are warned during freshman orientation that the Garrison Street regulars didn't tolerate the university. Spode and her friends were among those who blithely ignored the warning. Inevitably, one of them would do something so incredibly foolish—"I'm going to flash that cop. Watch!"—that it would be talked about for at least a week.

Spode was big and noisy and blonde. She'd been a varsity field hockey player at her high school back home in California. Her father was a movie producer, and her mother was a former supermodel who sold a line of beauty products for women over forty, designed to firm and tighten everything that needed firming and tightening. Spode was the exact opposite of Acacia, who was small and dark and quiet, yet they were good friends . . .

Upon meeting Acacia for the first time, Spode said, "Oh my God, you're so exotic! You look like Theda Bara. You know who that is?"

Acacia shook her head, never having heard of the silent film star.

"She was a big star back in the twenties. She was all sultry and mysterious. I can totally see you in a veil and loads of gold bracelets, riding behind Rudolph Valentino across the desert on an Arabian stallion."

"Thanks," said Acacia, amused.

"No, seriously, I totally can," Spode insisted. "Where are you from?"

"Newburyport."

"No, I mean originally."

"I was born in Newburyport," Acacia told her, which was true. So were her parents and her grandparents on both sides. Far back, some ancestor had come over from England, having originally come from someplace in the Middle East, either Syria or Saudi Arabia. The details had long been forgotten.

"Well, I think you're super-hot. If I was a lesbian, I would totally want to do you," Spode proclaimed. Then she launched into a complaint about how they weren't supposed to have microwave ovens in their rooms but screw that because she would die without a microwave and what did Acacia think of those stuck-up girls in Alpha Omega Pi? Weren't they the worst? Did she hear what they did to those two exchange students? It was supposedly an accident, but she wouldn't be surprised if they'd done it on purpose. She went on and on, cheerfully babbling about whatever came into her head. Acacia let Spode's words wash over her, happy that not much in the way of a response was required from her. It was relaxing, like hearing birds chirping or a fountain splashing.

The exchange students to whom Spode referred were Graziela Lombardi and Monika Luftheim. They'd been turned into toads during pledge week the previous year by members of Alpha Omega Pi, one of the sororities on campus. They remained toads despite all attempts by the faculty to restore them to their human state. On the morning of the day that Acacia hid in the library, an announcement was made in the dining hall that the sisters of Alpha Omega Pi would be having a bake sale in the lobby of the Wilmarth Student Center from 9 a.m. to noon, the proceeds going to supply Monika and Graziela with crickets and mealworms.

There were other announcements, the usual kind of thing, including that the west wing of the Halsey Building at the medical school had disappeared again. It was expected to return, having always done so in the past. In the meantime, students who had classes in the vanished wing were to consult the bulletin board outside the main lecture hall in Halsey for the location of their temporary classrooms.

The dean of students wished to remind everyone that doppelgangers had been sighted on campus. Students were advised that if they encountered someone who looks exactly like them to notify campus security.

"I wouldn't mind meeting my doppelganger," Spode told Acacia as they waited in line at the breakfast buffet. Acacia nibbled on a miniature cheese danish, trying to decide whether she really wanted to eat it or not. The food in the dining hall wasn't very good, and the pastry was stale.

"They're supposed to be a harbinger of death," Acacia told her. She decided against finishing the danish and threw it in the trash.

"Yeah, but if I met my doppelganger, I'd get her to turn around, so I could see if I should return these yoga pants or not. I think they make my butt look big. What do you think?"

"It looks fine but take them back if it bothers you."

"I will. They came from a store in Boston. I'm going there after my last class lets out. I'll probably stay overnight at this boutique hotel I found online. They've got a spa where you sit in a sauna until you're sweating like a pig and then you jump in a tub of ice water and then they beat you with sticks. It's supposed to detoxify your liver or something. You wanna come?"

Acacia told her she had to study. She hated not having enough money to pay her own way when she went places with Spode, even though her friend didn't mind paying for everything with the credit card and the generous allowance her parents gave her. Once she had successfully taken the book from the special collections room and given it to the man with the cement-colored eyes, Acacia would have plenty of money. The thought cheered her up, despite her apprehension about using the horrible objects given to her by the man who called himself Mr. Jones. (She doubted that it was his real name.)

Two naked young men, their bodies glowing with an eldritch blue light, edged into the buffet line in front of them, causing Spode to yelp, "Hey!"

They turned around, surprised. "No cutting in line. You're not invisible anymore. We can see you. Go put some clothes on," Spode told them.

The pair ran off, laughing nervously.

"A&P majors, probably," said Acacia, meaning *alchemy* and *pharmacy*.

"Idiots. They should have checked to see if anybody could see them before coming in here like that. I swear, this place is insane. My cousin goes to Bennington, and he says it's nothing like this," Spode told her, critically examining her teeth in the reflective metal hood over the buffet table.

Inside the special collections room, Acacia could hear the clock in the tower chime the quarter hour. Fifteen minutes past midnight. She could put it off no longer. Her nerves thrumming, she walked across the mosaic-tiled floor to the bookcase where the *Necronomicon* was kept.

Opening the glass door, she knelt, took off her backpack, unzipped it, and reached inside. Flinching, she drew out a pair of mummified hands. The skin was brown and dry and leathery, split in places to disclose ivory-colored bone. They ended in forearms that were cut off about five inches above the wrists, the stumps bound in black silk. They twitched in Acacia's grasp, and her lips drew back in an involuntary grimace of distaste . . .

"Not very nice to look at, are they? My suggestion is not to think of them as once having been part of a living human being. Think of them as tools, like salad tongs perhaps," Mr. Jones had told her, delicately licking powdered sugar from his fingertips.

Salad tongs for the Donner party, Acacia thought. A salad served with them would be likely to contain poisonous mushrooms.

Mr. Jones had been waiting for her on the previous afternoon when she left Orne Library. He was seated on one of the dark-green-painted cast-iron benches beneath the ancient sycamore trees that lined the flagstone walk between the library and Pabodie Hall, Acacia's dormitory. She had thought the man in the black suit, white shirt buttoned to the neck, and no tie must be an albino, so pale was his skin and so white was his hair. Then she drew closer and saw the eyes he turned to her weren't pink but the color of dry cement. He reminded her of photographs she'd seen of Andy Warhol.

"May I ask you something?" he said. His voice was a pleasant tenor with a distinct Southern accent.

"Sure," she replied, expecting to be asked for directions to the nearest ATM or if she knew what time the last bus left for Innsmouth. Around her, flocks of students eddied past. A black Labrador retriever with a red bandana around its neck barked at a squirrel. It was a busy, public place, and there was nothing threatening about the man, so she moved nearer, out of the way of two secretaries from the bursar's office who were striding determinately toward one of the food carts that were parked in the leafy shade beneath the trees.

"Would you like to make a lot of money?"

Acacia later wondered why she didn't turn and walk away. Men who asked college girls if they'd like to make a lot of money were usually up to no good, or at least, that's what she'd heard. But she was intrigued. This could be legit, one of those sudden, lucky windfalls that occasionally happen to people. If so, she'd be a fool to walk away without hearing more.

"Doing what?" she asked.

"Nothing too difficult," he said with a pleasant smile. He patted the bench next to him. "Have a seat."

She sat. He opened a white paper bag on his lap and extracted a puffy square pastry dusted with powdered sugar. "Care for a beignet? I got them at the Faneuil Hall Marketplace in Boston. They're not bad, but they're not nearly as good as the ones they make in New Orleans." He pronounced it as one word: *Nawluns.*

Acacia accepted a beignet. Powdered sugar rained down on her red T-shirt, and the man handed her a paper napkin. He chewed and swallowed. Then he licked his fingers daintily. "I'd shake hands, but my fingers are sticky. You can call me Mr. Jones. What's your name?"

Acacia told him her name.

"Unusual name, Acacia. Classical. Tell me, Acacia, I've noticed you leaving the library around this time for several days now. Are you by any chance employed there?"

So he'd been watching her. That was a little disturbing, but the man hadn't *done* anything; he'd just said he'd seen her leaving the library. Then there was the tantalizing offer of making a lot of money. It wouldn't hurt to hear him out. She could always refuse.

"I work there, shelving books. I'm on work-study," she said.

Mr. Jones smiled. Flecks of powdered sugar clung to his lips. His teeth were very white. Acacia wondered how old he was. He didn't look old aside from his white hair. His skin was unlined, and his jawline was firm. His cement-colored eyes were alert and focused as twin laser beams. She thought he could be anywhere between thirty and a well-preserved fifty.

"Are you acquainted with Ezra Greer, the head librarian?"

"I've met him," Acacia said, wondering where this was going.

Mr. Jones fished the last beignet out of the paper bag and ate it slowly, seeming to deliberate over his next words. When he finished, he folded the bag into a neat square and slipped it into the pocket of his suit coat.

"There are reasons I won't go into that I'm unable to enter Orne Library.

Therefore I need a surrogate. If you agree to act on my behalf and bring a book out for me, I'll pay you handsomely."

"You'll pay me to bring you a book?" Acacia wondered why he couldn't just check it out himself. Anyone with a library card could take out books; they didn't have to be students or faculty. Visiting professors, researchers, people from Arkham and the neighboring towns, just about anybody who could provide some form of ID was allowed to check out books, so why couldn't Mr. Jones? Maybe he'd taken books out in the past and had failed to return them and was banned from taking out any more?

"I'll pay you one hundred thousand dollars."

Acacia's eyebrows shot up in surprise. "Just for getting you a book?"

Mr. Jones nodded and patted the breast of his suit coat. "I have in my wallet a cashier's check for nine thousand, nine hundred seventy-five dollars. Banks must report transactions of any amount over ten thousand dollars, but that amount will cause you no difficulties by raising inconvenient questions about where it came from. I'll give it to you now if you agree to do this little task. Deposit it or cash it. It's yours if you say yes. Bring me the book, and you'll get the rest in a series of cashier's checks in similar increments so as not to ring any alarm bells with the FDIC."

The cement-colored gaze he turned to her was serene, as if what he was suggesting was nothing out of the ordinary although it sounded to Acacia as if it might be illegal. "Or I can give you the rest in cash. That would be ninety thousand and twenty-five dollars. I brought it with me in case the person I hired preferred cash."

Acacia thought about it. Clearly more was involved than going in and checking out a copy of *The Catcher in the Rye* or *DOS for Dummies*. No dummy herself, Acacia had a good idea what sort of book he wanted and that he didn't just want to borrow it; he intended to keep it.

"It's one of the books in the special collections room, isn't it?"

Mr. Jones showed his perfect teeth in a sharklike smile. "It's the *Necronomicon*."

Of all the grimoires and malignant manuscripts in the special collection at Miskatonic University, the *Necronomicon* was the most notorious. Every Miskatonic student knew the story of what it contained, though how much was true and how much was legend was open to conjecture. Written around 700 CE, it allegedly chronicled the doings of ancient beings called the Old Ones who once ruled the earth and hoped to someday to rule it again with the help of human followers who worshipped them. Only four copies were known to exist: one in the Vatican library, one in the British Museum, one in the Bibliothèque nationale de France, and one at Miskatonic.

In terms of rare books, it was among the rarest. Nobody checked out the *Necronomicon*. A few carefully selected scholars were permitted access to it, but it wasn't to leave the special collections room. Those were the rules that Acacia had been told by one of the senior librarians when she started working there, along with no gum-chewing allowed and no speaking above a whisper in the Waterfall Room. Anyone caught chewing gum was asked to dispose of it immediately. Anyone who spoke in a normal tone of voice in the Waterfall Room was in danger of being seized and eaten by whatever it was that lived in the cave behind the waterfall.

"You've heard of it?" Mr. Jones was watching the closest food truck to where they sat where a man in a Red Sox T-shirt leaned out of the window to hand an adjunct professor a can of Pepsi.

"Yeah, but the special collections room is locked, and I don't have the key, and besides I don't think I want to . . ."

Mr. Jones cut her off. "Nonsense. You'll never get another opportunity like this. One hundred thousand dollars for a few minutes work. I'll provide you with something to show the head librarian that will get you the key with no problems at all. I'll give you something else that will make removing the book perfectly safe. No one will know you did it. It will be fine. I promise. Do we have a deal or not?"

"Okay," Acacia told him. She'd never had more than two or three hundred dollars in her possession at one time in her entire life. With that much money, she could pay off her student loan and still have a lot left over.

Mr. Jones walked with her to a branch of Key Bank on Water Street where she had a checking account with a balance that hovered precariously around the thirty-dollar mark. True to his word, he gave her a cashier's check for just under ten thousand dollars, which she deposited, feeling a mixture of elation and apprehension. She'd taken the money. Now she was committed.

"There are a couple of things you'll need. Walk with me. They're in my car," Mr. Jones told her as they left the bank. They walked down busy College Street, Acacia dawdling as she looked into the front window of a chic little shop, the kind of place where Spode would casually pay four hundred dollars for a green cotton skirt with pink whales on it that she might only wear once. Acacia had been afraid to venture inside, so expensive was the merchandise and so haughty were the salespeople, but now she could afford to go in and buy anything she wanted.

In a space on the second floor of the parking deck behind the student center was a gleaming midnight blue automobile that stood out from the surrounding Fords and Volkswagens and Mazdas like a queen among peasants. It had a hood ornament of a woman leaning eagerly forward with her arms outstretched behind her, billowing cloth giving her the appearance of wings. Below it was a rectangular chrome plate with twin interlocked *R*'s, bearing the words Rolls Royce.

"It's a Phantom. Bespoke to my specifications. Lovely, isn't it?" Mr. Jones told her. He motioned her to walk around to the rear of the car and opened the trunk. Looking around to make certain they were alone, he rolled back a compartment on the floor made of highly varnished burled wood. There were two things in there: a black cloth drawstring bag about two feet long and a square, flat silver object slightly smaller than a CD case.

"This contains a mirror," Mr. Jones told her, picking up the silver square and handing it to her. "Don't look into it," he cautioned when she went to open it. "You're going to get the head librarian to look into it. Go to him tomorrow. Show him the mirror and tell him to open the safe in his office. He'll do it. Then tell him to take out the key to the special collections room and give it to you. He'll do that too. Then tell him you're going to borrow the key and that it's all right with him because he *wants* you to borrow it. Do you understand?"

Acacia understood. It was an enchanted mirror. She'd seen one demonstrated in her Applied Thaumaturgy class. The instructor had shown it to Chad Lowell, a stodgy member of the debate team, and had made him do the Russian dance where guys squat with their arms crossed and kick out their legs. It had been amusing to watch the normally slow-moving Chad exuberantly kicking his legs and shouting, "Ha!"

She looked down at the black drawstring bag. It was twitching. Mr. Jones saw her looking. "Ah, now this is something *really* interesting," he said, opening the bag.

The salad tongs from hell, as Acacia thought of them. Mr. Jones explained that they were necessary to pick up the *Necronomicon*. Anyone who attempted to touch it without using them would immediately die. They might burst into flames first; he'd heard about that happening once long ago.

"The author of the *Necronomicon* was said to be an Arab named Abdul Alhazred, though that seems to have been a nom de plume. Abdul means 'servant of' and Alhazred is a corruption of a place-name. Whatever his name was, he was killed by his enemies in Damascus, or so the story goes," he told her.

Acacia had heard all that before. What she hadn't heard was what Mr. Jones said next. "Before he was put to death, he had his servant cut off his hands and cut a piece of skin from his side, about so big." He held his long-fingered white hands with their manicured fingernails about eighteen inches apart to show her how big the piece of skin was.

"He put a curse on the book when he wrote it, saying that only his hands could touch it. When he knew he was done for, he made an addendum to the curse that not just the original manuscript, but all the copies that would ever be made could only be touched by his hands or with gloves made from his flesh. Quite a powerful fellow he must have been because it worked." Mr. Jones shook his head in admiration of the Arab and his ghoulish curse.

"Gloves made out of his skin?" Acacia couldn't take her eyes off the leathery brown hands that despite being dead were somehow quivering as if excited to be out and about. They were dreadful. Gloves made out of human skin seemed almost as bad. *It puts the lotion in the basket,* she thought, recalling a scene from *The Silence of the Lambs.*

"Oh, yes. Not entirely made out of his skin of course. There wouldn't have been enough of it to make more than a single pair. No, the gloves just had to have a strip of his tanned flesh sewn onto the palms. The head librarian, Ezra Greer, has a pair for use by anyone who's granted access to Miskatonic's copy. I daresay there are similar pairs somewhere in the Vatican library and in the libraries in Paris and London."

Holding the mummified hands by their silk-wrapped stumps, Acacia gingerly reached out with them to pull the *Necronomicon* from its place on the bookshelf. She recalled how Mr. Jones had replied when she asked him how he came into possession of the hands.

He'd smiled his sharklike smile and said, "I'm a collector. I have a great deal of money to devote to expanding my collection."

"Why did he have to collect mummified body parts and creepy old books?

Why couldn't he collect comic books or something like a normal person?" Acacia muttered as she held the book carefully between the hands' rigid fingers. The volume looked extremely old, its black leather cover was flaking, and its gilded pages were rippled as if they'd been wet at some point and inexpertly dried out. The book was almost to where she could lower it into her open backpack when the hands gave a violent twitch. She dropped them with a little cry and instinctively made a grab for the book before it could hit the floor.

Horrified, she thought, *I'm dead! I touched it, and now I'm going to die, burst into flames or just fall down dead! Oh God, I should never have done this!*

She waited, clutching the book, her heart pounding, but nothing happened. Thirty seconds ticked slowly by and then sixty. Still nothing. She let out her breath.

"Screw you, Mr. Jones. That was a lie. A con artist probably made up that story and sold you some mummy hands, and you fell for it because you wanted the fucking *Necronomicon* so bad."

She put the book and the hands into her backpack, zippered it, and slung it around her shoulders. "I'm outta here," she whispered, not liking the hushed, electric atmosphere of the special collections room.

The mirror hadn't been a lie. That part had worked like a charm . . .

She knocked on the door to Dr. Greer's office, intending to ask if he had a few minutes to spare to talk to her about a paper she was writing for her American Literature class about Mehitable Cabot, a minor poet about whom Greer had written his doctoral dissertation. Ms. Cabot was a contemporary of Emily Dickinson and Walt Whitman, and she'd carried on a lengthy correspondence with both. The two slender volumes of her poems were in the library's poetry section and were rarely checked out. The collection of her letters, published posthumously, was slightly more interesting. One of them to Ms. Dickinson contained an account of a picnic she'd attended in Amherst at which one of the guests had been bitten by a rabid raccoon. It went, in part, "It is well, dear Emily, that you remained within doors that day, or the fiendish thing might have savaged you also, and oh, my dear! The very thought makes me tremble with the utmost horror!"

Acacia really was writing a paper for American Lit, but it was about Jack

Kerouac, whom she found to be much livelier than the prim Ms. Cabot. She decided not to go into her little speech about writing a paper about Mehitable because once Ezra Greer started talking about her he tended to go on and on. Acacia would rather cut to the chase and see if the mirror worked or not.

Greer had gazed with a sweet, childlike intensity into the mirror's reflective service that Acacia held up before him as if whatever he saw in there made him very happy. Upon her request, he obediently unlocked the safe set into the oak-paneled wall behind his desk and handed her the key.

"I'll bring it back first thing tomorrow. Then you'll forget I ever had it," she told him.

"You'll bring it back first thing tomorrow, and I'll forget you had it. Okey-dokey," he told her with a big, sloppy grin. The enchanted mirror seemed to have caused him to have lost about seventy IQ points. Acacia hoped the effect was reversible.

She left the special collections room and walked downstairs to the door beside the loading dock. Letting herself out, she heard the clock in the tower strike twelve thirty. She passed a few late-night revelers, none of whom she recognized, on her way to the parking garage where Mr. Jones had said he'd wait for her.

She found him seated behind the wheel of his Rolls-Royce, eyes closed, apparently asleep. She tapped on the window to get his attention.

"How did it go?" he asked, getting out and stretching languorously. "Any problems?"

"No, but the thing about the hands was just a myth. I touched the book without them and I was okay."

He nodded. "Would you mind putting it in the trunk for me, along with the hands and the mirror? I have your payment in full."

She did as she was told, still grousing. "You said only the hands of Abba-dabba-do or whatever his name was could touch the book, or they'd die, but I touched it, and I'm fine."

He watched her as she stowed the hands in the drawstring bag in the compartment in the trunk and laid the book and the mirror beside them. Closing the compartment, he smiled his sharklike smile.

"There was a little more to it than what I told you. Alhazred made it so only his hands or the hands of his descendants could touch the *Necronomicon*. He was your ancestor. I was fairly certain of that before I approached you."

He handed her a heavy black nylon duffle bag, and she took it wordlessly from him. "It's all there in cash, just as you requested. Used bills, nothing larger than a fifty. You can count it if you like."

She shook her head, stunned. "What are you going to do with the book?"

"Nothing your ancestor wouldn't approve of. Thank you for your assistance. Don't forget to return the key to Dr. Greer."

He got into the car and drove off.

§

Jill Hand is a member of International Thriller Writers. Her Southern Gothic novel, *White Oaks*, won first place for thrillers in the 2019 PenCraft Awards. A sequel, *Black Willows*, will be released in the spring of 2020.

Between the Holes

Dani Atkinson

Naomi Ishii
Student ID #518105
OCCS 205
Essay topic #2: Interpreting the Necronomicon

Reading Between the Holes: A Reinterpretation of Omissions and Alterations in the Dee's English Translation

T HE ENGLISH TRANSLATION OF THE *NECRONOMICON* BY ELIZABETHAN occultist-mathematician John Dee has long been considered flawed and incomplete. Numerous rituals in the original Arabic document by mystic scholar Abdul Alhazred are omitted and come down to us only through other copies and translations such as the Latin and the Chinese (Liu, 459). In comparison, the "Dee's English" translation is considered manifestly inferior (Armitage, 762).

Some believe that the many gaps in John Dee's work were caused by damage in the intervening centuries between its creation and the present day. Several pages may have been torn out by the Cult of Yog-Sothoth who were in possession of it until the Dunwich Incident of 1928 (Armitage, 885). Others think that the missing rituals were accidentally left out in the process of the initial translation. Perhaps John Dee was somehow interrupted before having a chance to complete the work. Or Dee could have been working from an incomplete copy himself, possibly the rumored "missing link" Greek edition postulated by Penelope Cardison (Cardison, 12).

In this essay, I will put forward a new and radical hypothesis: the Dee translation is deliberately missing those rituals due to . . .

BRAINSTORMING SECTION

What the hell *is* my hypothesis here, fuck I'm so screwed, why did I wait until the last week before starting this stupid essay, why do I always do this to myself, I'm SO?? FUCKED?!?? Whatever, whatever, just keep writing. Come back and fix this later at 3 a.m. on the last day when your blood is more energy drink than plasma. It worked when I came up with that Greco-Roman History 101 essay where I claimed Brutus assassinated Caesar due to Freudian sexual jealousy. I still can't believe professor Whitmire bought that.

Possible Topics:

- ❖ John Dee was trying to protect us from the more dangerous rituals by leaving them out? Seems to be giving Dee more credit than he deserves. Plus he included that one spell that makes you vomit carnivorous slugs and piles of disembodied baby teeth. Dubious.

- ❖ John Dee was correcting flaws in the original rituals? Oh, HELL no. White savior Enochian bullshit. Probably what he THOUGHT he was doing. (Bullshit that Prof. Alistaire might eat up with a spoon tho? Come back to this later.)

- ❖ Parts of the *Necronomicon* are literally untranslatable into English? Hmm. Nuances do get lost and meanings shift whenever you translate anything. Grandpa says there are thoughts you can have in Japanese that you can't think in any other language. But I can read the Latin translations of the *Necronomicon* (or I could if my Latin wasn't shit and if literally EVERY OTHER COPY HADN'T ALREADY BEEN CHECKED OUT BY MY CLASSMATES, leaving me nothing but a transcript of the goddamn Dee, fuck me, why did I wait so long to start this). And I can read the second-hand sources with other people explaining what's in the Latin versions in English (ALSO ALL SIGNED OUT). So it doesn't seem like it should be impossible to write something out in

English . . . this feels weird enough that it'd catch the professor's attention though . . . in a good way? Bad way?

❖ The rituals in the *Necronomicon* are fundamentally different in different languages? Ooh, THIS one has legs . . . lots of legs, almost as many legs as that one bispecies kid in B-block dormitory with all the tentacles. Like I could DO things with this.

In this essay, I will put forward a new and radical hypothesis: the Dee translation is deliberately missing those rituals due to those rituals being radically different in function and form as a direct result of the nature of the English language itself, causing certain rituals to be merged into others, rendered completely unrecognizable, and thus assumed to be missing or made unnecessary and redundant . . .

Okay good, this is good, I THINK it's good, but how do I prove my case when I don't have another translation to work from (FUCK ME) (Ishii, 03). What's my word count so far, SHIT, only like 700 words, and most of that is babble that I'm gonna have to come back and delete later. THIS IS A THREE THOUSAND WORD ASSIGNMENT. I'm dead, dead, leave a note for my roommate and her colleagues in the reanimation track at the med school, new test subject incoming, so so dead. (Does she have her own copy of the complete Latin version with all the resurrection spells intact? Maybe I could borrow it . . . no, no, shit. Latoya is holed up at her parents' place all this week, and she took her books home with her. Never mind. Ray of hope gone. Still dead.)

Whatever whatever, keep writing, figure it out as you go.

The *Necronomicon* is unlike other books (Everyone, 01). Even when translating something as simple as a children's book or a recipe book, the text that emerges from the process is in effect a new and different work from the one you started with. Every act of translation is an act of transformation. But the *Necronomicon* is a book which transforms others . . .

No no, longer scholarly phrasing. Got to make word count.

The *Necronomicon* is a work of literature that itself enacts transformation on the world surrounding it . . .

Good. Oooh, good.

Okay, how do I DO this. Can I do this? The ideal way to proceed here would be to compare translations, like, get the Latin or some other translation and . . . well, several pages open to Google Translate and praying the prof doesn't realize my language skills aren't up to this. (Do teachers talk to each other about that, does he know I'm failing Professor Benedetti's Introductory Latin class?) Point is moot anyway, literally every single other library copy is signed out, and I am NOT paying campus bookstore prices for the damn thing. Shit. Taking a break.

Okay, another day and another dozen caffeine shots closer to doomsday . . . crazy idea time, what if *I* translated part of the Dee and compared THAT? Like, would a ritual still work if I rewrote it in my godawful high-school French or the snatches of Japanese I managed to drag out of Grandpa over the years? (Does the prof speak Japanese or any language more recent than Sumerian? Maybe he'll look at me and at my last name and just assume I know what the hell I'm talking about?)

I feel guilty about how little Japanese I know, but it's not like it's my fault Grandpa was so traumatized in his early years here that, by the time Dad came along, Grandpa was scared spitless to speak his own language around his own kids . . . it's not my fault Dad and I ended up trying to learn it together from online courses instead of growing up speaking it.

It's a little my fault that I keep putting off applying for my university courses until the last day and the beginner's Japanese class keeps filling up with anime nerds before I can get in. But only a LITTLE.

I did try auditing, but I swear half the guys in there are hoping to go to Japan to teach English just so they can score a Japanese girlfriend. They see me as a shortcut. I suck at Latin, but nobody in that class is learning it to try and bone Caligula.

Well, except Jordan maybe, but we try to ignore him. Seriously, all Latoya's classmates in reanimation studies are so weird. Tangent, tangent, off topic.

This essay shall demonstrate that the very act of translating certain rituals into a new language alters the function and nature of the ritual. One simple passage will be selected from the Dee's English translation and translated three times. Once into Pig Latin as a control, once into French, and once into Japanese. These different versions of the passage will then be compared with regard to their impact and effect, both literary and thaumaturgical.

For a test passage, we shall examine the brief *Pricking the Page* ritual, a simple divination that in the Latin and Greek sometimes provides a one-word answer to a single question if performed on the new moon. Dee's translation claims to contact angels and tends to produce a longer response but in gibberish. The Latin version is extremely well studied and familiar to even beginner students of the occult . . .

(Because you can bloody well bet every wretched soul on this campus knows a spell that has even a slim chance of giving you test answers. And hey, since tonight is the new moon, I can safely claim that I waited until the last night before the due date out of necessity and not a complete inability to adult.)

Dee's version runs:

A droppe of blood Vpon the Payge shall fall
From heauen's lips a droppe of wisdom call
Cnila mgleth torsvl ph'nglui ya.
(*Necronomicon*, John Dee trans.)

The described actions accompanying the ritual words require the sacrifice of a small animal such as a rat or a lizard as well as a few simple magical herbs and ritual objects. For the purposes of this exercise, the person conducting this experiment will be using laboratory rats generously donated by her roommate Latoya Mitchell . . .

(Sorry, Latoya. Desperate times. Though it's not like your rats haven't died like seven times apiece already.)

The seeker writes the words in specially prepared ritual ink and pierces her right pinky finger, allowing a single drop to fall upon the writing. She then slaughters the sacrificial animal, pours its blood upon the blank space on the page, and asks her question aloud. It is as yet unclear what entities the ritual is contacting. It is generally agreed that whatever Dee might have thought, angels are unlikely (Siddig, 66). Whatever those entities are, should they deign to respond, the blood of the animal is supposed to re-form itself into writing that answers the seeker's question. For the purposes of this exercise, the question shall be, "When will the sun rise?"

The ritual exactly as Dee wrote it provided the answer "OXOL OL OIAD TILAB." As near as the Enochian-English dictionary on my laptop can determine, this appears to mean roughly "Dance to the direction sinister" or in modern parlance "Shake it to the left."

For the record, the actual sunrise time in our time zone at this time of year is around six a.m. . . .

The ritual was then attempted in Pig Latin. The words used were all identical to the Dee but with any consonant sounds at the beginning moved to the end and -ay tacked on.

A-ay oppedray of-ay oodblay Vponay e-thay aygepay allshay allfay
Omfray eauenhay's ipslay a-ay oppeday of-ay isdomway allcay
Cnila mgleth torsvl ph'nglui ya.

The R'lyehan shall be left untranslated in all versions, though it should be noted Dee himself did alter some of the words himself from R'lyehan to Enochian "angel script." Many scholars point to this as the cause of the resulting inaccuracy of his version of the ritual (Yellowfly, 34).

The Pig Latin control, rather . . . confusingly, produced the answer "OXOLAY OLAY OIADAY ILATBAY, ADMAY OZIENAY OEAY OIADAY EXARPAY." Some editing back out of Pig Latin and running through the Enochian translator once again produced what appears to be the phrase "Shake it to the right, raise your hands up in the air."

The fact that the ritual works at all when scrambled in this manner is . . .

unexpected. The fact that it appears to give a longer answer, which is either an opposite response or a continuation of a previous response, is even less expected. The implications are beyond the scope of this essay, save to say that this does seem to indicate that the very act of translating a ritual, even when the "translation" is a simple scrambling with a playground code, can indeed alter the actual functioning of the ritual . . .

Shit.

I really wasn't expecting to actually get anywhere with this.

Maybe I won't flunk this assignment after all.

Assuming I finish before I pass out or class starts in the morning. Or have a heart attack from stimulant overdose. I'm on my third pot of tea, coffee, and canned energy shots boiled together, and things are starting to vibrate.

The French translation as I have translated it runs roughly . . .

Crud, this may take a while. I remember like nothing from high school, I blocked as much out as I could, like any sensible person would . . . online translation is saying like—

Une goutte de sang sur la page tombera,
Des lèvres du ciel, une goutte de sagesse appelée.

But I'm pretty sure that's wrong . . . *ciel* is just sky, I know that much—"lips of the sky" is just stupid. Don't they have a word for heaven in the sense of home of divine, holy, singing winged creatures with harps? (Which probably don't exist because they all got eaten by the scary tentacle things outside spacetime?) Also, Dee didn't just translate; he made the thing rhyme and have iambics and shit. Lessee, um. Okay, maybe . . . celestial lips? Des levres celestes? Lips of paradise? Or, um, what rhymes with *sang* . . . the word for tongue and language is like, um, *langue*, right? That sorta rhymes?

Sur la page il faut tomber une goutte de sang
Pour appelle un goutte de sagesse de la langue . . .

Wait, no, the adjective comes last, so it won't rhyme. If I stick *celeste* or *divine* after *wisdom*, like "heavenly wisdom," would that still work? It doesn't scan though . . . um, maybe *mortal* . . . drop of blood? Earthly page? FUCK it I'm running out of time here.

> Sur la page terreste doit tomber un goutte de sang
> pour appelle un goutte de sagesse céleste de la langue
> Cnila mgleth torsvl ph'nglui ya . . .

GOOD ENOUGH! I'm not sure if *terreste* is actually a real French word, but the crappy dorm wifi is conking out because OF COURSE it is, and now I can't Google it, so it can just sit there being wrong. Bring on the rat.

When the experimenter was able to stop her hands from twitching enough to perform the ritual, which took several unfortunate attempts and was not fun for either experimenter or sacrificial rat, there was a long pause before the rat blood on the page disappeared entirely. The experimenter then began speaking in tongues for several minutes. The experimenter was not actually able to tell whether this was the result of the spell or just from starting a fourth pot of boiled caffeine sludge.

Interestingly, though no words ever appeared on the paper, once the glossolalia symptoms subsided and the experimenter went to the dorm washroom to clean out her various nicks and scratches, she discovered in the mirror that words were written on her face. Enclosed is an attached file containing a selfie.

Looking at the selfie, I have just realized the words are actually written backwards. It was clearly legible in the mirror. The experimenter was too tired and wired to realize at the time that of course the words being frontwards in the mirror would mean they were backwards in real life. The words in the mirror: "Jamais. C'est la terre qui tombera."

Never. It is the earth that will fall.

Once again, the question was "When will the sun rise?" And the answer given by my phone's time and date app is . . . three hours from now, so chop chop, ominous or not, deadline's coming.

Translating the bad English translation back into a . . . frankly, even worse French translation appears to have restored some semblance of relevance to the results of the ritual. Is it because French is more closely related to Latin? The Latin version of the spell is the most common version currently used, though the original was in Arabic. Are there properties of Latin that make it and its descended languages more suited to this particular spell? But the Latin usually only gives a one-word answer. And the French version I wrote had . . . the Latin doesn't write on your face. Or . . . in it. On closer inspection . . . I . . . the experimenter . . . I'm . . . squinting at the mirror and zooming in on the selfie and I think the words are actually UNDER my skin, not on it . . . like veins burst and rearranged themselves or like something wrote the words . . . from the inside . . .

Three-minute dance break, fuck, I'm exhausted and not thinking straight, but I don't think I should risk more caffeine right now. Adrenaline from physical activity it is, trick that Latoya taught me.

Shake it to the left, shake it to the right, wave your hands up in the air like the sun ain't gonna rise . . .

Okay, I sorta feel better, but I sorta also feel worse because those silly words I just typed have appeared on my wrists in . . . is that Pig Latin French with Elizabethan English spelling? That had better fade out, or it'll look like the worst inspirational tattoo in history.

I should . . .

I don't . . .

It's nearly morning, and I'm gonna have to write a whole second draft without all the rambling and—

The experimenter has chosen to write her Japanese version of the ritual in the form of a haiku since the rhyming couplet is not a major feature of Japanese poetry, as it is in English and French (Authorname I Can't Remember, Page number I Can't Remember).

Page . . . peeji? That's just an English word imported. It feels like cheating.

Haiku supposed to have a word that tells you what season it is. Spring: rain, flowers? Chi = blood; kami = paper or also god depending on kanji used but fuck if I can remember the kanji right now.

These words, from red rain, wisdom blooms

kono kotoba   この言葉
akai ame kara   赤い雨から
chie ga saku   知恵が咲く
クニラムグレストルセヴィルフッングルイヤ

The experimenter chose to write the Enochian and R'lyehan phrase in katakana, the Japanese syllabic alphabet used to phonetically write out foreign words. The experimenter is down to her roommate's last rat, and the sun is coming up on schedule. Or the earth is going down—

—chi chi chi sang sang ga tombera allingfay sang ga sakimasu blood falling rising falling like rain rising like the sun itai itai the words are the words are blood and I am wounded I am je suis watashi wa eedingblay the words are spilling through the holes the holes

I was wrong Dee was wrong it's not translating it's getting it WRONG it's the gaps the gaps I DON'T SPEAK the Furansugo Japonaise I don't know the words and it's all the words I don't know *It's* coming in through the holes in my knowledge *It* needed the gaps it's a hole *It* can use *It They He She Il Elle* no wrong pronouns not the French for this the Japanese don't use pronouns unless they have to kimasu kimasu kiteimasu KITEIMASU I don't have the words not my fault NOT MY FAULT only a little my fault too many holes OJIISAN

The sun is rising there is a cloud across the east ridged and golden like a spine I want to take it between my teeth like a terrier with a rat tear it out the sky is le sora ciel wa the sky is a thin skin barely holding in the black blood the pulsing flowing vacuum and void

Crack the cloud bones pop the vertebrae between mes dents

Pull down the sky stretch and tan it scrape it to pale parchment write my conclusion on its skin step through the holes and write it backwards from the other side kara like me like they are doing to me I can feel the words appearing backwards inside my skin constellations in blood and ink exquisitely brushed calligraphy it's IT'S IN ME I'M IN IT IN CONCLUSION IN CON CLUE SHUN IÄ IÄ IÄ IÄ IÄ IÄ IÄ

Insert witty concluding sentence here.

WORKS CITED

Alhazred, Abdul. *John Dee's English Necronomicon*. Translated by John Dee, Miskatonic University Press, 1982.

Armitage, Henry. *The Lives of the Books of Dead Names: Provenance and History of the Copies of the Necronomicon*. Miskatonic University Press, 1936.

Cardison, Penelope. *Greek to Me: The Lost Copy that Dee Found*. Miskatonic University Press, 1957.

Everyone. *Literally Everyone Knows This*. Every Book Ever Written on the Subject, Infinity.

Ishii, Naomi. *Fuck Me and My Fucking Time Management Skills or Lack Thereof*. This Computer, 2017.

Liu, Xiaodan. *The Mad Arab in China: The Hidden Impact of the Necronomicon on Necromancers of the Qing Dynasty*. Mormington & Co. Ltd, 1962.

Siddig, Rasheed. *Enoch or Oh Noch: The Human Origins of Angelic Script*. Sherry L. Abrams, 1989.

Yellowfly, Frieda. *Arrogance and Imperialism and its Effect on the Transmission of Arcane Knowledge*. Elbow River Books, 1999.

Insert Author Name. *Insert Book Name*. Publishing junk here.

Insert Author Name. *Insert Book Name*. Publishing junk here.

Insert Author Name. *Insert Book Name*. Publishing junk here.

Teacher's note: In general, we prefer that students hand in a more polished draft. Also, we prefer that the polished draft be printed in its entirety on plain white paper rather than partially on the student's dormitory walls, carpet, and shed oozing skin. However, we do tend to grade more highly whenever a student helps future generations of Miskatonic scholars by discovering a new item to add to the forbidden activities list in the student handbook. Also, the small rift in the eastern sky over the school has inspired exciting new collaborations between the occult, astronomy, physics, and medical school faculties as they attempt to determine whether an injury to the fabric of space can be sutured like a wound. The linguistics faculty are already attempting to replicate some of your results and three grad students majoring in various foreign languages have disappeared. Assuming you are still alive and are ever found again on this plane of reality, B–.

Professor Walter Alistaire.

§

Dani Atkinson is a writer and artist in Alberta, Canada. She's bounced around doing day jobs ranging from English teacher in Japan to ice cream parlor clerk in the Canadian Rockies. Between day jobs, she writes stories, comics, plays, poetry, and zombified murder ballads. Her school didn't offer occult studies, which is probably for the best, or she absolutely would have taken that class and doomed us all with something she summoned for midterms. Her short fiction has appeared in *Daily Science Fiction* and *Cast of Wonders*.

The Kingdom of Is

Matt Maxwell

RYAN KNEW NOW WHY EVERYONE WAS SCARED OF THE LINGUISTICS Department at Miskatonic, why physicists and computer scientists, even the weirdos in the biological sciences, cleared a path when the linguists walked the halls.

"Never mess with the linguists," he had been told his first day on campus. "They're feral."

The thought bit down into his skull, those exact words branding themselves onto his brain until they became real and inescapable. He laughed, trying not to maniac-giggle about it as he turned over the paper. His hands were sweat-sheathed, and the note was as sticky as if he'd had frog fingers.

He giggled despite trying to choke the laughter back.

The air above Arkham had grown heavy and dense, starting that morning. Now it was stifling as a coffin lid.

He almost believed that it was the freakish weather driving his perspiration. Down inside, in a place that he refused to acknowledge rationally, he knew that it was fear.

Not the fear of the unknown but of something too well known now, too tangible to be written off as freak lightning strikes or gas main ruptures. He knew what had happened ten years ago at the Petersen Obelisk of MU. He knew that it wasn't any of the desperately mundane explanations that had been used to wallpaper over events.

He focused on the page before him, finding the tiny mark that indicated the top, which way to hold it. That mattered. He stared at the symbol, and it almost made sense.

Ryan wished that he hadn't erased the copy of the sign that had been chalked at his feet not even an hour before. But he had no way of knowing then. And even if Elizabeth had told him, he wouldn't have believed it. Not until he'd seen what a word could do.

His fingers closed around the stick of bright pink chalk in his pocket, and he started scratching out a crude copy of the symbol. Before today, he'd prided himself on his retention and precision, the directness and rationality of his argumentative approach and his grasp of any of the sciences. Now he was hard-pressed to hold a stick of child's sidewalk chalk.

The sun's trek to the horizon made the heat worse, light rippling through the burdened atmosphere like molten glass. But it wasn't just the weather. It was more than that. The way the sky itself rippled and bulged like a tumor.

It was becoming.

He put the thought out of his head and kept working, grinding the chalk to a stump.

A sound slithered through the air, like a snake on a glass window, a susurrus of scales. He froze in place, suddenly feeling cold despite the heat. Elizabeth had told him to expect this, only she'd used her weird way of talking, avoiding the dread word *is.*

Ripples and vibrations of possibility and potential resolved themselves into nightmare.

The monster went from "maybe" to "was."

It looked like a mucoid rainbow, a spectrum itself given tumorous lesions and left to bubble over into iridescent meaninglessness. A multitude of seven-segmented arms unfolded along its length, hundreds of them in assemblage. Tipping each one was an uneven pair of claws or blades, each snicking against the other in a horrific chain of whispers. The thing oozed through the air itself, undulating and tearing.

It felt him there. It was hungry.

Ryan tried to force himself to say the word from the postcard aloud. He had to be careful. Once used, the word would lose any power. There were only so many words, just like bullets in a clip.

"S-s-s," Ryan hissed. He couldn't speak. The creature swam through water that was not there, an echo of undersea motion. In the last of the sunlight, it radiated gold with a thousand colors beneath.

He gave up and instead wrote the word in crude block letters, each one as tall as his hand. *S*. His fingers scraped against the asphalt such that the last letter, also a capital *S*—curves made angles in haste—became darkened with blood.

It was close now, close enough that its legs or cilia or claws—whatever they were, the definition didn't matter—were close enough that he could feel the air displaced as they whipped past him. Ryan sucked in a breath and spoke from his diaphragm like he'd learned in debate club.

"Squamous. You *are* squamous!"

The leg that raked across and snagged his hoodie was semitransparent and smelled of saltwater and boiled crab shells that had made him sick as a boy behind his uncle's restaurant. Ryan hated seafood and always would. The thing tugged the fabric a little before he crossed out the word with a savage motion of his arm. His knuckles went to fire, but he held tight to the little stub of chalk.

As he crossed through the letters, the thing was un-made. Pieces of glistening shell fell away and rainbow ooze dripped out, evaporating before it hit the asphalt. The legs, once choreographed with an alien grace, fell to twitching and spasming. The thing's proportions snapped, as a whip in the hand of a giant, and it went straight. The last pieces of it, carapace and scissor feet and undifferentiated jelly and chitin, all of it dropped to the ground and ceased to exist.

He stared at it in astonishment. This thing, whatever it was, its trip to the land of *is* was over now. It never was.

"Never screw around with a linguist," he whispered to himself.

Ryan looked down at the sigil in chalk, eyes lingering at the dark streak of blood on the final strokes. If someone had told him that he'd bleed for Elizabeth Stokes and be glad for it, even a few days ago, he'd have said that person was insane.

Not so much now.

The sun was down, but the sky still burned orange as if the earth had stopped turning at this moment and the light wouldn't change anymore forever. Over in the direction of the rebuilt obelisk, the highest point on campus, the sky still roiled, and the sunlight came through it like nearly transparent oil in a vortex.

She was still over there with her postcards and chalk and her lighter.

At least he hoped she was. He started to run despite not being accustomed to it. In twenty steps, his sides ached, but he kept running, stopping only to take off his sweatshirt emblazoned with "Miskatonic Phys Ed."

He ran toward the roil. It would be there. She hadn't been wrong yet.

A few days before.

"Welcome to the Land of Is," Elizabeth said. She stood in front of the chalkboard, which was so anachronistic that Ryan had stared at it for a full ten seconds before realizing what it was.

She had the same phrase written on the board. But then this was a social sciences class, so repetition was going to be key for these dullards to retain anything.

Yes, he was angry that he was being forced to take a course outside his major. Not even something useful like applied mathematics. But linguistics. Theory, outside of any manner of useful application, was anathema. It was about what could be done with a discipline that mattered. Arguing about the fundamentals was useless navel-gazing. But still, he'd dodged the requirement for as long as he could.

He only ended up here when he'd heard that the linguists were insane, and he thought there might be some kind of a challenge. Instead, it was nothing but tautology and emptiness.

But Dr. Stokes was supposed to be a good lecturer, even after her long absence from the school and teaching. An absence that had begun not long after the toppling of the original Petersen Obelisk some ten years ago.

The chalk squeaked as she drew on the board, underlining the *is*. "I hope you have come to class prepared," she said. Her voice was direct, ringing a unique tone, one of clarity.

Ryan was sure her eyes rested on him for a moment, but nobody else seemed to notice.

"We will spend this semester unlearning some things and, hopefully in the process, open up to learning new things." The chalk fell into the metal tray with a *tak*.

"Language is how we fabricate the world, describing, codifying, hammering into consensus an agreement as to what constitutes reality.

"Language shares in a power that we used to accord to magic."

Ryan stifled a laugh, though no one else in class seemed to get the joke. Magic. Ugh.

She was older than any of the graduate fellows he'd seen. She didn't look like Mom back home with her tremendous wrinkles. Rather, the maturity evidenced itself in her stance, her directness. Though there was something more beneath, which he picked at but could not figure out.

"We shall examine existence under the tyranny of the great king *to be*, which has proven itself to be a burden and even more has served as accomplice to mistruths and misrepresentation.

"In short. Nothing human *is* beyond being human. I can say that I *am* a teacher, but perhaps you sit in a better position to judge. I *am* a woman, what lays beneath these Levis not mattering. I *am* a percussionist in a band called Anathaid, which means 'unknown' in Irish, but do you see a drum in my hand?"

Tautology and navel-gazing. And how she harps on the point, ridiculous.

There were perhaps ten other students in the lecture room, all of them lost in rapt attention, hanging on her every word.

"*Am* and *be* counterfeit a permanence that humans simply do not possess the capability for. These verbs suggest chains and solidity that do not exist."

Oh enough.

"But I *am* here," Ryan grouched. "I am sitting in this chair, which is in this room."

Elizabeth paused, a smile flickering across her face but that died quickly. "You sit in this room. You sit on that chair."

Her red hair shone with a faint patina in the fluorescent light of the room, skin taking on a greenly radiant cast, unearthly when coupled with her weird speaking cadence and disregard for mere being.

Ryan scooted his chair and let the screech echo a moment. "I *am* in this room." He let his voice go sour. "I am a man."

Her smile flickered again. "You appear old enough to buy alcohol legally, yes. We'll leave it at that." She crossed her arms in front of her. "I gather that you do not agree with the thesis of this class, which may or may not reflect my personal beliefs. Or the use of *is* as commonly accepted.

"Where lies your objection? Excessive formality? Over-precision? Disregard for convenience? I have received that last one more than once."

Her smug expectation made him seethe.

The class stared into their notebooks and laptops, wondering if this was part of the lecture or something else.

"I reject the entire notion. You're doing away with *being*! I've never heard anything so ridiculous."

"Everything that I have said sustains proof. I do admit that this view brings with it a certain . . . rigidity.

"But you have come to this classroom to learn, yes?" She didn't point or glare or accuse. She only said her piece with a stone confidence.

The same confidence that the insane possess. She really is crazy. Maybe the rumors were more than that.

"Yes. I am here to learn."

Her eyebrow arched. "You exist in this place to learn? Intriguing. And a bold statement."

The chuckle that ran through the classroom shamed him in his seat.

"Enough of that, please," she said, loud enough to be heard in the back. "Mockery brings nothing to our experience here. Instead, Mr., ah . . . Kolnik, yes?"

Ryan nodded, not knowing how she knew.

"Mr. Kolnik has brought us to a place that I'd hoped to steer us toward. And in this moment, you will find the key to the class and, not without coincidence, your grades."

Another chuckle from the class, this one more nervous.

"The next time you feel hungry, do as my kin in Ireland have said. My elder kin at any rate. Please say the following when your stomach growls.

"'Hunger is upon me.' Not 'I *am* hungry.' If you don't wish to sound like a Hibernian grandmother, then try 'I feel hungry,' or 'Let's get lunch.' Shift from the tyranny of *is* to something more open yet precise."

The cadence of her voice and dodging around the simplest verb in the universe ate at Ryan. She couldn't say it without mockery. This was ridiculous. He was hungry. He was sitting in the classroom hungry. He was pissed off that he had to take this stupid class from this dingbat woman who was rumored to have spent several years institutionalized. Perhaps that was part of the glamor.

It was intolerable.

"Shake off the shackles of eternal being," she said with a laugh. "And share in a world that contains more vividness and strangeness than the Kingdom of Is." She hissed out a short breath.

"Now let us take this moment to introduce ourselves to one another before we start into our analysis of Lowery's rejectivist theory of grammar and construction."

It was going to be a very long semester.

But perhaps Ryan could find a way to cut it shorter.

The reconstructed Petersen Obelisk scratched against the tangerine sky like a scalpel, dimpling the skin but not yet slicing. Ryan could see a pattern in the heat ripples and whorls of the atmosphere, not just a pattern but a malignance. It filled him with dread, but he wouldn't allow it to be dreadful. He'd learned that much.

He wondered if it had looked like this ten years ago. He'd never found many pictures. That was before everyone started carrying cameras in their pockets and selfies and patchwork recorded history spit out on a minute by minute basis. Just a few tiny photos, hairy and unrecognizable from digital compression and resizing. There weren't any pictures of Elizabeth at the center of the strange storm. But he knew she'd been there. A little digging had uncovered that. She'd been here before her involuntary institutionalization, lasting more than eight years and returning to school only last semester.

She'd told him herself. She even said that she had been there, dipping her toe into the Kingdom of Is.

He kept walking and saw glimpses of distorted faces in the sky above. Whatever existed there, it grew closer. But then she was calling it down to do just that.

Ryan's research showed the original Petersen Obelisk had stood in the central plaza at Miskatonic for nearly ninety years before it had been destroyed in a weird accident. An accident described as a lightning strike during a freak storm early in the fall semester. Though there were no fatalities, a postdoctoral student in the linguistics department had been incapacitated and remanded to the custody of state mental health authorities and then bounced from private clinic to private clinic.

The paper trail was hazy as was the digital one. But Ryan knew that characterizing this as an accident was an error. Elizabeth had been responsible for it. The why of it eluded him.

The more she talked about language and magic in class, the more he wondered. Once was a time that Miskatonic had been famous for the occult: back before transatlantic flight, penicillin, the moon landing, and the internet. Now it was another mid-Atlantic private college, using this mythology to sell sweatshirts and kitschy glasses.

And paperweights. Glass paperweights bigger than a closed fist, a cluster of multicolored globules and trailing tentacles, all made with some abstract blowing technique, all marked with the MU Cephalopods. A funny joke and a very popular souvenir, even if he couldn't identify exactly what kind of cephalopod it was supposed to be (and he'd spent an hour or two familiarizing himself with them).

Ryan had watched Elizabeth buy several of them since he started following her after class.

Just like he was right now.

He knew it was creepy and strange but no less than she was. She was up to something, finishing the work that she'd started years ago. She was still insane, only masking it now.

Not very well. This was the third seemingly identical paperweight she'd purchased this trip. It didn't make any sense. Nor did her selecting postcards out of a spinner rack, apparently by random. She'd spent an hour doing that once, and he'd almost gotten bored of it.

The purchases had to be random because she had her eyes closed when she gave the wire rack a turn, fingers fumbling over it as it came to a stop, selecting cardboard images by touch.

Miskatonic in the winter, the hurricane gates, a clutch of daffodils in a colonial-seeming graveyard. If she came up with one displaying the obelisk, she shuffled it away and never on a rack that it had come from. It didn't make sense.

This trip, she bought her latest paperweights and two buckets of sidewalk chalk from art supplies.

He fought with himself over confronting her. But if it was magic, like she blathered about in class, then where was the harm in it? Magic wasn't *real*.

His mind turned to the newspaper picture of the toppled obelisk, and he thought that she'd been interrupted last time. And how it looked more like it had been flattened by a titanic blow than struck by lightning. If that had come from being interrupted, then what would she be working toward this time?

He chickened out and watched as she walked out with her plastic bag filled with supplies, stopping only to pick up her full backpack from the cubbies out front.

The roiling sky above swelled and pulsed like a heart outside the body. Surging power flowed through it as something seemed to squeeze between the layers in the air like jelly pressing through a screen door, jelly that slowly reassembled itself into something like eyes and mouths, both open and hungry. It was a tornado of appetite bound together only loosely by a string of words that Ryan reached for in description.

He had been well-read once, though he traded that in for the comforting solidity and regularity of code. Code defined a world that could be controlled and harnessed, even if it was through tricks and hacks. As the thing in the sky materialized above him, he reached for words to describe and contain it and found himself without the language to carve it into being.

It could not be named.

He ran again despite the furnace burn inside his ribs.

Pieces in the air moved against one another, diamond facets but organic and shuddering as if sickened. Their translucence made it impossible to tell if there was just a thousand or a million or billions of them, compounded and amplified and . . .

He fell into it, staring, feeling his feet come to a leaden halt, unable to move ahead, not even wanting to any longer. It was the thing that was. It had always been. It would always be. It was a totality, the only thing that mattered, the emptiness of possibility. And it was the king.

Ryan wasn't even a subject, wholly beneath its notice, but would be obliterated all the same when the king came.

The bookstore had been ready to close, and Ryan had to be sneaky, embody the essence of the thought in order not to be seen by Elizabeth as she checked out.

The obelisk had been toppled ten years ago to the night. He couldn't think about anything other than that and how she had done it. Perhaps his irritation at inconvenience had started this thing. Perhaps it was just that. But that had only been the start. It had grown into a thought that crowded out all others.

He was the only one who could stop her. She was going to do it again. She was going to take the whole school with her this time. Whatever force she had called on the last time, she was going to do it a hundred times over now. She'd been to the far side of crazy and hadn't ever come back, just pretended. That's why she couldn't *be* sane or *be* normal. It was pretending. It was all so obvious.

She was going to do it tonight.

And he would stop her. Even if he didn't know how.

She walked along into the early evening, stopping to open one of the tubs of chalk as she paused at one of the granite benches that littered the campus. She carefully removed a blue stick and wrote something out on the bench itself.

Ryan stuck to the shadows and the cover of the greenery as she left, trying to see her work. There was a symbol on the bench, something he didn't recognize but received a sensation from. He was uneasy as he regarded it, unsettled as surely as if he'd been standing on a boat and a wave had risen and fallen beneath his feet. More than that, he was moved, feeling a press of unseen force, gentle but firm, emanating from the sign.

He shook it off and kept following.

She paused and marked several other spots on campus, never the same symbol twice but variations. She consulted a notebook as she drew some of them but not always. She worked quickly but not in a hurry. She never saw him.

The largest of the symbols, one she had to work from her notes or plan or spell or whatever it was, was drawn out in pink chalk at the top of the Chambers Stairway that led to the main ring of Miskatonic's architecture.

The marking was a welcome mat. He knew this as sure as he felt the temperature rise even though the sun was approaching the horizon. The weather change was weird and sudden as a car crash, atmospheric density increasing as if something was rushing in, displacing the air itself.

Ryan looked down at the symbol and a feeling surged in him: disgust or horror or righteousness or all of them. He took the toe of his sneaker and rubbed at the chalk lines. A minute of effort and he wiped out everything but a ghostly afterimage.

He smiled at his work. He thought about wiping out the other markings, really knocking her out, but this sort of paranoid fantasy was easily upset. Just the one would be enough, he thought.

He sweat some as he walked but kept his hoodie on, throwing the hood up, armoring himself. He was ready to face her.

The restored obelisk was marked off with a precise circle as wide around as the statue itself was tall. The rocks in the border were made of the crushed remnants of the original, a memorial or tribute, not destroyed but transformed.

She kneeled within that circle, inside another chalk marking. Beside her was the collection of glass paperweights. She took one of them in both hands, lifted it up as high as she could from her kneel, and dropped it. Ryan saw that it chipped but did not shatter.

Apparently satisfied, she did that with another. And then the third.

"You lost, you know," he gloated as he walked to the tip of the obelisk's shadow. It was the only place to be, filled with portent even if it was meaningless babble. Perhaps it would have an effect on her. "Your game *is* over."

She kept arranging her chipped paperweights in the chalk circle.

"And you're right. *Is* means permanence. Like. 'Your magic circle *is* erased.' The one over at the Chambers Stairway."

She refused to turn, and Ryan grew impatient.

"Haven't you heard me, you crazy bitch? It's over." He shocked himself with his own words. He'd never called anyone that to their faces. In text, online, sure. All the time. But that wasn't real.

"I heard you," she bit.

"Well?" Ryan stamped his foot, begging a reaction.

"I didn't think any of it worth responding to. More pressing matters now." She made a minute adjustment to the paperweights and stood, stepping carefully over the drawing and outside it.

"Aren't you going to do something? I broke your spell! I won! Whatever you did ten years ago and tonight? It's over."

"Ryan, your umbrage at having to endure my class has revealed some strange truths. More about you than me, I'd add." She half-smiled.

The sky went from boiling to transparent eruption. A great swirling commenced, and the wind kicked up, skittering leaves across the plaza like bones scraping against the concrete. Her drawing with the chalk must have sounded the same, desperate and scratching.

Her reaction was saved for the sky and whatever was in it.

"You *are* insane," he said.

"That judgment does not alter me, Ryan. Nor does it—"

The clap of thunder sounded more like the sky slapping into the whole of the earth. The wave reverberated through Ryan's bones, and he had to fight not to be put to his knees.

When he regained his footing, he saw something rush out from the sky toward the two of them. A multitude of wings, all of them grotesque and diaphanous, buzzed and swooped. They were all clustered to a central object, like a mouth with three arms grabbing into the air, plucking and feeding. It was as big as a car, impossibly flying, impossibly charging toward them. The voice that came from it was hollow and mocking, meaninglessly insane.

"You! You are gibbering and ichorous!" Her voice cut through everything with a dread finality. He'd never heard her say *are* without anything but ridicule or subversion. She was making the thing real. She was bringing it into the kingdom of *is* and then destroying it.

She held a pair of postcards in one hand. In the other, there was a burning lighter. She played the flame over the cards as the thing angled from Ryan to her, arms working in synchrony as its wings beat and blurred. The cards were consumed in fire, and she dropped them to her feet where they landed as a rain of curling ash.

The thing of wings ceased to be. Like a heat mirage when you step too close, it simply was no longer there. There was a residual humming and smell of burnt honey and bile in the air but nothing else.

"What the hell was that?" Ryan shrieked.

"Two words. I shouldn't have used both. One would have worked. Stupid."

"What was that thing?"

"The word made real," she said like it meant something.

"But it's gone now?"

"That one disappeared, yes. But there will be others." She stepped toward him, simmering with anger but focused and under control.

"Now tell me exactly, precisely which of my sigils you fucked with, young man. In doing so, you have assumed responsibility for repairing them." The firelight on her face transformed her. Whatever gentleness had been there once was lost in the sharp contrast of firelight and setting sun.

"Like I said," he confessed, "the big one at the top of the stairs. I . . . erased it."

"Congratulations. You have enabled *that*," she said as she pointed to the sky.

"That thing that I just unmade? You enabled that as well. This would have been controlled without your interference. Ten years of work nearly ruined." She set her jaw and waited for a reply.

"I thought you were insane, and I didn't know it was . . ."

"Real? It only possesses half-reality, Ryan. I tried to unmake it ten years ago.

"I failed then and paid for it."

The dusk light on her face revealed depths that she had hidden before, depths he could have fallen into. He dry-swallowed, tasting only shame and fear.

The look was gone now, no regret, only certainty. "And I will not allow one pissy graduate student who put his foot in the wrong mess to prevent me from succeeding this time. Now put out your hand," she snapped as she turned away from him and back to her bag of supplies.

"What do you want me to do?"

"Take this," her voice sounded as steel. She shoved a piece of pink chalk into his hand, thicker around than a roll of quarters. "And take this paper and copy this symbol, right side up. Note the orientation on the original. Draw it where the one you erased lay."

"If I don't?" he offered and didn't believe the bluff himself.

"Then your failing my class won't matter. In fact, you won't even remember taking it. But you'll have shown me up.

"So decide what you value more."

He nodded firmly.

She told him what to do if he was attacked. She even gave him a list of words to work from but told him to be careful. Each was only good once, and they needed to save as many on the list as they could for the big one. His way had been opened, and he had been trapped for ten years. Tonight he was strong enough to escape fully into the world, to take his kingdom back.

Ryan stood without any ability to move. He could only stare at what was becoming. It was too late. Certainty filled the moment and expanded outward, becoming hard as diamond. The crushing weight of inevitability bore down on him like a thousand dead stars. He had unmade a lesser creature spawned by the greater, but the chains had been put on reality.

It was, entire and whole. The nature of the thing didn't matter, only its being. Wind-borne debris flowed around it like a tornado mashed flat and spread on a picture plane. At the center of that was the translucent jelly-mass of unidentifiable organs and appendages as meaningless as colored globs trapped.

Trapped in glass.

A tiny voice called to him, miles away. He dimly recognized it. Stokes. Elizabeth. The crazy linguist.

"Come on, Ryan!" she called. "Don't believe the lie. Don't fall for certainty!"

He tried to move, but the weight was too great.

The voice was right next to him now. "You *are* a smart kid even if it exhibits as a dumb kind of smart."

He felt pride in spite of himself, the heat of that flushing into his veins. He raised his left hand, still stinging from the scrape earlier.

"Right. Good job."

Then the weight was gone. He stood, sweat slicked and feeling empty inside.

"Emptiness fills me," he said.

"You have it now. Come on, and let's put a finish on this job."

He heard her speaking with the same precise cadence, almost singsong and lyrical. "The words, Ryan. These words give us power. The whole of my only meaningful teaching, what I learned when I had been broken for those years. The words make the real."

"And those words can unmake."

"You have brought me understanding," he said. "I am . . ."

"Be present, but don't be a word." She pressed a small sheaf of postcards into one hand, all flipped to the back side, each having a different word written on them.

"Do not speak these words until you are ready to destroy them."

"What do we do?"

"Cataloguing. Definition. Destruction or at least entrapment." She sounded hopeful but not positive.

The whirling sky howled, and the thing within it struggled to be, struggled to evade precision. It remained glutinous, an aggregate of indistinct appetites, reaching toward solidity.

"Where did you get these?"

"I made them." She marched to a stop near the chalk lines.

Ryan realized that he had only been a few feet away, but it seemed like miles or more. "No, no. Where did you get the words themselves?"

She flicked open the lighter, spilling its yellow glow. "From books. Books I read once and realized they illuminated not a doorway but a set of locks. Locks that had been opened long ago. These protections lay buried under camouflage, the masquerade of fiction. These words, wrought from magic, make keys to relock the doorways left dangerously open."

"And you can transfer that from the word to the thing up there?" Ryan allowed himself to be directed by her, marched over to a nearby wire wastebasket, nearly empty but lined with transparent plastic.

Above them, the thing breathed out the smell of sweet and baking rot as it ate the sky.

"If we hurry and have focus." She stood beside him. "Now do as I do."

She raised her head to address the king in the sky. "You are cyclopean!"

As soon as the syllable rang, she set the lighter to the postcard as before and dropped it into the basket. "Now you," she urged with a quiet resolution.

"You are moldering!" he shouted and added the flame and dropped the card into the bin.

"You are octopodan!"

"You are mammoth!"

"You are pseudopodal!"

"You are recrudescent!"

The fire grew. The words continued in a stream, not mere syllables but things of power themselves.

The sky shuddered in response, electrified and convulsing. The eyes blinked in spasms, but its flailing was only partially real, only half here.

"You are squamous!" she shouted.

"I used that one. Sorry."

She picked the next one without pause. "You are sluggish!"

Vaporous, unclean, yonic, fungous, acrocephalic, antediluvian, bilious, membranous, heaving, oleaginous, nonsensical. All these words and more. Each one of them pinning down and peeling away another bit of its power. This continued for minutes, each word stunning and slowing its vast and drab majesty, squatting in the dusk sky.

Above their heads, the thing seemed to shrink and vibrate, faster and faster, bound to the rhythm of the speech and definition, each of their pronouncements and additions to the fire burning off more of the thing. All it could do in reply was howl and shriek. Uncounted tentacles glistened in the stalled dusk, flailing and skinned into flayed remains. Their castings shone prismatic, like rainbow-hued snail trails peeled off the sky and rained down.

"You are anomalous!"

"You are batrachian!" Ryan flipped the last of his cards into the fire in front of him. The light from it played over him and Elizabeth and the base of the obelisk. "Done."

"You. Are. Zymotic," she intoned. The voice that poured out of her could fill the world, replacing the dreadful certainty of the alien god with possibility, with chance and opportunity. The Land of May. Freedom.

Protective cilia and organelles all but shriveled and destroyed, the failed king flopped and twisted, contorting and shrinking. Its true nature revealed, its form condensed to a single and unblinking eye rendered out of transparent jelly, the king fled. It could not survive here any longer.

The wind sucked inward and held for a moment.

"Hold on!" she yelled and grabbed his hands in hers.

The dusk closed as a massive presence evacuated itself from the atmosphere, rushing past them tangibly. The eye blinked out of existence as something rustled in the collection of paperweights.

Ryan heard the sound of glass on stone and opened an eye.

"I believe it worked," she said and quickly disentangled herself from his grasp. She bent down and picked up one of the rounded globs of glass. There was a faint anti-light within it, not green, not blue, not yellow.

"Is it there?" Ryan asked.

She sighed. "That word again. It *resides* there. It *endures* entrapment there. But it does not *embody* the totality," she laughed. "Honestly. And here I believed that you'd grasped the concept. You may not pass my course at all."

Her laughter was welcome.

§

Matt Maxwell was born in California, sometime between the JFK assassination and the moon landing. Lived there his whole life. Learned to drive stick shift in the parking lot of the ziggurat that you see in Roger Corman's *Death Race 2000* and went to school where they filmed all those soft brutalist sets in *Battle for the Planet of the Apes*. He's worked in video arcades and think tanks, been an animator, taught sociology, thanatology, and ethnomethodology.

His past writings include work for Blizzard Entertainment and, from Broken Eye Books, the novella *Queen of No Tomorrows* and a story in the anthology *Tomorrow's Cthulhu*. He's self-published a number of books, both nonfiction/commentary and short/long fiction and was also the writer and publisher of the weird western comic *Strangeways*.

Sure. He'd love to be on your podcast. You can find him online at highway62press.com and on Twitter at @highway_62.

The Last Observer

Erica L. Satifka & Rob McMonigal

T HE WHISTLE OF FLASHBANGS ACROSS THE QUAD HURRY Caryn's WALK TO
Professor Matsumoto's office. *That would explain why the campus police
aren't doing anything. They're a part of it now,* she thinks, stepping up her pace.
A woman with a bandanna drawn across her face jostles Caryn with an elbow.

"Can you watch it?" Caryn rubs at her side, more annoyed than hurt.

"Do you believe?"

Caryn strides away without a word.

"I said, do you *believe*?"

Caryn feels something hit the back of her neck; the bandanna woman has
thrown a small rock at her.

"You've gotta pick a side!"

"Jesus fucking *Christ*, lady," Caryn says. She throws the rock back in the
protestor's general direction and takes off for the professor's lab like an antelope.

As she reaches the door, she realizes she's been spotted. The two factions of
campus protestors, who've been locked in an intense struggle for the past three
weeks, surround her. Bats thump into bloodied palms, tattered signs flutter
in the wind. Caryn feels a tug on her collar as she's pulled into the physical
sciences building.

"What the *hell* were you doing out there?" Professor Helena Matsumoto
stands with her hands on her hips, and Caryn thinks she might actually be
angry.

"It's not that dangerous," Caryn says. She touches the back of her neck, and a line of blood comes away in her hand. "Okay, maybe it is."

The professor shakes her head and stalks down the hall. "Well, come on. If you've made it this far, I might as well show you the images."

The images. Deep-space photography beamed back from a satellite launched before Caryn was even born. *And they arrived just in time for the world to go to shit,* Caryn thinks.

Three other students are in the lab, each one transfixed by the images, which have been projected on the wall in stunning detail. Caryn opens up her own computer.

"What's that smudge?" a male student says, aiming a laser pointer at a spot on the wall.

The professor squints at the spot. "It's a blemish in the film. It's nothing."

"Are you sure?" one of the other students asks.

The professor zooms in on the quadrant containing the "blemish." It really does look like just a blur, and Caryn feels vaguely disappointed.

"Now since we don't have a very big class today, I'll open it up to questions." The professor's voice rings against the walls of the lab, which had been intended to seat around three dozen.

"Where are these from?" the third student in the lab asks. His too-small NASA T-shirt has a stain. *Could be blood,* Caryn thinks, *or maybe it's chocolate.*

"Galaxy GN-z11," Professor Matsumoto says, "the most distant galaxy known to mankind. As well as one of the oldest."

The other female student starts to ask a technical question about the specs of the satellite but is interrupted by a loud boom from outside. A chorus of cheers rises up, followed by a round of guttural chanting.

"I don't know how I'm expected to work like this." The professor throws up her hands and exits the lab, leaving the four students behind.

The guy who found the smudge gets up and slides in next to Caryn. "So which side are *you* on?"

She gives him what she hopes is a dirty look. "The one you're not on."

"Patrick," he says, extending a hand and ignoring the insult. Caryn cautiously takes it. "I'm with you for what it's worth. I stopped following the protests a long time ago."

"It hasn't been that long," Caryn says.

"Three weeks is pretty long."

"Protests always have a shelf life. Look at how fast the marches against the president went from millions to thousands in only a few months. We'll be back to worrying about grades and frat parties in no time."

"Before or after the mass funerals?"

Caryn studies Patrick's face. He's not going to let go of this. She changes the subject. "Hey, maybe we should go check on the professor."

Caryn and Patrick enter the hall, leaving the other two students to puzzle over the images still on the wall. They find the professor in the next lab over, huddled on the floor. She's muttering in a language that neither recognizes, slapping her ears. Caryn exchanges a brief glance with Patrick and sits beside her.

"Are you all right, Professor Matsumoto?"

"Please," she says, still hitting herself, "leave me alone. Class dismissed."

Patrick's shoes squeak away, but Caryn can't make herself go, not while the professor is shaking in a corner. "What's wrong? Is it the protestors?"

"It's nothing. You'll all be marked present for the day. Go back to the dorms, uh—"

"Caryn."

"And be careful." The professor peeks out of a window, wincing as the chanting intensifies. "Whatever you do, don't listen to *him*."

Caryn wonders if she means Patrick. But there's no way to ask as the professor crawls away on her hands and knees, smearing her own blood into the cracks of the tile floor as she scuttles like a crab escaping a predator.

On Wednesday, Caryn makes the trek back to the astrophysics lab. She holds her own bat in her hands, though she can't imagine using the thing.

"Caryn!" She turns to see Patrick. "You're going to Matsumoto's class, right? Come on. Let's walk together."

They cross in front of a line of trash cans that have been set aflame. A student barely out of puberty with a face painted yellow climbs upon a makeshift rampart and begins to swing a chain.

"Hastur approaches! Do you hear me, my brothers?"

A not-especially loud whoop emanates from the crowd of onlookers.

"I said, *do you hear me*?"

A projectile slices through the air, and before Patrick yanks her away, Caryn sees another person with a painted face. A woman this time, holding a Nerf gun. Despite herself, Caryn laughs.

"On *this* campus, we worship the Beast." She strides over and with one fluid motion, punches the yellow-painted student into a fiery trash can. "Mighty sorrowful one, we beseech you!"

The screams of the burning student ring inside Caryn's ears like klaxons, and she knows immediately that she'll never forget them. She won't forget the smell either.

"*Hurry*, Caryn!" Patrick runs up the steps of the physical sciences building, shoving a random protestor who'd jumped in his path.

Caryn points at the garbage can, ignoring the woman who'd fired the Nerf gun, now dancing an arrhythmic little victory jig. "We need to help him. He's dying!"

Students start to advance on her with dead, zoned-out eyes, and she quickly enters the building behind Patrick.

"Why are you even here?" asks Caryn, leaning against a wall to catch her breath. Her hand touches a fading sign for a tolerance rally.

"I could ask you the same question." Before Caryn can reply, Patrick continues. "I need to know what that 'blemish' is. If I'm going to die at the hands of a children's-toy-wielding maniac, I want to see if we've found interstellar life first."

Caryn stares at him. Is that why she's here too? To have some sense of normalcy? Because the truth matters? She doesn't get a chance to share her side; Patrick's already on his way to class if you could call it that.

There's only one student in the lab this time; Mr. NASA Shirt is absent. Not that the professor, who's leaning unsteadily against the podium, seems to mind.

"Bourbon," Patrick says, sniffing the air.

"You're all still here," she says. "Shouldn't you all be out there saving the whales or whatever you kids do?"

"I want to look at those images again," Patrick says. He hasn't yet sat down and neither has Caryn.

"Me too," Caryn says.

Professor Matsumoto waves a hand. "Okay, okay. Here you go. You were right by the way."

The three students look around for a bit. "Me?" Patrick asks.

"That spot. It wasn't a blemish. We have updated photos sent to us in real time from Hawaii. It's getting closer. Fuck if I know what it is." The professor collapses into a chair. "Welcome to college, children. We swear here."

Caryn moves closer to the photograph. The spot, which had been so far away before that she'd barely been able to make it out, is now roughly the size of a dime. "Does anyone know how fast it's traveling?"

Professor Matsumoto snores.

"I'm taking this back to the dorm." Patrick lifts the professor's laptop into the air and gently disconnects it from the cords. "You're welcome to join me."

"I can't let you steal her computer, Patrick." Caryn looks back to the other student for backup, but her eyes have taken on a curious glazed expression Caryn's starting to recognize all too well.

"She's not using it," he replies. He stuffs the laptop into his backpack, puts it on, and holds out his hand. "Well, you coming?"

Caryn thinks about the dot, and the scene on the quad. No ambulances have pulled up. They haven't for some time. "All right. But you better not just be trying to get in my pants."

"Are *you* thinking about sex right now? Because I'm sure not."

Hand in hand, they push their way through the crowd, which has now descended on the physical sciences building. Caryn allows her gaze to fall on the trash cans. Mr. NASA Shirt is there, his clothing tinted with a different kind of stain.

"On *this* campus, we worship the Beast." Then he bites a hunk out of an especially long femur bone.

Patrick's dorm room is spartan, the only features of note a high-end coffee maker and a wall calendar that looks like it came from an insurance company.

"Here're some blankets for the floor," he says, throwing a pile of them at Caryn.

Such hospitality, she thinks. *Well, it's better than him inviting me into bed.* "Don't you have a roommate?"

"Haven't seen him since . . . you know."

"We need to look at those pictures. I think you're right about that thing getting bigger."

"I know I'm right," he says, setting the professor's laptop on a rickety side table, booting it up. "I'm just not sure what it is."

As Patrick logs in to the server that hosts the satellite pictures, Caryn goes to his window. Peeking through the drapes, she sees protestors encircling what looks like a statue of an octopus made out of papier-mâché. All of them have the yellow paint on their faces.

"Patrick, what's going on?"

"Uh, the image in the pictures is—"

"Not that. All of this. The protests. The violence. A woman on Fox News slit the throat of her own senator on national TV! What's happening to us?"

He shrugs. "I don't keep up with politics."

"This isn't politics."

"If you say so." Patrick shrugs and tries to get the Internet back online. At least the power hasn't gone out.

In the opposite building, the women's dorm, someone unfurls a banner painted in red and black. Scrawled letters like that of an ancient language adorn every bit of the surface, creating an effect much like a scream. As Caryn attempts to decipher it, a spike of pain blooms in her head, an instant migraine. Without thinking, she slaps herself in the ear.

"Why are you crying?" Patrick asks, momentarily distracted from the images.

She hadn't realized she's crying, not until he says it. "My head hurts. I'm going to bed." Caryn burrows into the mound of blankets, pulling one over her head, which is still swirling with the bizarre graphemes of the banner. She lies awake for several hours as Patrick clicks away.

At last, she slips into dreams.

"You've made an excellent choice."

Caryn whirls around. There's a man behind her, a tall man, with only shallow indents where his facial features should be. His skin is silver and highly reflective, and his long coat drags along the ground as he walks slowly toward her.

"You're what they're fighting about." She takes a few steps backward, coming up against the tree line, against the edge of the dream.

"I have many names," says the man, ignoring her. His voice spills forth not from the dimple in his face but from all around Caryn. "The Crawling Chaos, the Dweller in Darkness, the Haunter of the Dark, Nyarlathotep. But you may call me the Beast. *They* all do."

"Get out of my head," Caryn says. "You aren't wanted here. Or anywhere."

"I am wanted everywhere." If the man had a mouth, he would have been smiling.

Caryn crosses her arms across her chest. "They're just a bunch of dumb college kids. They don't know what they're doing."

"Oh yes, they do. This is exactly what humanity wants—to rip and tear and burn anyone who disagrees with them. I'm not like the others, Caryn. I dwell not in the stars but on the Earth's surface. I'm a man of the people." The thing laughs smarmily.

"I'll never follow you."

"Greater ones than you have fought me and failed. Give in, wretched creature." The Beast towers over her; she can see her own image reflected in the mirrored flesh. "Give in and receive all of the wisdom I have to offer. That's first-rate wisdom, no money down!"

Caryn gropes for one of the trees, breaking away a branch in her hand. She shoves it at the giant, gaunt man. Instead of ducking, he pushes his body into the branch, allowing it to spear his chest.

The branch bobs in the man's reflective body, which close up has the consistency of blubber. As Caryn watches, the branch transforms into an arm sprouting several hands, all of which open up to reveal jagged mouths. They all cackle in unison.

"Make your choice, Caryn. Ticktock. Don't delay. Supplies of my generosity are running out. The Unspeakable One's prices are far higher than mine." The voice comes not from the mouths but again from all around her, and underneath the advertising pitch, she senses a deeper language. An ancient one whose rough texture scrapes against her soul like sandpaper. "I know you'll join the winning team. *She* did."

Caryn bolts awake. She claws the blanket from her face and swivels to look at Patrick who's fallen asleep in his computer chair.

She creeps to the window. Fighting has broken out again, or maybe it never stopped. The yellow-painted students swing sticks at the other faction who wear long trench coats and robes adorned with mirrors. Plastic ones, mostly, from makeup cases. *That's new,* she thinks. An outbreak of fires leers back at her from the glittering ornaments, making her head spin. She feels her hands ball into fists but resists the urge to self-harm. Caryn doesn't dare look back at the banner.

"It's not politics," she says to Patrick's sleeping form before climbing back into his bed.

"We need to go back to the lab," Caryn says.

Patrick hands her an espresso from the fancy machine. "Have you looked outside?"

"I haven't been doing anything else," she replies with a scowl. She's not going to tell him about the dream.

"Then you'd know that they're killing each other out there. You *saw* what happened yesterday. It's too risky. Not like anyone is going to class anymore anyway."

Caryn gulps down the coffee in one fluid motion. "Professor Matsumoto is. We need to get her to safety. Or at least give her back her computer."

"Look," Patrick says, angling the laptop toward her. "The object. Because that's what it is, not a star or a smudge or anything else. It's accelerating. A goddamn *U-F*-fucking-*O*."

The object slash blemish has increased from the size of a dime to at least a sixth of the total screen area; since Patrick has it zoomed in though, it's hard to tell if the image is really so big as all that. Caryn can almost make out features of the strange item, squiggles that look like—

"I think I'm getting sick again," she says, slumping back down to the bed.

"Maybe we'll make it." Patrick shrugs. "Or maybe not. But if she means that much to you, we'll try it."

"She's a fucking *person*," Caryn says, trying to keep the edge out of her voice. *I have to save her.*

Patrick equips himself with a large Bowie knife—"my grandfather's," he says, "but I've never used it"—and Caryn makes do with a tennis racket stolen from the roommate's side of the cramped space. More rummaging reveals a set of oil paints, and Caryn smears the contents of one of the tubes over her face.

"Put this on," she says, throwing him the tube.

"Cadmium," Patrick says. He squeezes a little onto his fingers. "Yellow."

"I think it'll protect us. At least as far as the building anyway."

He paints his face, though he does a terrible job of it. "Let's go," he says, sliding the knife into his jacket pocket.

A series of small fires have broken out again, and from across the quad, Caryn can hear the sound of another flashbang. She grips Patrick's hand a little tighter.

Are we the only ones left? she thinks. *Surely there must be others holed up in their dorm rooms afraid to catch . . . whatever this is. The whole world can't be descending into chaos, right?* Caryn looks up at the windows of the dorms on either side of them as if she could catch the eye of a sane person from fifty yards away.

"Watch out!" Patrick yells, and Caryn instinctively ducks. Something hot just barely misses her, but the smell of burnt wood is unmistakable. She winces.

"Flaming arrows, *really*? Is this the Middle Ages?"

"We'd better run," he says, ignoring the jab, and takes off for the physical sciences building, not even bothering to hold her hand.

It's almost time for class, but of course, Caryn doesn't expect any other students to be there. She's a little surprised that Professor Matsumoto is. From the emptied liquor bottles around her, she's been there quite a while.

Caryn slips an arm around her. "We're getting you to safety."

The professor jerks out of her grip and points her finger at Caryn's face. "You're with *them*! The Yellow Sign!"

"We're not with anyone, we—" But before Caryn can finish her statement, the astrophysicist has taken off in a drunken stumble, heading for the doors.

"Oh no you don't," Patrick says. They both go into the hall, which is littered with discarded papers and office supplies, and Patrick easily overtakes the professor, wrestling her to the ground. "You have a problem, Professor Matsumoto."

She barks a laugh. "We *all* have a problem, Mister . . . oh, I don't know what your name is, and I don't care. That object? It's something all right. It's the end of the world."

"Is it a meteor?" asks Caryn.

"You're gonna *wish* it was a meteor." The professor tries to get back on her feet, but Patrick keeps her pinned down. "Galaxy GN-z11. Seven times older than the Milky Way, only on our radar for the last two years. When we sent that damn satellite." She releases a vodka-infused belch.

"So the object is what's making everyone so crazy?" Caryn asks. "Is it some kind of drug or—"

"Science was wrong," Professor Matsumoto says as if Caryn hasn't spoken at all, "and religion was right. But not any of the religions practiced on Earth. Not anymore anyway. What's on that object . . . *that's* a true god."

"Hastur," Caryn says, remembering the chanting, and her dream from last night crystallized in her mind.

"The Unspeakable One," the professor says with a nod. "And I doubt he's the only creature on that rock."

Loud pounding echoes from the doors as from a battering ram. Fighting the urge to ask more questions, Caryn tries to bring her back to whatever passes for reality. "Neither of us is affected for lack of a better term. Patrick's dorm is safe, and we want to take you there."

Professor Matsumoto laughs bitterly. Dried tears, blood, and alcohol flake from her skin and shirt. "You tell yourself that if it helps. Not affected, ha! I know the truth." She shoots Caryn a knowing look.

Caryn stares at the professor. Will she reveal Caryn's dream to Patrick? How could she even be aware of it?

"This is the end for me," Professor Matsumoto continues, knocking Caryn from her thoughts. "The scientific method's shot to hell. Tyson announced the Earth was flat and shot himself. These aren't the rules I'm used to." She coughs up blood, bile, and a bit of hamburger. "Plus," the professor says, looking straight at Caryn, "I made a bad deal."

Caryn shivers. "They'll *kill* you if you stay, Professor!" Caryn looks over to Patrick for backup, but he's already loosened his grip.

"If this is what she wants, let her go. I told you this was a dumb idea."

The professor stands up, dusts herself off, and heads toward the sound of the approaching mobs. "Go out the back while they're distracted. And don't leave the dorms once you're there. Stay inside. Oh, and get that damned paint off. As for my computer—"

Patrick holds up a hand. "It was me."

"My notes are on there. The password is *Nyarlathotep*."

Caryn lurches backward, nearly falling on the mess of fluids slowly leaking from Professor Matsumoto. "*That's* your password?!"

"Nonsense word, isn't it? Came to me in a dream." The professor pushes her way through the doors and is instantly engulfed by a mass of painted people with their sticks and Nerf guns, their signs and banners, all of which are etched with those same migraine-inducing glyphs.

And then Caryn takes off ahead of Patrick for once, running like hell for her life. As if there would be anything left after this disaster that could be called a life.

"Dinner," Patrick says, flipping an individually wrapped packet of saltines to Caryn.

"How charming," she replies before jamming them into her mouth. "Well, get the computer out. Let's look at her notes. We can't let the professor die for nothing."

Patrick boots it up and accesses the restricted section of the laptop. There are pictures not included in the professor's class presentations. He zooms in on the object, now hundreds of light-years away from its starting place, Galaxy GN-z11. "It's got a tail."

"A yellow tail," she says, instantly dismayed. *Professor Matsumoto was right,* Caryn thinks. *The creatures on that rock are coming for Earth, and there's nothing we can do to stop them.* Caryn feels an overwhelming urge to go out there herself, join one of the murderous little campus organizations, and let this all be over.

Patrick walks over to the window and draws the curtains aside. Even from her spot on his bed, Caryn can hear the whoops and hollers of the students, campus cops, and faculty as they pledge allegiance to their respective new gods. "What are we going to do, Caryn?"

"As if I *know*?" she snaps back, immediately regretting it. Caryn opens her phone to see that the wireless signal is weak and that her Twitter feed is nearly empty. "It's crazy everywhere, and not even the news feeds are posting reports anymore. Hell, they stopped reporting the names of the dead almost ten days ago because there wasn't enough time."

"So we're fucked then?" Patrick asks, biting down on the last of his cracker.

Caryn pauses, thinks. It's hard because no matter what she does the buzzing of ancient, otherworldly tongues haunt her ears. "It didn't affect us," she says, turning off the phone to save the battery. *Sort of.*

"Which means there might be others." Patrick takes another gander out the window, looking across to the women's dorm. "We need to find anyone else who wasn't affected. We need to band together."

"The professor said we shouldn't leave, and I don't think it's a good idea either. The violence is getting worse." As if to illustrate Caryn's point, a loud crash sounds from below them, followed by screams. Some people are driving stray cars into the opposing factions and ramming the vehicles together at top speed. She can just make out twisted metal covered in blood through the smoke.

"It'll be safe. You wait here." Patrick freshens his yellow makeup, slips the knife back into his coat, and heads out before Caryn can even attempt to restrain him.

He's not looking for survivors, she thinks. *He's committing suicide. Just like the professor did, just like I should.* She curls up on his bed underneath the blankets and allows herself to cry. After what seems like hours, she sleeps.

An inhuman screaming jolts her awake.

"What is it *this* time?" she says, throwing off the covers, going back to the window.

A black, shriveled creature, not unlike a flying jellyfish, sails through the air and lands on the glass in front of Caryn's face with a plop. The thing peels back a few of its way-too-numerous limbs and unsheathes pointed talons that glint in the moonlight.

Too late, she realizes the thing is cutting a hole in the window like a cat burglar breaking into a house.

Caryn reels, gasping at the yellow-brown smoke that is permeating the room. The jellyfish is gone, replaced by a hooded man in an ill-fitting robe. He gestures to her, but she doesn't dare move from her spot against the far wall of the dorm.

"You're the other one," she says. "Here to recruit me."

The thing inclines its head slightly, which can't quite be interpreted as a yes or a no.

"I won't follow you," Caryn says. "Either of you. Or anything else that's on that meteor."

"You were very kind to send that satellite to us."

"I didn't send anything!" Caryn shouts at it, realizing too late it just saw her as yet another feeble creature, and the specifics mattered as much to it as which ant first found a hole in the kitchen mattered to her.

"We'd lost contact with this planet long ago. Thought we'd never find it again."

Science summoned these gods, Caryn thinks. Somewhere, William Jennings Bryant was laughing from his grave. "It was a mistake."

The hooded man chuckles. Caryn's skull starts to pound. "Child, this is no tragedy. This is the experience of a lifetime! Mi-go, flock to me." He holds out his arm, and three creatures that look like excised tumors with bat wings land on it.

Bile runs down the back of Caryn's throat. "What are those things?"

"The mi-go. My little brain collectors." He pets one of the monstrosities under what Caryn assumes is its chin, and she can swear she hears a coo. "They used to be allied with that silly old Beast, but I won them away in a game, but that cheat shrunk them first. Would you like them to take you out for a spin?" He pokes one of the creatures in what might be its side. "Yuggsy, go open up that lady's brain case."

"No!" Caryn yells and flails her arms, though the mi-go doesn't make any attempt to fly at her.

Hastur lets out a great belly laugh. "It's not just you, you know. You're not that special."

"I never thought I was." *And yet,* Caryn thinks, *I must be. Because why would I still be sane?*

"Keep telling yourself that. It doesn't matter if you walk on two legs, four, or even swim with the deep ones. Anyone who resists thinks they're *special.* The chosen one if you will, set to save their kind. But they never do. Revolutions come and go, but absolute power—the power that I control—remains."

Caryn looks from the hooded man to the mi-go and back to the hood. If there's a face in there, it's buried too deep in the cloth to make out. "Why are you fighting against Nyarla—fuck it, the Beast? You're both just trying to kill us. Why the factions?"

"It was the best way to harness humanity's . . . let us say *unique* energy. Your species gravitates toward hyper-polarization. Give a human two options, both equal in every way, and they will choose one and immediately consider the human who chooses the opposite his mortal enemy." A lip-smacking sound echoes from within the endless hood. "Delicious."

Caryn doesn't want to admit that the Unspeakable One is right, but the being can already read her mind. "Then take me, Hastur. Recruit me. I don't *want* to be special. I just wanted to be the first person to discover a new world in space. It's why I kept going to class. Look, I'm already wearing your colors. Just—"

The horror with the three bird-like mi-go attached to his arm seems to grow smaller, and more smoke envelops the room. Caryn gasps for breath. Is this how it ends?

Slowly, she realizes nothing is happening. "But you're so *good* at it, Caryn," he resonates. "Look at your noble attempts to save Professor Matsumoto." A cacophony of avian noises that sound like they've been played backwards in a tape recorder drown out the end of his message, and then all is smoke, and Caryn wakes up, the daylight on her face and the window unbroken.

Patrick still hasn't returned.

She waits.

And she waits some more.

And then it is night once again.

On the third day since Patrick took off to locate survivors that may not even exist, Caryn steels the courage to look at the feed of the object. It's now or never as the internet and electricity have become increasingly rare. She takes five tries to spell "Nyarlathotep" correctly, but the password-protected page opens, and more secrets spill out like the faces on the Beast. Mocking her.

The meteor or comet or whatever's rate of acceleration is exponential. It's less than fifty light-years away. And at the rate it's continuing to gain speed, it won't take fifty years to arrive.

Caryn's stomach rumbles, and her eyes swim with black dots. She'd already eaten the peanut butter and stale pizza Patrick kept in his dorm mini-fridge, but that isn't enough. She needs to go out.

She's armed with a butter knife, but strangely, the quad is silent and empty and clean now that the perpetual smoke is gone. No hint of the otherworldly carnage that had persisted for weeks is visible. Not even an overflowing trash can or so much as a fast-food wrapper blowing in the wind.

More disturbingly, there are no other people. "Patrick?" Caryn calls as she rapidly makes her way to the cafeteria. "Professor Matsumoto?"

At the entrance to the dining hall, she finally spots some people. Unpainted people who don't catch her eye. She opens her mouth to say hello but thinks better of it.

This détente won't last, Caryn thinks. *The meteor with Hastur and all his friends will soon be here and so will Nyarlathotep and all the slithering horrors of Earth itself. Posing as enemies but uniting as friends. To devour us. To suck out our brains even.*

"There's no difference between the two sides!" she shouts and laughs while the others scuttle away into the corners, their trays and plates rattling an unholy chorus.

She walks behind the counter and heads for the industrial-sized refrigerators. She purposely does not take any food that resembles meat.

When she's finished her salad—her very big salad—Caryn slides the tray back to the workers' area even though nobody there will ever clean it. She takes a slow survey of the cafeteria but sees nobody she recognizes. Not even Mr. NASA Shirt.

"Something for the road," she mutters under her breath as she fills her coat pockets with stale bread.

The sun is high overhead as she leaves the cafeteria, but it's been tainted with a sickly gray haze. Caryn looks up, squinting, and locates the pinhole-sized object now just about visible to the naked eye.

A coo bubbles up from the eaves of the physical sciences building. Caryn glances at the mi-go, gives it a sharp nod, and walks a little faster.

Whether Caryn likes it or not, she'll be around to see the end.

§

Erica L. Satifka's short fiction has appeared in *Clarkesworld, Shimmer,* and *Interzone.* Her novel *Stay Crazy* won the 2017 British Fantasy Award for Best Newcomer, and her rural cyberpunk novella *Busted Synapses* will be released soon by Broken Eye Books. She lives in Portland, OR, with her husband (and co-writer) Rob and several adorable talking cats.

The only secret monster at **Rob McMonigal's** university was an off-the-record smoking lounge. He's Site Editor and Head Writer for Panel Patter (www.panelpatter.com), an Eisner-nominated comics criticism site. He's also been been published in *Fireside Magazine* issue 12 ("Not So Super") and lives in Portland, Oregon, with his award-winning co-writer Erica Satifka and entirely too many cats.

I just keep meeting more and more utterly fascinating individuals during my explorations of Arkham!

My Miskatonic:
A Who's Who of Arkham

Matthew M. Bartlett
(art by Yves Tourigny with
introduction by Scott Gable)

A NOTHER YEAR, ANOTHER ARKHAM.
But I suppose that implies change where there really isn't any. At least no more than the usual amount for any given population. Though probably less actually.

No, I mean you discover more layers. Layers that were always there but that you only see now that you're well acquainted with the area and its people. Perhaps truths were being actively hidden from view, or perhaps it was just a matter of not knowing enough to see what was right there, always there to see if you knew how. But you learn, and you establish trust, and suddenly, you wake up to a whole new world. The odd sights and strange coincidences are just the commonplace now. Everyone has their strange rituals and quirks of personality. But try to find anywhere that isn't true.

But it's comforting after a while, the people and their ways. It's home. You find that you just start knowing things—things you were sure you were never taught—and accepting of one another's secrets, the ones that have been shared and the ones that haven't but are surely there, just out of sight. And not getting all fussed about the little things that you can't control, like why it's always a good ten degrees cooler in the blocks around the bank, why the cod catch is always so much better here than other nearby communities, and why spring storms often seem tinged with rust.

It's just life, and it's sometimes messy and unexplainable. But you'll probably find a different explanation from every soul you meet . . .

Stacey Boquet

Shows of cops and robbers were a staple on the television in the Boquet household; young Stacey Boquet frequently raised her hand, finger pointed, thumb up, at the screen and mimicked the gunfire with bursts of air from her pursed lips. She participated with great relish in meet-your-local-police days, toured the station and the jail, rode in police cars, not even putting her hands over her ears to cushion them against the siren's howl. She attended Quinnipiac University down in Connecticut and found herself enamored with college life—to the detriment of her studies. Upon graduation, she returned home and was promptly hired on at MU as Public Safety Officer.

Her job involves mundanities, like jump-starting stalled cars and delivering packages. She prefers the foot patrols, dealing with conflicts, things that make the day go by. She likes less the incidents she is told by her supervisors to leave alone. There was the hunched human figure skirting the fenced-in soccer field at dusk, unclad and with a strange, ox-like tail. The flames flickering in the locked student-center radio station at 3 a.m. The chanting in the astronomical observatory. The professor reported for unseemly, deranged muttering on the hill behind the quadrangle. One day, a concerned parent called dispatch requesting a welfare check on their daughter; Officer Boquet knocked on the dormitory door, and it opened, revealing a group of students involved in a spirited game of spin the bottle . . . only it was not a bottle that was being spun. Disgusted and sickened, she called for backup, static her only reply. Somewhere in that static, she heard strange, chirping music and maybe a voice under that. She has been reassigned to cafeteria duties, serving up lasagna and limp pizza and pancake dinners. At night, she still watches police shows and dreams.

Brathwaite

Brathwaite, who prefers to be addressed sans honorific nor second name, has in her sprawling Queen Anne at the corner of Saltonstall and East Streets a private library, legendary even in Arkham. It is said that her collection rivals that of MU and puts to shame any number of antiquarian bookshops. The curious reader—admitted by appointment only—will find, behind glass, books on every conceivable topic: endocrinology, esoteric surgery, cookware of 16th-century Holland, obsolete sex practices of lesser known New England witchfinders, private writings by the likes of Machen, Dickens, Jameses Henry and M.R. One might surmise such a house to be the target of thieves. In fact, only one attempt was made, in 1950, when Brathwaite was traveling abroad, acquiring new volumes. The miscreants picked the locks and were immediately set upon by a squadron of cats: Birman and Bombay, Manx and Munchkin, Tabbies brown and blue, Tuxedo and Tonkinese. The thieves incurred grave damages: lost eyes, torn septa, mutilated tongues, ripped-off fingernails, shredded lips. Brathwaite returned to find the cats lounging in their usual places, purring with adoring avidity, delighted at Brathwaite being home again. The only signs of the intruders were blood-sopped floors, the damaged lock, and one human ear left sweetly on Brathwaite's pillow.

Passersby peer at the intersecting hipped and gabled roofs, at the bay windows reflecting the muted sunshine, and wonder at the store of knowledge behind those walls and at the keeper of that knowledge. For when the curious enter, they encounter neither Brathwaite nor cats, just a platter of pastries and a servant of alarmingly advanced age who watches silently, his surly expression a warning to wash one's hands and to handle the books with great care.

Daniel van Buren

It is fitting that Daniel van Buren was born during a party. The lavish gathering, put on by Rechemey and Bardolph van Buren, was an orgy of dancers in daring outfits and masks, liquor running across the floor like a pungent river system, bare-chested men and women spinning in the air over trampolines, trailed by tassels, chanting, and parlor games of an unseemly variety. At the height of the howling frenzy, Rechemey crumpled to the floor, bellowed over the pounding music, and ejected Daniel onto the parquet where he slid four yards through the stomping feet of the revelers, miraculously unharmed. They washed him in the fountain and carried him above their heads. The party went on.

Today, Van Buren Party Planning, run out of an office on the fourth floor of a mostly vacant office/apartment building, is the place to go for searchers after creative revelry, whether of a bent occult, celebratory, mournful, or otherwise. He has an in with all the finest restaurants in Arkham; knows the clowns (those who are suitable for children and those who are decidedly not); has ties to dancers, acrobats, musicians, magicians, and even warlocks and undertakers for those who wish to bring their soiree to unthinkable places. One might also come to Daniel for party supplies and decorations: shrunken heads, candles, figurines from thimble-high to fifty feet tall, statuary, balloons, garland, paper lanterns, noisemakers, enchanted objects, talismans, and totems. There is something to be said, Daniel will tell you if you ask him or if he's in his cups and you don't, for living in one place for one's whole life. Travel can be mind-expanding, but home is home, and if you know the people there and they know you, you never do a drop of work a day in your life.

Kelly Cadiere

Once MU's most charismatic and engaging student tour guide, Kelly Cadiere continued the role through her graduate studies and beyond and currently provides the service on a strictly volunteer basis despite demanding full-time work as a biomedical consultant. The on-the-books tour includes the library, the student center, the cafeteria, a dormitory (one of the quieter ones), and several academic buildings. She fields questions, offers advice, and talks up the best qualities of the school. Many of those who take her tour apply; a few are accepted.

After the main tour, she offers to certain handpicked tourers what she calls a look at "the real" Miskatonic. In this unofficial tour, she leads her charges through the tucked-away nooks and less-than-hallowed halls of the campus, refusing to field questions; in fact, her charges are forbidden to speak at all, lest they be ejected. Students are shown the underground classrooms, the hidden outdoor amphitheater, the heavily fortified entrance to the real rare book room, the small cafeteria solely for three professors and two administrators with obscure, unsavory, possibly illegal appetites. The tour ends just past dusk with a peek from a disused, darkened floor of Edward D. Beene Academic Hall through binoculars at the building that houses some of the school's professors. Through the windows can be seen Mr. Grenphoal, reclining in his nightly milk bath, and robe-clad Professors Garden and Dantham in a red-lit hall, bowing in supplication to a statue of a three-headed stag micturating absinthe into a shell-shaped basin. To those students who are still interested, she offers a full scholarship as long as they sign a contract on the spot and agree to be initiates in a certain school society whose very name is a closely guarded secret.

Darien Dennis

The daughter of Zebadiah Dennis, the famed deep-sea fisherman lost with his crew off the coast of Gloucester in the terrible storm of '62, Darien developed a simultaneous terror of and fascination with the ocean. Her mother, from the wealthy Johanson family, provided an unthinkably large allowance, a significant portion of which Darien used to purchase and install in her Carriage Street home a number of wall-to-ceiling fish tanks.

These are filled with fish of all categories, but her favorites, the cuttlefish, she keeps in a tank with brittle stars and hermit crabs in her capacious bedroom, attended by a staff of five. These handsomely paid attendants are charged with skimming protein from the water, maintaining separate tanks of crabs and prawns with which to feed Daren's favorites, and watching and forestalling incidents of cannibalism. She reads to the fish a section of the infamous play "The King in Yellow," four pages of which she'd won at auction for a hefty sum. Often she'll wake at night and see in the shimmering blue phosphorescence the image of her father, standing in the tank, tatters of fish-chewed flesh floating on bone, the cuttlefish circling him. She cannot tell if his countenance bears a look of proud approval or of wrath. After these disquieting incidents, she often motors to the shore and gazes out upon the fearsome ocean to offer a prayer to both her father and to the deep ones she knows frolic out there somewhere, that they might keep her father and feed him and tend to his watery needs. But his return to the cuttlefish tank in the deepest hours of night is inevitable. It fills her days with anxiety and terror. And also with anticipation.

Don Donaldson

Don Don is the garishly clad proprietor of Tuck-In Tiki, the most notorious bar in all of Arkham, so dubbed due to its constantly being shut down by the city and state for various violations of hygiene and standards of decency. Don Don's idea was to merge the tiki theme with a bedtime theme. Thus the floor and the kitchen are lit only by glow-in-the-dark stars. The tables bear pillows and blankets. The waitstaff wear Hawaiian-themed pajamas and bathrobes. A fake river runs through the establishment, on which menu items float on miniature beds for the patrons to scoop up. The river is routinely dirty and green and smells of . . . something. The palm trees are real and rife with insect life, assailed by Fusarium wilt. The drinks have a suspicious chlorine odor.

Don Don bears the constant strife with a great, gleaming grin and good humor and appears to work willingly to make improvements. All he wants—all he ever wanted—was to be the congenial host, to draw a college crowd and impress them with his dark bar and his strong drinks. And his singing. For Don Don himself takes the stage every Friday in a tuxedo shirt and coat, grass skirt, and mirrored sunglasses and croons Satanic ditties of his own invention to the crowd. Though reactions to the food are mixed, the drinks are strong, and the signature Hawaiian nachos—sweet-potato triangles piled with pineapples and olives and coconut mango salsa and dripping with jack cheese—draw admirers from around the globe.

Casey Gohlke

Criminal justice was always Casey Gohlke's thing. Her stepfather—a thug and a goon whose assaults she'd ducked assiduously since he came shouting and cursing into her life when she was fourteen years old—was finally apprehended at the house after a series of armed robberies, during which the jerk was caught on camera. More than once. She quizzed the cops when they came to the house, befriended them, plied them with questions.

She was eighteen at the time and had just been accepted into MU despite middling grades. She had always been a curious cat, full of questions. What was the source of the weird colors coming from the neighbor's basement windows? What could account for the curious tentacle-shaped clouds that rose above the 1986 forest fire on the eastern side of town? Who was that one-legged man with the three eyes who always occupied the corner seat at Archibald's Diner but never ordered anything other than room-temperature coffee? College brought more mysteries to be solved. Why did worms gather and form themselves into strange symbols in the cement alcove behind the library? Who was that creep with the overstuffed backpack who stood stark still and staring oddly at certain academic buildings? What was the source of the wheezing screeches that echoed around the dormitory quadrangle every third Tuesday in September?

With each class, she gains new tools of detection, and her professors are certain that one day the notebooks she fills with her theories and the results of her rogue investigations will be available for study to future generations of students. She was last seen just yesterday, holding down the backpack man, the pack itself open like a gaping mouth and the contents within spread across the sidewalk. Another case solved by the legendary Casey Gohlke.

Dr. Daphne Heitner

Arkham's most popular veterinarian, Daphne Heitner, helms a small practice devoted specifically to cats, though in her days back in California she cared for all sorts of animals. She'd drug tested racehorses and vaccinated zoo animals, but one day, she encountered a human-interest news feature about the unusual number of felines in Arkham, and there she found her niche. She's helped Nickels, a tuxedo cat owned by Brathwaite, the city's notorious book collector, when the feline presented with a urinary blockage, and she repaired the leg of Chicken Nose, an injured tabby belonging to Professor Roger Gist. She sees to the cats of Arkham's wealthiest residents, and they in turn helped fund the building and ongoing maintenance of an annex to help store specialty foods, toys, and medicines.

Cats are her life's work to the exclusion of all else, so she offers on-call services twenty-four hours a day, including holidays. Some of her emergency house calls do become exceedingly strange though. She once detached from a Russian Blue kitten a curious leech with a terrifyingly human face. The cat was fine afterward (and the leech interred in a local crematorium), though she's developed a new habit of trying (and on occasion coming very close) to mimicking human speech. One night a taxi driver called from a pay phone, saying his cab had struck a cat, and she'd come out only to find not a cat but some kind of curious, amorphous grey hairless thing with three eyes and a small mouth with an extruding tangle of marble-like teeth. She'd done what she could, but the thing deflated and died in her arms. And she once pulled a sixty-foot bright-red worm from the posterior of an obese black cat named Satan.

Ted "Red" Jasper

Roustabout, trouble-seeker, and habitué of both emergency room and city lockup, Theodore Jasper is the sort of man loath to sit still and stew. He is often known to stand in the median at the intersection of Aylesbury and Water Streets and holler at the traffic, warning them in a shrill voice and portentous tones of the dark doings of his neighbors and fellow townsfolk, calling them diabolists and devils and worse. The fevered, paranoiac editorials he regularly pens rarely end up in the pages of the *Advertiser*, suffused as they are with dangerous rhetoric and words that border on libel. In one that somehow managed to see print, he blamed the city's residents for his ailments and injuries: suppurating blue-red rashes, aching joints, sudden jolts of pain in his neck and underarms, dropsy. Even his ingrown toenails he blamed on Elias Cull, a next-door neighbor who, upon spying him unleashing one of his jeremiads to passersby, gave him the evil eye and waggled his long fingers at him in a "diabolical" aspect. The local constabulary treats him with exasperated patience. The hospital has, on more than one occasion, had him removed when he refused to leave after treatment.

Recently, in a terrible accident, Jasper was struck by a sedan piloted by Glenn Mardyce, son of noted religious leader Edmund Mardyce. Jasper consulted a personal injury lawyer in a bid to sue Mardyce (and inexplicably, his father) for assault. Not even the subsequent swelling of his tongue and loss of his voice has prevented him holding signs on the streets and wielding his poison pen. It is said by some that he simply cannot be stopped and by others, darkly, that Jasper's troubles have only just begun.

Dr. Elymus Linwood

Born to clothiers in an upscale Arkham carriage house, Elymus Linwood was decidedly not the type one might expect to become a doctor, being at a young age capricious and whimsical and not at all studious. But after an accident with a kitchen knife when he was eight years old, his father found him on the kitchen floor happily drawing faces in the spilt blood. Fascinated by this copper-scented liquid of life itself, Elymus committed himself to its study. He excelled in the sciences and mathematics, got by in English and the humanities, and through a generous scholarship attended medical school in Portsmouth, New Hampshire. He worked as a hematologist at St. Mary's, specializing in white blood cell disorders, until he was ejected under the suspicion of theft.

Not long after, police raided his house to find each room furnished with multiple refrigerators, each one stocked with jars containing blood and other fluids of unknown provenance. The house itself was surrounded by generators, and the electrical system was amateurishly reworked. After searching the house and finding blood-penned messages under the carpets and on the ceilings, investigators plugged in a lamp for a better look, but sparks erupted from the electrical socket, followed by flames tearing across the ceiling and setting alight the valances and the curtains. In seconds, the whole house was an inferno of blue flame and black smoke. Only four of the fifteen policemen escaped with their lives, and the odor of boiling blood and cooking flesh can still be detected on humid days. The remains of Elymus were not found, but blood still goes missing from St. Mary's, and shadows in the form of a man are often seen sliding along the white walls and ducking under doorjambs into the stairwells.

Carolyn Mandrill and Swanson

People are leery of Arkham bookkeeper Carolyn Mandrill, or more accurately of Swanson, the parrot who rides on her shoulder like a colorful hitchhiker. It is not that Swanson has ever so much as pecked at anyone nor said an ill word; it's that it seems, the townsfolk say, he is about to. Carolyn, who loves the bird fiercely as a companion, a sounding board, a friend, and a confidant, scoffs at this assessment. Her officemates have met in secret with supervisors and human resources, demanding that the strangely leering psittacine be banished from the office on the grounds of uncleanliness, allergies, unpredictability, whatever objections their imaginations can raise. Management is sympathetic to a fault, reassigning people to other floors if ultimatums are delivered, but otherwise they refuse to ban the bird. It is speculated that they fear the parrot might . . . say something about them. Divulge a secret, speak aloud their private thoughts. Carolyn bears all of this with good cheer and is unfailingly kind to those who she knows disparage her beloved pet behind her back. Kill them with kindness. For his part, Swanson looks this way and that in that jerky way birds have of moving their heads, occasionally makes snicking sounds that seem to mimic suppressed laughter, and parades about on Carolyn's shoulder like a joyous grand marshal.

It is only at night, in Carolyn's home, where he is comfortable saying what he really feels and what his plans are to deal with his enemies. Carolyn is kind, gently encouraging, feeding him seeds, dates, and struggling insects from a jar with holes in the lid. It is a good existence, and the future holds such wonders for both of them, so the oracles and omens say, once Swanson begins to execute his plans.

Mary-Kate Mellor

Mary-Kate Mellor inherited her father's charcuterie after he died of a massive heart attack. Mellor's was known for flavorful sausages with taut natural casings and no gristle. But Mary-Kate was a creative sort, so she began offering sausages with exotic and unexpected ingredients. Cherries. Sun-dried tomatoes. Curry. Basil and cumin and saffron. Before long, lines were out the door. People came from as far as Leeds and Fitchburg, insulated totes in hand to buy in bulk. But Mary-Kate was not satisfied.

She began using the strange powders and gels from her father's old desk, having hired a locksmith to open it. The papers with strange designs and impenetrable notes she shredded. Whatever her father had been into in life, with his curious compatriots and their murmuring meetings in his office, she wanted nothing to do with. The new sausages, which she offered with names she'd made up, such as greemshan sausages and freoogh sausages, sold well. If people asked the ingredients, she was circumspect, muttering something about special spices and herbs from the farthest reaches. Before long, customers who had purchased these mysterious items locked themselves up in their homes, sending emissaries to purchase more on their behalf. Mary-Kate often wondered what became of them, especially once the whispers started up. She dismissed it as typical Arkham gossip. Deformities, extra limbs, distended lips and curious bulges in the stomach and thighs—the stuff of nonsense and surrealist silliness. Finally, one day, she sampled the sausages. The flavor was odd, off somehow, flinty and copper-like. After a week of eating nothing else, she glanced in the mirror one day and something was terribly amiss with the color of her eyes. Soon after, the shop was boarded up, and passersby can still hear strange sounds from within.

Graham Morgan

Graham Morgan is such a common sight on the grounds of MU that most simply assume he is a student or maybe a professor. One day, he's trudging with his grubby, overstuffed backpack across the common, another sitting at the back of Professor Rosas's trigonometry class in dark glasses, avidly taking notes. In fact, Morgan has no official connection to the university.

If you see him in the cafeteria, he's sneaked up the back stairs for a free meal. If you see him in a classroom, it is a large class, too big to take attendance. He sleeps in his conversion van in one of the lots restricted to faculty and staff, having forged an official decal. He had applied to the university as a young man and been rejected, largely on the basis of his personal essay, which was far too personal and far too strange for the admissions committee. Even Miskatonic, which is known for its eccentricities and strange courses of study, has its limits. Among a small group of students in the Department of Criminal Justice, he is the source of much speculation. What, for one, is in that backpack? What is his plan? And these are pertinent questions. For Graham has a grudge. The backpack contains a Post-it–strewn bible, acetone, fertilizer, detonators, small screws and nails, and a timer. It also contains several notebooks with page after page tracking the movements of certain professors and administrative staff. He hates the place. Hates its shadows and its mysteries, its frat houses of dark worship, masquerading as derelict properties marked for demolition. He hates the age of the place. When his plan comes to fruition, he will be doing the world a favor.

Destiny Sloane

Destiny Sloane, even as a young girl, assumed the mantle of the schoolteacher. Out by the rusting swing set at the stone wall that bordered the elementary school, children would gather around to hear her tell tales of the region's dark history, of grifters, robbers, sadists, and shamans who roamed the Arkham alleys even as far back as colonial days. She told of buried bodies, hidden troves of jewels and gemstones, and seeming gimcrack trinkets that in fact held great power.

She ended up teaching history at that same district; for four years, she took up residence teaching a variety of classes at the high school. She seemed immune to the complaints of parents; administrators shielded her, promising to the parents she would face harsh discipline and penalties financial and professional while instead fawning over her, offering her promotions, indulging in laudanum and quaaludes at her midnight gatherings in the teachers' lounge. At similar afterschool get-togethers, it was whispered, she would teach classes of her own devising where no topic was off-limits, no matter how salacious, obscene, or grotesque. Those, anyway, were the rumors. And despite those rumors, her students excelled, not only in her classes but in their studies as a whole. They went on to hold prominent positions in Arkham government agencies, to command the attention of occult luminaries in faraway Europe, to lead their own covens and cloisters. Some, it was said, cavorted with devils. Ms. Sloane, now a fully tenured professor of fine repute at MU, still attends their meetings, a secretive smile on her face, a cane clutched in her hands, a twinkle of mischief and malfeasance in her eyes, and danger in her bearing.

Trevor Thomas

Arkham native Trevor Thomas had set his sights on MU as far back as middle school. And on being a teacher at an even younger age, note his parents, hearing him proclaiming late one night in his bedroom and finding him holding class, attended by his stuffed animals, the writing in colored chalk on the board behind him presumably a misbegotten attempt at depicting mathematical symbols. He was six.

After he found an MU yearbook in a used bookshop, his parents, despite their (admittedly half-hearted) exhortations to look at colleges farther afield, resolved themselves to the fact that his heart and mind were set. He drew the university's crest on his notebooks and requested an official T-shirt from their shop for his fourteenth birthday. By the age of sixteen, he'd written reports on New England myths and folklore and on alien conspiracies and the farther reaches of the universe and what might dwell there. He turned them in at school but also, unbeknownst to his parents, mailed them to the university, care of the Department of English. He received very good marks from his high-school teachers along with cautionary notes suggesting he develop more wide-ranging and uplifting interests. At these, both Trevor and his parents scoffed. He never did hear back about the reports he'd mailed but was delighted to find he was accepted within four days of having applied. Before long, he was a TA, and a beloved and admired one at that. He had had so much potential, it was said after . . . everything happened. He could have—likely would have—ended up as the president of the school. His picture still hangs in the student center in a place of honor under a plaque of the university's mission statement.

Tommy Tuchman

Tommy Tuchman is generally known for his foul mouth, his ill temper, and his fondness for absinthe and soda crackers, but in Arkham, he is known as Tuckered Tommy, host of *Arkham by Night*, the local NBC affiliate's public access show. Airing after Irv Wasserman's *Hot Takes and Record Reviews*, Tommy sat on a threadbare set, just a few stools and plastic plants in front of a red velvet curtain, interviewing a host of Arkham luminaries, opining on current events local, national, and sometimes international. He was reliably uninformed, and his outrage was in direct proportion to his ignorance. No one knows what precipitated the change in his show, but it came in the late nineties. One night, it was an interview with Archibald Robey about omelets and a rambling diatribe about the CIA; the next . . . well, it was by all accounts just odd.

The show opens with the title, and the lights fall on an empty set. The curtain ruffles from time to time, and if you turn up the volume all the way, you can just make out a tentative whimper. Then Tommy slithers out from underneath, naked as a jaybird. He tilts his head up to the camera, and a station worker bolts out and throws a bathrobe at him. Tommy stands, covering his parts as best he can, and glares at the camera. The cameraman zooms in on his face. Closer. Closer. Soon his nose fills the screen. A small red hand reaches from the nostril, and slam cut to black.

The remaining half hour was a monologue of nonsense, foreign phrases yelled out, causing feedback, and odd xylophone music. One sharp viewer noted strange patterns in the blackness. Tommy's shows after that only got stranger. They still air even today. One is strongly advised not to tune in.

Averill Watkins

On a dark September day when the clouds fell from the sky to roll across the land and the mighty Miskatonic River seethed and raged like an angry drunkard, Averill Watkins and Tommy Beene were out in the thick of it in defiance of their parents, and Averill, in a moment of mischievous whimsy, pushed Tommy into the roiling black waters where he sank like a bag of cats. Averill sat howling by the shoreline for a long time as the fog washed over him and the rain pelted his neck and back, and finally he made his way home. When the Beene family telephoned, Averill said they'd parted ways at the river, which was, in certain sense, true. Averill grew up, as people do, went to high school, barely passing, eschewed college in favor of grease-monkeying at Gritley Automotive and Fabrication, drinking vodka at Willoughby's.

Throughout the years, he saw Tommy Beene at many places. He saw him sitting in the back of a crushed Ford Falcon, a bloated thing in overalls and rags, tongue out, eyes bulging like accusations. He heard the lashing of leaves in the treetops and looked up to find Tommy floating through the branches like a dinghy in the surf, looking just as he did before he flew flailing over the mossy riverbank. He heard the clink of snifter touching bottle and glanced over to see Tommy at the dark end of the bar, winking at him over a brandy. Averill was born in Arkham and died in Arkham, and the last thing he saw as he faded away in his hospital bed was Tommy, livid, pale, hungry, reaching for him with river-swollen hands, and Tommy was the Miskatonic itself, Arkham itself, brooding, mad, suffused with shadows.

Dr. Gwendolyn Wettlaufer

A graduate of Tufts University's School of Medicine after a four-year residency in emergency medicine at the Brigham, Gwendolyn Wettlaufer took a position as an emergency doctor at the Miskatonic Regional Medical Center. Having seen all the medical television dramas, she was surprised, especially after the nurses' warnings that Arkham was a particularly strange city in which to work, at how mundane things were, at least for the better part of the first year anyway. There were children hurt playing in the summer, football injuries in fall, winter car wrecks and slip-and-falls, one-car accidents in the spring when joggers first reappeared to distract winter-exhausted male drivers, food poisoning incidents from Archibald's Diner year-round.

She has garnered a reputation for being attentive despite having a large number of patients in her care, responsive and soothing to anxious relatives. She is respected by nurses, and though conflicts with other doctors occur, they never result in employment difficulties. Her first strange case was Samuel Paneuf, brought in with his chest wide open, heart in his hands, crying out that he was the victim of black magic. The EMTs had found him that way. He died in her arms. Then Bill Mardyce came in with burns all over his body—burns in the shape of frogs. Over the years, there have been plenty more. Carrie Kisk staggered through the doors, her right arm withered to a thread. One night a screaming ambulance smashed through the double doors, the vehicle empty of people but stuffed full of bats. Old Bill Carnker was brought in by his angry wife, his belly swollen strangely; in surgery, a book was removed from his gut. Despite its half-digested condition, both Carnker and his wife insisted on keeping it afterward. Gwendolyn handles all of this, it is said, with stolid equanimity.

Richard V. Weyer

A staff photographer for the *Advertiser*, Richard V. Weyer covers sports events, political rallies, and human-interest stories, but in his off time, he chooses more artful—and grimmer—subjects for his portfolio. His more notorious photographs depict such scenes as the bloody aftermath of a street fight; a five-legged cat standing on its hind legs in an alley, the remains of a squadron of mice scattered before it; the famed cultist Edward Mardyce clad in a robe with glittering Satanic insignia, wielding a curved knife and a dripping chalice, sheathed in orange fog; a bent, gnarled figure, bellowing at the cotton-and-charcoal sky in an ancient churchyard; a cloud-eyed child in a sawdust-coated warehouse, dressed in a cassock and clerical collar, holding up the desiccated remains of a chipmunk. His goal was to capture the essence of the outré, the ineffable, and the uncanny and, by doing so, to somehow both capture their power and divest them of their power. His ultimate goal was to take a picture of the mi-go, whose bodies, composed of alien material, could not be captured on regular film. He'd tried to do so by magic, rubbing the film with hawthorn and the fur of bats, by having it touched by the anointed fingers of Glimstergge, the blind, mad wizard of Kingsport, and finally (rumor had it) by astral travel to Yuggoth itself to find material suitable to capture the image of these mysterious beings. Arkham's underground paper, *The Truth-Teller*, reports that Weyer has recently met with mysterious intermediaries in the back room at the Cat & Fiddle and that he mutters in his cubicle of strange things, of interstellar travel, dangerous surgeries, and other worlds. Most recently spotted staggering along East Street, he looked unkempt and exhausted, but his eyes blazed with the ecstasy of secret knowledge.